'You really are the most extraordinary creature,' Hainford said.

Ellie opened her mouth to deliver a stinging retort, and then realised that his lips were actually curved in a faint smile. The frown had gone too, as though he had puzzled her out.

'So, not only am I a *creature*, and an *extraordinary* one, but I am also a source of amusement to you? Are you this offensive to *every* lady you encounter, or only the plain and unimportant ones?'

'I feel like a hound being attacked by a field mouse.'

He scrubbed one hand down over his face, as though to straighten his expression, but his mouth, when it was revealed again, was still twitching dangerously near a smile.

'I had no intention of being offensive, merely of matching your frankness.'

He made no reference to the *plain and unimportant* remark. Wise of him.

'You are unlike any lady I have ever come across.'

'But?' Ellie held her breath.

Hainford looked up, the expression in his grey eyes either amused or resigned, or perhaps a little of both. 'B⟋ ⟍u to Lan⟋

Author Note

Do you ever wonder where the ideas for a novel come from? I do too! Quite often they seem to appear mysteriously in my head—but occasionally I can trace at least some elements of a story back to its inspiration.

Marrying His Cinderella Countess was a marriage of more than my hero and heroine. I knew quite a lot about Ellie already, and I also knew just how Blake came to be injured at his club, but it took a little while to realise that the two of them belonged together. And then I went to the Romantic Novelists' Association annual conference at one of Lancaster University's rural campuses, built around an old farmstead. The lovely farmhouse had become part of the dining hall, and after several days of eating my lunch outside its front door I began to wonder who had lived there.

It was when I imagined Ellie there that the parts of this story all fitted at last. I hope you enjoy Blake and Ellie's tale—and if you are thinking about visiting Lancashire I can promise that it really doesn't rain all the time. That was 1816, which was *not* a good year for the weather!

MARRYING HIS CINDERELLA COUNTESS

Louise Allen

MILLS & BOON

Published in Great Britain 2017
by Mills & Boon, an imprint of HarperCollins*Publishers*
1 London Bridge Street, London, SE1 9GF

© 2017 Melanie Hilton

ISBN: 978-0-263-92594-4

Printed and bound in Spain
by CPI, Barcelona

Louise Allen loves immersing herself in history. She finds landscapes and places evoke the past powerfully. Venice, Burgundy and the Greek islands are favourite destinations. Louise lives on the Norfolk coast and spends her spare time gardening, researching family history or travelling in search of inspiration. Visit her at louiseallenregency.co.uk, @LouiseRegency and janeaustenslondon.com

Books by Louise Allen

Mills & Boon Historical Romance

The Herriard Family

Forbidden Jewel of India
Tarnished Amongst the Ton
Surrender to the Marquess

Lords of Disgrace

His Housekeeper's Christmas Wish
His Christmas Countess
The Many Sins of Cris de Feaux
The Unexpected Marriage of Gabriel Stone

Brides of Waterloo

A Rose for Major Flint

Stand-Alone Novels

Once Upon a Regency Christmas
'On a Winter's Eve'
Marrying His Cinderella Countess

Visit the Author Profile page
at millsandboon.co.uk for more titles.

For AJH. You know why.

Chapter One

London, May 1816

As the burning ball of the sun sinks into the shimmering azure of the Mediterranean and the soft breezes cool the heat of the day I lie in the cushioned shade of the tent, awaiting the return of the desert lord. The only sound besides the lap of the wavelets and the rustle of the palm fronds is the soft susurration of shifting sand grains like the rustle of silk over the naked limbs of...

'*S*usurration... Drat!' Ellie Lytton thrust her pen into the inkwell and glared at the words that had apparently written themselves. She opened the desk drawer and dropped the page onto a pile of similar sheets, some bearing a paragraph or two, some only a few sentences. She took a clean page, shook the surplus ink off the nib and began again.

> *I can hardly express, dear sister, how fascinating the date palm cultivation is along this part of the North African coast. It was with the greatest excitement that I spent the day viewing the hard-working local people in their colourful robes...*

'Whatever possessed me?' she muttered, with a glance upwards to the shelf above the desk.

It held a row of five identically bound volumes. The gilded lettering on the red morocco spines read: *The Young Traveller in Switzerland*, *The Youthful Explorer of the English Uplands*, *Oscar and Miranda Discover London*, *A Nursery Guide to the Countries of the World* and *The Juvenile Voyager Around the Coast of England*. All were from the pen of Mrs Bundock.

Her publisher, Messrs Broderick & Alleyn, specialists in 'Uplifting and Educational Works for Young Persons', had suggested that Oscar and Miranda might fruitfully explore the Low Countries next. Edam cheese, canals, tulip cultivation and the defeat of the French Monster would make an uplifting combination, they were sure.

Ellie, known in the world of juvenile literature as the redoubtable Mrs Bundock, had rebelled.

She yearned for heat and colour and exoticism, even if it came only second-hand from the books and prints she used for research. She would send young Oscar to North Africa, she declared, while secretly hoping that the Barbary corsairs would capture him and despatch the patronising little prig to some hideous fate.

What she *really* wanted was to write a tale of romance and passion to sell to the Minerva Press. But separating the two in her head for long enough to complete Oscar's expedition—and earn enough from it to subsidise several months of novel-writing—was proving a nightmare. No sooner had the beastly boy begun to prose on about salt pans and date palms than her imagination had filled with the image of a dark-haired, grey-eyed horseman astride a black stallion, his white robes billowing in the desert breeze.

She pushed back the strands that had sprung out of her roughly bundled topknot and jammed in some more pins.

After luncheon, she promised herself. *I will start on the sardine fisheries while the house is quiet.*

Her stepbrother, Francis, who had not returned home last night, was doubtless staying with some fellow club member, which meant that all was blissfully peaceful. With only Polly the maid in the house she might as well be alone.

The rap of the front door knocker threatened her hopes of an uninterrupted morning. Ellie said something even more unladylike than *drat*, and tried to ignore the sound. But it came again, and there was no sign of Polly coming up from below stairs. She must have slipped out to do the marketing without disturbing her mistress at work.

Ellie cast a glance at the clock. Nine o'clock, which meant that it was far too early for any kind of demanding social call, thank goodness. In fact it was probably only Francis, having forgotten his key again.

She got up, wiped her inky hands on the pinafore she wore when writing, jammed a few more hairpins into her collapsing coiffure and went out into the hall, wincing as her damaged leg complained from too much sitting. She tugged at the front door and it opened abruptly—to reveal not Francis, but a tall, dark, grey-eyed gentleman in dishevelled evening dress.

'Miss Lytton?'

'Er… Yes?'

I am dreaming.

She certainly seemed to have lost the power of coherent speech.

I have only just shut you safely in the drawer.

'I am Hainford.'

'I know,' Ellie said, aware that she sounded both gauche and abrupt. *Where are the white robes, the black stallion?* 'I have seen you before, Lord Hainford. With my stepbrother Francis.'

But not like this. Not with dark shadows under your eyes. Your bloodshot eyes. Not white to the lips. Not with your exquisite tailoring looking as though it has been used as the dog's bed. Not with blood staining—

'Your shirt… You are bleeding.'

Ellie banged the door open wide and came down the step to take his arm. It was only when she touched him that she remembered she was alone in the house. But, chaperon or no chaperon, she couldn't leave a man out there, whoever he was. Losing blood like that, he might collapse at any moment.

'Were you attacked by footpads? Do come in, for goodness' sake.' When he did not move she took his arm. 'Let me help you—lean on me. Into the drawing room, I think. It has the best light. I will dress the wound and as soon as my maid returns I will send for Dr Garnett.'

She might as well have tugged at one of the new gas lamp posts along Pall Mall.

'I am quite all right, Miss Lytton, it is merely a scratch. I must talk to you.' The Earl of Hainford, standing dripping blood on her doorstep, looked like a man contemplating his own execution, not a shockingly early social visit.

He was going to fall flat on his face in a moment, and then she would never be able to lift him. Worry made her abrupt.

'Nonsense. Come in.'

This time when she grabbed his arm he let himself be pulled unresisting over the threshold. She shouldered the door closed and guided him down the hallway, trying not to let her limping pace jar him.

'Here we are. If you sit on that upright chair over there it will be easiest.'

He went willingly enough when she pushed him into the drawing room, and she realised as he blinked at her that he was very tired as well as wounded, and possibly rather drunk. Or in the grip of a hangover.

'You *are* Miss Lytton?'

No, not drunk. He sounded perfectly sober.

Something fell from her hair as she put her head on one side to look more closely at him and she caught at it. Not a hairpin, but the quill she had misplaced that morning.

'Yes, I am Eleanor Lytton. Forgive my appearance, please. I was working.'

And why am I apologising for my old clothes and ink blots? This man turns up at a ridiculously early hour, interrupts my writing, bleeds on the best carpet... So much for fantasy. The reality of men never matches it.

'Please wait here. I will fetch water and bandages.'

The Earl had extracted himself from his coat by the time she got back. The state it was in as it lay on the carpet was probably not improved by her spilling water on it in agitation as he began to wrestle with his shirt.

He is wounded, she reminded herself. *This is not the moment to be missish about touching a man's garments, let alone a man.*

'Let me help.'

It was probably an indication of the state he was in that he sat down abruptly and allowed her to pull the shirt over his head. She took a sharp breath at the sight of the furrow in his flesh that came from below the waistband of his breeches at the front and angled up over his ribs to just below his armpit on the right-hand side. It was not deep, but it was bleeding sluggishly and looked exceedingly sore as it cut across the firmly muscled torso.

Ellie dropped the shirt, then picked it up again and shook it out, pulling the fabric tight as she held it up to the light.

'That is a bullet wound in your side.' She had never seen one before, but what else could make a hole like that?

He nodded, hissing between his teeth as he explored the raw track with his fingertips.

'But there is no hole in your shirt. And the wound starts below the waistband of your equally undamaged breeches. You were shot when you were *naked*?'

Hainford looked at her, his eyebrows raised, presumably in shock at a lady saying *breeches* and *naked* without fainting. 'Yes. Could you pass me some of that bandage and then perhaps leave the room so I can deal with this?'

He gestured downwards. The bullet must have grazed his hip bone, and the chafing of his evening breeches, even if they *were* knitted silk, must be exceedingly painful. He would certainly need to take them off to dress the wound. There was already far too much of the Earl of Hainford on display, and she realised she was staring in appalled curiosity at the way the light furring of dark hair on his chest arrowed down and...

'Here.' Ellie pushed both basin and bandages towards him. 'Call me when you are decent—I mean, *ready*—and I will bring you a clean shirt.'

She was not afraid of the sight of blood, but she had absolutely no desire to get any closer to that bared body, let alone touch it, even though as a budding novelist she ought to know about such matters. Writing about them was one thing, and fantasising was another, but experiencing them in real life...

No.

She closed the door behind her and leaned back against the panels while she got her breathing under some kind of control. The man she had glimpsed a few times with Francis—the one who had become the hero of her future novel and the disturber of her rest—was in her drawing room. Correction: was half-naked and injured in her drawing room.

How had he been shot like that? By a cuckolded husband catching him *in flagrante* with his wife, presumably. She could think of no other reason for a man to be wounded while naked. If it had been an accident in his own home his servants would have come to his aid.

She could visualise the scene quite clearly. A screaming female on the bed, rumpled sheets, Lord Hainford scrambling bare-limbed from the midst of the bedding—her imagination skittered around too much detail—the infuriated husband brandishing a pistol. How very disillusioning. One did not expect to have one's fantasy arrive on the doorstep in reality, very much in the flesh, and prove to be so sordidly fallible. Her desert lord was, in reality, a hung-over adulterer.

And, naturally, life being what it was, fantasies did not have the tact and good timing to arrive when one was looking one's best. Not, she admitted, pulling a rueful face at her reflection in the hall mirror, that her best was much to write home about, and nor did she actually want to attract such a man. Not in real life.

Ellie had few illusions. After all, at the age of twenty-five she had been told often enough that she was plain, gawky and *'difficult'* to recognise it was the truth. And now she was lame as well. A disappointment to everyone, given how attractive Mama had been, with her dark brown hair and petite, fragile appearance. Ellie took after her father's side of the family, people would tell her with a pitying sigh.

Her best gown was three seasons old and she had re-trimmed her bonnets to the point where they were more added ribbons and flowers than original straw. Her annual allowance, such as it was, went on paper, ink and library subscriptions, and her earnings from Messrs Broderick & Alleyn seemed to be swallowed up in the housekeeping.

None of which mattered, of course, because she was not out in Society, lived most of her life in her head, and had a circle of friends and acquaintances that encompassed a number of like-minded and similarly dressed women, the vicar and several librarians. Giving up the social struggle was restful...being invisible was safe.

It was Francis who had the social life, and a much larger allowance—most of which went, so far as she could tell, on club memberships, his bootmaker and attempting to emulate his hero, Lord Hainford, in all matters of dress and entertainment.

She did not enquire any more deeply about just what that 'entertainment' involved.

At which point in her musings the door she was leaning on opened and she staggered backwards, landing with a thud against the bare chest of the nobleman in question.

He gave a muffled yelp of pain as Ellie twisted round, made a grab for balance and found herself with one hand on his shoulder and one palm flat on his chest, making the interesting discovery that a man's nipples tightened into hard nubs when touched.

She recoiled back into the doorway, hands behind her back. 'I will fetch you a shirt.'

'Thank you, but there is no need. I will put mine back on. Please, listen to me, Miss Lytton, I need to talk to you—'

'With a shirt on. And not one covered in blood,' she snapped, furious with someone. Herself, presumably.

As she negotiated the stairs to Francis's bedchamber she wondered what on earth Lord Hainford could want to talk to her about. An apology was certainly due for arriving in this state, although probably he had expected Francis to be at home—not to have the door opened by some idiot female who was reduced to dithering incompetence by the sight of a muscular chest.

She snatched a shirt out of the drawer and went back down again. Hainford got to his feet as she came in, the bandages white against his skin, the dark hair curling over the edges.

'Here, that should fit.' Ellie thrust the shirt into his hands and turned her back. She closed her eyes for good measure.

'I am respectable again,' he said after several minutes of flapping cloth and hissing breath.

Ellie turned back to find the Earl once more dressed, his neckcloth loosely knotted, his bedraggled coat pulled on over the clean shirt. His own shirt was bundled up, the blood out of sight. 'Thank you,' he added. 'Your maid—'

'Is still not back. She cannot be much longer and then she will go for the doctor.'

Something in her bristled defensively at his closeness and she gave herself a brisk talking-to. He was a gentleman, and surely trustworthy. And he was hurt, so she should be showing some womanly nurturing sympathy. At least the Vicar would certainly say so.

Her feelings, although definitely womanly, were not tending towards nurturing…

'There is no need. The wound has stopped bleeding. I am concerned that you are alone in the house with me.'

You are concerned?

'You think I require a chaperon, Lord Hainford?' Ellie used the back of the chair as a support and sat down carefully, gesturing at the empty chair. 'Or perhaps that you do?' Attack was always safer than showing alarm or weakness.

'No, to both.' He ran his hand through his hair, his mouth grim as he seemed to search for words. 'I have bad news for you, and I think you will need the support of another woman.'

'My maid will soon be here,' she said. Then what he had said finally penetrated. 'Bad news?'

That could only mean one thing. Her parents and her stepfather were dead and there was no one else, only her stepbrother.

'Francis?' Her voice sounded quite calm and collected.

'Sir Francis…there was an accident. At the club.'

'He is injured?'

No, if he was I would have been called to him, or he would have been brought here.

She seemed to be reasoning very clearly, as though this was not real—simply a puzzle on paper to be solved. 'He is dead, isn't he? How? Did you kill him? Was it a duel?'

Over a woman?

That was all she could think of, given that Hainford had been naked when he was shot himself.

'No. I did not shoot him. It was an accident. Someone was shooting at me, and Francis was standing at my back.'

'And you had no clothes on,' she said, her voice flat.

She must have fallen asleep over her work—this had all the characteristics of a bad dream. Certainly it made no sense whatsoever.

'Which club was this?'

Perhaps *club* was a euphemism for brothel? Or something else—something not legal. She read the newspapers, had some glimmering of what went on between certain men, but she hardly knew how to ask.

'The Adventurers' Club in Piccadilly.'

A perfectly respectable gentleman's club, then. Not a... What did they call them? A molly house—that was it. It would not completely surprise her if Francis had gone to one—out of curiosity, if nothing else—but this man? Surely not. Although what did she know?

Her silence was worrying the Earl, judging by his expression and the way he leaned forward to look into her face, but she was not sure how she was expected to act, how she should feel. Perhaps this was shock.

'Look, let me fetch you some brandy. It is dreadful news to take in.' He was halfway to his feet again when the door opened.

'Miss Lytton, I'm back! Oh!' Polly stood staring, her arms full of loosely wrapped parcels. An onion dropped to the floor and rolled to Ellie's feet.

'Polly, this is Lord Hainford and I believe he needs a glass of brandy.'

'*I* do not.'

He was on the verge of snapping now—a man at the end of his tether. She should have wept and had the vapours. Then he could have produced a handkerchief, patted her hand, said, *There, there* meaninglessly. He would have felt more comfortable doing that, she was sure.

'Fetch your mistress a cup of tea,' he ordered.

'And brandy for Lord Hainford. The hair of the dog might be helpful,' Ellie suggested mildly.

Yes, this was a bad dream. Although…could one faint in a dream? The room was beginning to spin and close in…

She closed her eyes and took a deep, steadying breath. Fainting would not help. When she opened them again Lord Hainford was still there, frowning at her. The crumpled shirt was still at his feet. Francis had still not come home.

'This really is not a dream, is it?' she asked.

'No. I am afraid not.' *Simply a nightmare.*

Blake saw the colour flood back into Miss Lytton's cheeks with profound relief. Things were bad enough without a fainting woman on his hands and, ungallant as it might seem, he had no desire to haul this Long Meg up from the floor.

Her figure went up and down, with the emphasis on *up*, and showed little interest in anything but the mildest in-and-out. Even so, his ribs had suffered enough, and lifting plain women into his arms held no appeal.

He studied the pale oval of her face, dusted with a spectacular quantity of freckles that no amount of Lotion of Denmark, or even lemon juice, would ever be able to subdue. Her hair was a bird's nest—a flyaway mass of middling brown curls, ineptly secured with pins. The wide hazel eyes, their irises dark and dilated with shock, were probably her best feature. Her nose was certainly rather too long. And there was the limp... But at least she had managed not to swoon.

The girl came back with a tea tray and he gestured abruptly for her to pour. 'Put sugar in your mistress's cup.'

'I do not take sugar.'

'For the shock.' He took a cup himself and gulped it sugarless, grateful for the warmth in his empty, churning gut.

The maid went and sat in a corner of the room, hands folded in her lap. He could feel her gaze boring into him.

Miss Lytton lifted her cup with a hand that

shook just a little, drank, replaced it in the saucer with a sharp click and looked at him.

'Tell me what happened.'

Thank heavens she was not some fluffy little chit who had dissolved into the vapours. Still, there was time yet for that…

'I was at the Adventurers' last night, playing cards with Lord Anterton and Sir Peter Carew and a man called Crosse. I was winning heavily— mainly against Crosse, who is not a good loser and is no friend of mine. We were all drinking.'

Blake tried to edit the story as he went—make it somehow suitable for a lady to hear without actually lying to her. He couldn't tell her that the room had smelled of sweat and alcohol and candlewax and excitement. That Anterton had been in high spirits because an elderly relative had died and left him a tidy sum, and he and Carew had been joking and needling Crosse all evening over some incident at the French House—a fancy brothel where the three of them had been the night before.

Blake had been irritated, he remembered now, and had wished they would concentrate on the game.

He had just raked in a double handful of chips and banknotes and vowels from the centre of the table and called for a new pack and a fresh bottle

when Francis Lytton had come up behind him—
another irritation.

'Your stepbrother appeared, most agitated, and
said he wanted to talk to me immediately. I was on
a winning streak, and I certainly did not intend to
stop. I told him he could walk home with me afterwards and we would talk all he wanted to then.'

Miss Lytton bit her lip, her brow furrowed.
'Agitated?'

'Or worried. I do not know which. I did not pay
too much attention, I am afraid.'

'You were drunk,' she observed coolly.

It was a shock to be spoken to in that way by a
woman and, despite his uneasy sense of responsibility, the flat statement stung.

'I was mellow—we all were. And we were in
the middle of a game in which I was winning con-
sistently—Lytton should have seen that it was a
bad time to interrupt. We began to play with the
new pack. Crosse lost heavily to me again, then
started to shout that I was cheating, that I must
have cards in my cuffs, up my sleeves. That I had
turned away to talk to your stepbrother in order
to conceal them.'

*That red face, that wet mouth, those furious,
incoherent accusations.*

The man had scrabbled at the cards, sending
counters flying, wine glasses tipping.

'Cheat! Sharper!'

Everyone had stopped their own games, people had come across, staring…

'I told him to withdraw his accusations. So did the others. He wouldn't back down—just kept ranting. It seems he was on the brink of ruin and that this bout of losses had tipped him over the edge. He was so pathetic I didn't want to have to call him out, so I stripped off my coat, tossed it to him to look at. He still accused me of hiding cards. I took off my waistcoat, my shirt. Then, when he overturned the table shouting that I had aces in my breeches, I took those off as well. Everything, in fact. He'd made me furious. Francis stood behind me, picking things up like a confounded valet. People were laughing…jeering at Crosse.'

He paused, sorting out the events through the brandy fug in his head, trying to be careful what he told her.

Everyone had been staring, and then Anterton had laughed and pointed at Blake's wedding tackle, made some admiring remark about size. *'Hainford's hung like a bull!'* he'd shouted. Or had it been a mule?

He had laughed at Crosse.

'Not like your little winkle-picker, eh, Crosse? The tarts wouldn't laugh at his tackle like they did at yours last night at the French House—would they, Crosse?'

'Crosse fumbled in his pocket, dropped something, and went down on his knees, groping for it. Then I saw it was a pistol. He was shaking with rage.'

I thought I was going to die—stark naked in the wreckage of a card game.

As the club secretary had pushed his way to the front of the crowd Blake could recall wondering vaguely if you could be blackballed for being killed in the club like that.

Conduct unbecoming...

'Crosse pulled the trigger. The thing was angled upwards, so the bullet scored the track you've seen across my ribs and hit Francis, who was still standing behind me.'

Miss Lytton gave a short gasp, cut off by a hand pressed to her mouth. She was so white that the freckles across her nose and cheeks stood out as if someone had thrown a handful of bran at her.

'He really is dead?' she managed.

Very. You don't live with a hole like that in you.

'It must have been instant. He will have felt a blow to the chest, then nothing.' He thought that was true—hoped that it was. Certainly by the time he'd knelt down, Lytton's head supported on his knees, the man had been gone.

'Where is he now?'

She was still white, her voice steady. It was the unnatural control of shock, he guessed, although she didn't seem to be the hysterical type in any case. She had dealt with a bleeding man on her doorstep calmly enough. An unusual young lady.

'At the club. There was a doctor there—one of the members. We took him to a bedchamber, did what was necessary.'

They had stripped off the wreckage of Lytton's clothes, got him cleaned up and dressed in someone's spare nightshirt and sent for a woman to lay him out decently before any of his family saw him.

'I have his watch, his pocketbook and so on, all safe.'

'I see.'

Miss Lytton's voice was as colourless as her skin, and that seemed to have been pulled back savagely, revealing fine cheekbones but emphasising the long nose and firm chin unbecomingly.

'He must come here, of course. Can you arrange that?'

He could—and he would. And he would try and do something about that mass of blood-soaked papers with a hole through the middle that had been stuffed into Lytton's breast pocket. There was no way he could hand those back as they were.

'Certainly. It is the least I can do.'

The dowdy nobody of a woman opposite him raised her wide hazel eyes and fixed him with an aloof stare.

'I would say that is so. If you had listened to your friend when he was obviously anxious about something, instead of drunkenly goading that man Crosse, then Francis would not be dead now. *Would* he, my lord?'

Chapter Two

Her hostility had hit home—visibly. Ellie suspected that if he had been himself, alert and not in pain, Lord Hainford would have betrayed nothing, but she saw the colour come up over his cheekbones and the bloodshot grey eyes narrow.

'If your brother had not come to the club, yes, he would be alive now, Miss Lytton.'

'My *step*brother Francis is...*was*...the son of my mother's second husband, Sir Percival Lytton. I took his name when she remarried.'

She could hardly recall her own father, the Honourable Frederick Trewitt, an abrupt man who had died when she was eight. Her mother's remarriage had given them much-needed financial stability, although Sir Percival had shown little interest in his stepdaughter at first—so plain and quiet, where her mother had been vivid and attractive.

Not at first.

As for Francis, three years her senior, he had ignored her until, his father and stepmother dead, he had needed a housekeeper.

She had felt no affection for him, waiting for him to turn out like his father, but as time had passed and he'd shown her nothing but indifference she had begun to relax—although never to the point of leaving her bedchamber door unlocked.

The use she could be to her stepbrother had given her the only status that Society allowed a plain young woman of very moderate means and no connections—that of respectable poor relation.

'You were close, of course. This must be a dreadful shock for you...a great loss.' The Earl had reined in his irritation and was clearly ransacking his meagre store of conventional platitudes. 'I quite understand that you are distressed.'

'If my stepbrother had removed himself to some remote fastness and I had never seen him again I would not have shed a single tear, my lord,' she said. 'That does not mean I do not grieve the fact that he met his end in such sordid circumstances, thanks to someone else's selfish neglect.'

She would have felt pity for *any* man killed like that, let alone a relative.

'Madam, neither the place nor the circumstances were sordid, and Lytton was in a club where he might have safely passed the time with any number of acquaintances while he waited for me to be free.'

Hainford got to his feet and regarded her with something very like hauteur.

'That he chose to insinuate himself into the middle of a fracas was entirely his choice, and the result was a regrettable accident. Unless you have an undertaker in mind I will engage a respectable one on your behalf. I will also establish how the Coroner wishes to proceed and keep you informed. Good day to you.'

Polly scrambled to reach the front door before he did, and came back a moment later clutching a small rectangle of card. 'He left this, Miss Lytton.'

'Put it down over there on my desk, please. I know perfectly well who he is.'

She had made it her business to find out the identity of the grey-eyed man whom Francis had idolised. William Blakestone Pencarrow, third Earl Hainford, was twenty-eight, owned lands in Hampshire, Yorkshire and Northamptonshire, a London townhouse of some magnificence in Berkeley Square and a stable of prime bloodstock.

He was also in possession of thick black hair, elegantly cut, a commanding nose, rather too large for handsomeness, an exceptionally stubborn chin and eyes that were beautiful even when bloodshot. His shoulders were broad, his muscles, as she was now in a position to affirm, superb, and he easily topped Francis's five feet eleven inches.

To Francis, silently worshipping, he had seemed a god—a *non-pareil* of style, taste and breeding who must be copied as closely as possible, whatever the cost.

Altogether Hainford had seemed the perfect hero for her book. It did not matter in the slightest that in real life he had proved to be impatient, arrogant, self-centred and shameless.

Something fell onto her clasped hands. She looked down at the fat drop of water that ran down to her wrist.

Poor Francis, she thought, feeling sympathy for her stepbrother for the first time in her life. He deserved something more than one tear from her. He deserved that she exert herself for this final time for his comfort and dignity. He hadn't been able to help being his father's son, and probably hadn't been able to help being insensitive and foolish either.

'Polly, please see that the front room is cleaned thoroughly for when the…for when the master is brought home. The blinds and drapes must be closed in all the rooms. And then we will look at mourning clothes.'

* * *

Gradually the shock wore off. In a strange way it was a relief to feel loss as well as anger, and to cling to the rituals of death that Society prescribed. The black ribbons on the door knocker, the drawn blinds, the hasty refurbishment of the mourning blacks last worn when her stepfather had died—all occupied Ellie's time.

A letter had arrived from the Earl, informing her that the inquest had been arranged for the next day. It seemed surprisingly prompt to Ellie, and she was grateful for the Coroner's efficiency until she realised that it was probably due to Hainford's influence.

The undertaker he had selected called on her, sombre and solemn as he delicately discussed the funeral details.

'The Earl did not want you to be troubled with any tiresome detail, Miss Lytton.'

'How kind,' Ellie said thinly.

Managing, autocratic, domineering... Or perhaps he is feeling guilty, as he should.

The day of the funeral passed in a blur, until finally she was able to join Mr Rampion, the family solicitor, in Francis's study. He seemed ill at ease—but perhaps he rarely dealt with women. He stood when she entered the study, as did the man sitting to one side of the desk.

'Lord Hainford is here at my request, Miss

Lytton. After he spoke to me earlier I thought it advisable.'

Tight-lipped, Ellie sat down, fighting against her resentment at the intrusion. No doubt it would all become clear. Something to do with the inquest, perhaps. She needed to be calm and businesslike.

'Very well. Mr Rampion, if you would proceed.'

'The will, as it stands, holds no surprises in its terms,' the solicitor said, still looking inexplicably unhappy. 'The baronetcy and the entailed land pass to Sir Francis's cousin, Mr James Lytton, who resides in Scotland. There are bequests to family retainers, and the residue of the estate to you, Miss Lytton. Sir Francis had, as you know, under the terms of his father's will, been the sole trustee of your investments.'

'Well, I suppose it will not make any difference that I have no trustee now. I am hardly a wealthy woman with complex affairs to control. I assume I will receive my quarterly allowance as I always have.'

Mr Rampion took off his spectacles, polished them, put them back, cleared his throat. 'That is why Lord Hainford is here. Perhaps you should produce the documents, my lord...'

Blake took the wedge of papers from his pocket. Jonathan, his secretary, had washed the pages, and that had got the worst of the blood out, leaving a pencilled scrawl visible on the wrinkled paper. He had ironed each sheet, smoothing out the ragged edges in the centre where the bullet had passed, and had transcribed what could be made out of Sir Francis Lytton's frantic calculations.

'These notes were in your stepbrother's breast pocket, Miss Lytton.' He felt like a brute for being so direct, but there was no way of edging delicately around this.

She went pale as she took in the significance of the damage and made no move to reach for them. 'What do they concern?'

'I believe this is what Lytton wanted to talk to me about. He had, it seems, made major investments in a canal scheme near the Sussex coast. I knew of it—a hopelessly overblown and oversold scheme that has now crashed. The stock is worthless.'

'Why would he have wanted to speak to *you* about it, Lord Hainford?'

She had not realised at all what this meant. He could see that. She was still puzzling over the detail.

'He knew I had myself made a success of a series of investments in various canal schemes. I think Lytton had come to suspect that something was very wrong with the one he had put money into, and wanted to ask my opinion.'

'And if he had spoken to you? Would it have made any difference?'

Miss Lytton was leaning forward. Hearing the question in her voice, watching the thoughts so transparently obvious on her face, Blake realised that this was an intelligent woman who was striving to understand what had happened. Curiosity animated her face and he almost revised his opinion of her as wan-faced and uninteresting. *Almost.*

'If he had sold the next morning he would have made a small profit or just about broken even. But by the close of business that day things had fallen apart.'

'I see.'

She met his gaze, her hazel eyes cool and judgmental. She did not have to say the words—if he had left the card game, spoken to her stepbrother there and then, not only would Lytton still be alive but he might have salvaged his investment by making immediate sales the next day.

Now it only remained to deliver the really bad news and she would go from despising him to hating him.

The solicitor spoke before Blake could. 'I am afraid it is worse than that, Miss Lytton. It appears that not only did Sir Francis invest all his available resources in this scheme, but also yours.'

'Mine? But he could not do that.'

'He could,' Blake said. 'And he did. He had complete control of your finances. Doubtless he thought it was for the best.'

She took a deep, shuddering breath, her hands clenched together tightly in her lap, and Blake braced himself for the tears.

'I am ruined,' she said flatly.

It was not a question and there were no tears.

'The investments have gone, and this house, as you know, is rented,' Rampion said. 'There is nothing remaining of your liquid assets—nothing to inherit from your stepbrother. However, you do own Carndale Farm in Lancashire. It was part of your mother's dowry, if you recall, and tied up in ways that prevented Sir Francis disposing of. It is safe. That is nothing has been sold and it still brings in rents…although a mere two hundred a year.'

'Lancashire,' she murmured faintly. And then, more strongly, 'But there *is* a house?'

Any other lady would have been in a dead faint by now, or in strong hysterics, Blake thought. Certainly she would not be wrestling with the essentials of the situation as this woman was. It occurred to him fleetingly that Eleanor Lytton would be a good person to have by one's side in an emergency.

'Yes, a house—although it has been uninhabited since the last tenant left a year ago. The farm itself—the land—is leased out separately.'

'I see.' She visibly straightened her back and lifted her shoulders. 'Well, then, the furniture and Francis's possessions must be sold to pay any remaining debts. Hopefully that will also cover his bequests to the staff. I will move to Lancashire as soon as possible.'

'But, Miss Lytton, an unmarried lady requires a chaperon,' the solicitor interjected.

'I will have a maid. I think I can afford her wages,' she said indifferently. 'That must suffice. My unchaperoned state is hardly likely to concern the Patronesses of Almack's, now, is it? Perhaps we can meet again tomorrow, Mr Rampion. Will you be able to give me an assessment of the outstanding liabilities and assets by then?'

She stood and they both came to their feet.

'I think I must leave you now, gentlemen.'

She limped from the room, a surprisingly impressive figure in her dignity, despite her faded blacks and the scattering of hairpins that fell to the floor from her appalling coiffure. The door closed quietly behind her and in the silence Blake thought he heard one gasping sob, abruptly cut off. Then nothing.

'Hell,' Blake said, sitting down again, against all his instincts to go and try to comfort her. He was the last person she would want to see.

He was trying his hardest not to feel guilty about any of this—he was not a soothsayer, after all, and he could hardly have foreseen that bizarre accident and its consequences—but his actions had certainly been the catalyst.

'Indeed,' the older man re-joined, tapping his papers into order. 'Life is not kind to impoverished gentlewomen, I fear. Especially those whose worth is more in their character than their looks, shall we say?'

'Why does Miss Lytton limp?' Blake asked.

'A serious fall three years ago, I understand. There was a complex fracture and it seems that she did permanent damage to her leg. Her stepfather suffered a fatal seizure upon finding her. I imagine you will want to be on your way, my lord? I am grateful for your efforts to make these notes legible. I can see I have some work to do in order to present Miss Lytton with a full picture tomorrow.'

'I will leave you to it, sir.'

Blake shook hands with the solicitor and went out, braced for another encounter with Miss Lytton. But the hallway held nothing more threatening than scurrying domestics, and he let himself out with a twinge of guilty relief.

'That is the last of the paperwork concerning Francis Lytton's death.' Jonathan Wilton, Blake's confidential secretary, placed a sheaf of documents in front of him.

Blake left the papers where they lay and pushed one hand through his hair. 'Lord, that was a messy business. It is just a mercy that the Coroner managed the jury with a firm hand and they brought a verdict of accidental death. Imagine if we were having to cope with Crosse's hanging. As it is, he's skulking in Somerset—and good riddance.'

Jonathan gave a grunt of agreement. He was Blake's illegitimate half-brother—an intelligent, hard-working man a few months younger than Blake, who might easily have passed for a full sibling.

Blake had acknowledged him, and would have done more, but Jon had insisted on keeping his mother's name and earning his own way in the world. It had been all Blake could do to get him to accept a university education from him. He had gone to Cambridge, Blake to Oxford, and then Jon had allowed himself to be persuaded into helping Blake deal with the business of his earldom.

In public Jon was punctiliously formal. In private they behaved like brothers. 'Lytton was a damn nuisance,' he remarked now.

'What I ever did to deserve being a role model for him, I have no idea.' Blake made himself stop fidgeting with the Coroner's report. 'He irritated me. That was why I was so short with him that evening, if you want the truth. I didn't want him hanging round me at the club.'

'Not your fault,' Jon observed with a shrug as he slid off the desk and picked up the paperwork.

'I could have talked to him—made him see he was acting unwisely.'

He couldn't shake an unreasonable feeling of guilt about the incident, and Miss Lytton's courage in the face of bereavement and financial ruin had made him feel even worse. He did not like feeling guilty, always did his rather casual best not to do anything that might justify the sensation, and he managed, on the whole, to avoid thinking about the last time he had felt real guilt over a woman.

Felicity...

The woman he had driven to disaster. The woman he had not realised he loved until too late.

As usual he slammed a mental door on the memory, refused to let it make him feel...*anything*.

There was a knock on the study door. Blake jammed his quill back into the standish. 'Come in!'

'The morning post, my lord.'

The footman passed a loaded salver to Jon, who dumped the contents onto the desk, pulled up a chair and began to sort through it.

He broke the seal on one letter, then passed it across after a glance at the signature. 'From Miss Lytton.'

Plain paper, black ink, a strong, straightforward hand. Blake read the single sheet. Then he read it again. No, he was not seeing things.

'Hell's teeth—the blasted woman wants me to take her to Lancashire!'

'What?' Jon caught the sheet as Blake sent it spinning across the blotter to him. 'She holds you responsible for her present predicament...loan of a carriage...escort. *Escort?* Is she pretty?'

'No, she is *not* pretty—not that it would make any difference.'

I hope.

'Eleanor Lytton is a plain woman who dresses like a drab sparrow. Her hair appears never to have seen a hairdresser and she limps.' He gave her a moment's thought, then added for fairness, 'However, she has guts and she appears to be intelligent—except for her insistence on blaming *me* for her stepbrother's death. Her temper is uncertain, and she has no tact whatsoever. I am going to call on her and put a stop to this nonsense.'

Blake got to his feet and yanked at the bell-pull. 'Lancashire! She must be even more eccentric than she looks. Why the devil would I want to go to Lancashire, of all places? Why *should* I?'

'The sea bathing at Blackpool is reckoned quite good—if one overlooks the presence of half the manufacturers of Manchester at the resort,' Jon said with a grin, ducking with the skill of long practice as Blake threw a piece of screwed-up paper at his head.

Chapter Three

'Lord Hainford, Miss Lytton,' Polly announced.
So he had come.

Ellie had known from the moment the idea had occurred to her that it was outrageous. In fact she had been certain he would simply throw her letter into the fire. But she had lain awake half the night worrying about getting herself and her few possessions to Lancashire, about how she could afford it, and how she would probably have to dismiss Polly in order to do so.

The loan of a carriage would save enough to keep her maid for two months—perhaps long enough for her to raise some more money and finish her book—and an escort would save them both untold trouble and aggravation on the road. She had written the letter and sent it to be delivered before she'd had time for second thoughts.

'Good morning, my lord. Polly, I am sure his lordship will feel quite safe if you sit over there.'

'Good morning. I feel perfectly safe, thank you, Miss Lytton. Confused, yes—unsafe, no.' The Earl sat down when she did so, and regarded her with a distinct lack of amusement.

He looks like an elegant displeased raven, with his sharply tailored dark clothes, his black hair, his decided nose, she thought.

There had been no apparent soreness when he sat, so presumably the bullet wound was healing well.

'Confused?' Ellie pushed away the memory of the feel of his naked torso under her palm and folded her hands neatly in her lap.

'I am confused by the reference to Lancashire in your letter, Miss Lytton.'

She had been right—he was not going to be reasonable about his obligations. Not that he would see it that way, of course. Probably he still did not recognise his responsibility in the way Francis had behaved. But why, then, had he called? A curt note of refusal or complete silence—that was what she had expected.

'My lord—'

'Call me Hainford, please, Miss Lytton. I feel as though I am at a meeting being addressed if you keep my-lording me.'

I will not blush. And if I do it will be from irritation, not embarrassment.

'Hainford. My brother was your devoted disciple. He spent money he could ill afford copying your lifestyle and your clothing. He invested money he most definitely could *not* afford, and some he had no moral right to, in a scheme inspired by your dealings. And then, when he came to you for help and advice, you turned your back on him and neglected your friend for the sake of a card game.'

'Francis was an adult. And an acquaintance, not a friend. I never advised him on his clothing, nor his horses or his clubs, and most certainly not on his investments.' His eyes narrowed. 'Are you implying an improper relationship, by any chance, Miss Lytton?'

'Improper?'

It took her a heartbeat to realise what he was referring to, and another to be amazed that he would even *hint* at such a thing to a lady. Probably he did not regard her as a lady—which was dispiriting, if hardly unexpected.

'Polly, kindly go and make tea.' Ellie got up and closed the door firmly behind the maid. 'No, I am not implying anything improper, and it is most *improper* of you to raise such a possibility to me.'

'I am attempting to find a motive for your blatant hostility towards me, Miss Lytton, that is all.'

'Motive? I have none. Nor am I hostile. I merely

point out the facts that are at the root of my disapproval of your behaviour.'

Attack. Do not let him see how much you want him to help.

It had been dangerously addictive, the way he had stepped in after Francis's death and arranged matters. She should have too much pride to want him to do so again. And, besides, the less she saw of him, the better. He was far too attractive for a plain woman's peace of mind—unless one had a bizarre wish to be dismissed and ignored. There was this single thing that she asked of him and that would be all.

'Why do you attempt to recruit me to escort you the length of the country if you disapprove of me so much?'

He sounded genuinely intrigued, as though she was an interesting puzzle to be solved. The dark brows drawn together, the firm, unsmiling mouth should not be reassuring, and yet somehow they were. He was listening to her.

'I am impoverished thanks to my stepbrother's foolishness and your failure to him as a... as an acquaintance and fellow club member. To reach Lancashire—where I must now be exiled— I face a long, expensive and wearisome journey by stage coach. The least you can do is to make some amends by lending me your carriage and your escort.'

'Do you *really* expect me to say yes?' Hainford demanded.

He was still on his feet from when she had got up to close the door and, tall, dark and frowning, he took up far too much space. Also, it seemed, most of the air in the room.

'No, I do not,' Ellie confessed. 'I thought you would throw the letter on the fire. I am astonished to see you here this morning.' She shrugged. 'I had lain awake all night, worrying about getting to Carndale. The idea came to me at dawn and I felt better for writing the letter. I had nothing to lose by sending it, so I did.'

'You really are the most extraordinary creature,' Hainford said.

Ellie opened her mouth to deliver a stinging retort and then realised that his lips were actually curved in a faint smile. The frown had gone too, as though he had puzzled her out.

'So, not only am I a *creature*, and an *extraordinary* one, but I am also a source of amusement to you? Are you this offensive to *every* lady you encounter, or only the plain and unimportant ones?'

'I fear I *am* finding amusement in this,' he confessed. 'I feel like a hound being attacked by a fieldmouse.'

He scrubbed one hand down over his face as though to straighten his expression, but his mouth, when it was revealed again, was still twitching dangerously near a smile.

'I had no intention of being offensive, merely of matching your frankness.'

He made no reference to the *plain and unimportant* remark. Wise of him.

'You are unlike any lady I have ever come across, and yet you are connected—if distantly— to a number of highly respectable and titled families. Did you not have a come-out? Were you never presented? What have your family been doing that you appear to have no place in Society?'

'Why, in other words, have I no good gowns, no Society manners and no inclination to flutter my eyelashes meekly and accept what gentlemen say?'

'All of that.'

Lord Hainford sat down again, crossed one beautifully breeched leg over the other and leaned back. He was definitely smiling now. It seemed that provided she was not actually accusing him of anything he found her frankness refreshing.

You are entirely delicious to look at, my lord, and lethally dangerous when you smile.

'If you want it in a nutshell: no parents, no money and no inclination to become either a victim of circumstances or a poor relation, hanging on the coat-tails of some distant and reluctant relative.'

'A concise summary.' He steepled his fingers and contemplated their tips. 'My secretary will tell me I am insane even to contemplate what you ask of me...'

'But?' Ellie held her breath.

He was going to say yes.

Hainford looked up, the expression in his grey eyes either amused or resigned, or perhaps a little of both. 'But I will do it. I will convey you to Lancashire.' His gaze dropped to his fingertips again. 'If, that is, we do not find ourselves compromised as a result.'

'Polly will come with us.'

'A maid? Not sufficient.'

'Lord Hainford, do you think I am plotting to get a husband out of this?'

He looked at her sharply.

'Because I am not looking for one—and even if I were I have more pride than to try and entrap a man this way. A maid is a perfectly adequate chaperon. No one knows me in Society. I could be observed in your carriage by half the Patronesses of Almack's, a complete set of duchesses and most of the House of Lords and *still* be unrecognised. I can be your widowed distant cousin,' she added, her imagination beginning to fill out the details of her scheme. 'A poor relation you are escorting out of the goodness of your heart.'

His mouth twisted wryly.

Yes, she realised, he *had* been wary that she was out to entrap him. From what she had heard he was exceedingly popular with the ladies, and had managed to evade the ties of matrimony only with consummate skill.

'I could wear my black veils and call you Cousin Blake,' Ellie suggested helpfully.

A laugh escaped him—an unwilling snort of amusement that banished his suspicions—and something inside her caught for a moment.

'You should write lurid novels for a living, Miss Lytton. You would be excellent at it.'

'You think so?' she asked eagerly. 'Oh, I see. You are teasing me,' she added, deflated, when he shook his head.

'What? You would aspire to be one of those ink-spattered blue stockings, or an hysterical female author turning out Gothic melodramas?'

It seemed he had forgotten the quill in her hair and the ink spots on her pinafore when they had first met—clues that might well have given her away. But then, Lord Hainford had had other things on his mind on that occasion.

'No, I have no desire to be an hysterical female author,' she said tightly, biting back all the other things she itched to say.

Ranting about male prejudice was not going to help matters. Hainford's reading matter was probably confined to Parliamentary reports, the sporting papers, his investments and Greek and Latin classics.

That little stab of awareness, or attraction, or whatever it was, vanished. 'When do you wish to set out?'

'How long do you need?' he countered. 'Would six days give you enough time?'

'That would be perfect. Thank you... Cousin Blake.'

He stood. 'I will be in touch about the details, Cousin Eleanor.'

'Ellie,' she corrected, rising also.

'I think not. Ellie is not right for the character you will be playing in this little drama. Eleanor is serious, a little mournful. You will drift wistfully about under your floating black veils, the victim of nameless sadness...'

So what is Ellie?

She did not dare ask—he would probably be happy to explain in unflattering detail.

'Tell me, Cousin Blake, do you make a habit of reading Minerva Press novels or do you have a natural bent for the Gothic yourself?'

'The latter, Cousin Eleanor. Definitely the latter. Dark closets, skeletons...' There was no amusement in his eyes.

'Will you not wait for tea?' She rose, gestured towards the door.

'I think not.'

He caught her hand in his and lifted it to his lips, his breath warm as he did not quite touch his mouth to her fingers, which were rigid in his light grip.

The door opened and Polly edged in, a tea tray balanced against one hip.

'Lord Hainford is just leaving, Polly. Put the tray down and see him out, if you please.'

And leave me to recover from having my hand almost kissed and from the knowledge that I am about to spend several days in the company of such a very dangerous man.

She would be quite safe, she told herself. Polly would be with her, would sleep in her room every night, and an earl would stop at respectable inns—inns with locks on the bedchamber doors.

The problem was, he was not the danger—*she* was. Or rather her foolish imagination, which yearned for what, quite obviously, she could never have.

Ellie stood at the foot of the stairs and regarded the sum total of her personal belongings. One trunk with clothes and books, one hat box containing two hats, one valise with overnight necessities, one portable writing slope. And one umbrella. Nothing so frivolous as a parasol.

Polly had almost as much luggage.

Somewhere upstairs an auctioneer was going

round with Mr Rampion, making an inventory and sorting the furniture into lots. The solicitor had managed to locate enough money and small items of value to discharge the debts and the legacies to old servants, which was a weight off her mind, but she would get no recompense from the sale for her losses.

The new baronet was inheriting nothing more than a title.

Polly was peering through one of the sidelights framing the door. 'He is here, Miss Lytton. The Earl, I mean.'

'I guessed that was who you meant,' Ellie said wryly, and took a firm hold on the umbrella, feeling like a medieval knight arming himself for battle.

What did she know about this man? That he spent a great deal of money on his clothing and his boots, his horses and his entertainment. And most of the entertainment, she gathered, was hedonistic and self-indulgent but not, as a perusal of the gossip columns had told her, undisciplined.

Lord Hainford might enjoy gaming, racing... all matters of sport. He might be seen at every fashionable event and he might enjoy himself very well in other ways, as sly references to 'Lord H' and 'renowned beauty Lady X' being 'seen together as we have come to expect' betrayed, but there were never any reports of riotous parties, scandals at the opera or heavy gaming losses. He was not married, betrothed or linked to any respectable lady who might have expectations—which was interesting as he was now twenty-eight and had his inheritance to consider.

And when he smiled she thought there was something behind the amusement—as though he could not quite bring himself to surrender to it. Her imagination, no doubt…

Polly opened the door a fraction before the groom's knock. 'All these,' she said pertly to the man, with a wave of her hand to the small pile of luggage.

'It will go in the baggage carriage,' the groom said, and Ellie saw there was a second, plainer vehicle behind the Earl's glossy travelling coach with his coat of arms on the door. 'Is there anything you would like to keep with you, Miss Lytton?'

'Thank you, no.' She had her reticule, holding her money, her notebooks, a pencil and a handkerchief. 'Polly, run upstairs and tell Mr Rampion that we are about to leave.'

By the time the solicitor had come down Lord Hainford was out of the carriage and the luggage was loaded. She shook hands with the solicitor, took the letter he handed her with details of the house that would be her new home, and gave him, in return, the keys of the London house.

She had lived there for more than five years, and yet she could feel no particular sadness at leaving it. The companionship of her friends, the bookshops, the libraries—yes, she was sorry to lose those. But in this place she had been no more than a glorified housekeeper, the poor relation. At least now she would be mistress of her own house.

My own hovel, more likely.

All it would take was the willingness to endure the company of the Earl of Hainford for a few days.

He stood waiting to hand her into the carriage and she balked on the doorstep, the reality of being in such an enclosed space with a man making her stumble. She gripped the railing and limped down to the pavement, exaggerating the hitch in her gait to account for that moment of recoil.

Courage, she chided herself. She was not going to allow the past to rule her present, her future. And this man was the bridge to that future—whatever it held.

'Miss Lytton, may I introduce my confidential secretary, Jonathan Wilton?'

Jon got to his feet, stooping under the roof of the carriage. 'I do beg your pardon for not getting out to greet you, Miss Lytton. I did not realise you were ready to join us.'

Blake noticed the fractional recoil before she held out her hand, and the sudden loss of colour in her cheeks, and yet she was perfectly composed as she greeted Jon. Was she simply unused to the company of men? He supposed that might be the case, if she had not made her debut and had led a somewhat isolated existence. Then, as she sat and looked up, seeing Jon's face properly for the first time, he saw her surprise, carefully but not perfectly masked.

'We are half-brothers,' he said, settling himself next to her, opposite Jon.

The little maid scrambled up and sat opposite her mistress, a battered dressing case clutched on her knee.

'It is something recognised but not spoken about. With the typical hypocrisy of Society Mr Wilton, my secretary, is perfectly acceptable, whereas Jonathan, my somewhat irregular brother, is not.'

'Which can be amusing, considering how alike we are.' Jonathan, three inches shorter, brown-haired and blue-eyed, grinned. 'Acceptable as in a suitable extra dinner guest in emergencies, but not as a potential husband for a young lady of the *ton*, you understand.'

'Yes, I quite see.' Eleanor Lytton nodded. 'One day everyone will be judged only on character and ability, but I fear that is a long way off.'

'Are you a radical, Miss Lytton?' Blake asked as the carriage moved off. He noticed that she took no notice of their leaving, and did not send so much as a fleeting last glance at her old home.

'Cousin Eleanor, is it not?' she reminded him. 'I suppose I *might* be a radical—although I would not want change to be driven by violence. Too many innocents suffer when that happens.'

Blake was intrigued. There was plenty of room on the carriage seat and he shifted a little so he could study her expression. Most ladies, other than the great political hostesses and the wives of politicians, would be appalled at the suggestion that they might have an opinion on politics, and even those who did would be obediently mouthing their husband's line.

To have radical leanings was quite beyond the pale, and indicated that she both read about such matters and thought about them too. What a very uncomfortable female she was to have around— and yet somehow refreshingly different from his usual female companions.

'I agree with much of what the radicals advocate—both the need for change and the perils of making it happen,' he said, jerking his thoughts back from his recent amicable parting with Lady Filborough, his latest mistress.

A gorgeous creature, and yet he had become bored very rapidly with her predictability. He had no desire for a mistress who would try and plumb the depths of his soul—far from it—but he did prefer one who engaged his brain as well as his loins.

'People need bread in their stomachs before peaceable progress can be made.'

'Bread in their stomachs and books in their hands. Education is critical, don't you think?'

Her earnestness was rather charming, Blake decided. She was so unselfconscious, so passionate. Such a pity that she had no looks, he mused as he settled back into his corner. That passion combined with beauty would be truly...*erotic*. Good Lord—what a peculiar word to think of in conjunction with this woman.

Jon was ready to launch into his own opinions on working class education, he could see. A discussion of that all the way to Lancashire was going to be distinctly tiresome.

'I hope you will excuse us, Cousin Eleanor, but we must go through this morning's post.'

'Of course.'

It was like blowing out a candle. All the intensity went, leaving only a meek spinster effacing herself in her corner.

'Polly, pass me the book from my case, please. I have my notebook here.'

By dint of dropping his gloves, Blake managed to get a glimpse of the spine of the volume. *Agri-*

cultural Practices of the Mediterranean Lands.
He sincerely hoped that she was not going to try
and impose those on the farm labourers of Lancashire or she would soon come to grief.

What a strange little female she was. Or not so
little—she must be all of five feet and nine inches,
he estimated, before he reached for the first letter Jon passed him and became lost in the detail
of a land boundary dispute affecting a property
he was buying.

Chapter Four

To be closed in with not one but two gentlemen had almost caused her to back out of the carriage in instinctive panic. Ellie was quite proud of herself for not only standing her ground but greeting Mr Wilton with composure. No one would have noticed anything amiss, she was sure.

And, curiously, the secretary's presence made things easier. He was not as good-looking as his half-brother—more of a muted version—and the fact that the men had soon become engrossed in their work had helped her to relax. She did not like being the centre of attention under any circumstances, and now Lord Hainford—*Cousin Blake*—had a perfect excuse for virtually ignoring her, and she was sure he much preferred to do so.

She looked up from her book. The carriage was luxurious beyond anything she had travelled in before, with deeply buttoned upholstery and wide seats which meant that she could sit next to Blake without touching him or his clothing. Even though she told herself it was irrational, she had dreaded being shut up in a closed carriage, pressed against another body—or, worse, sandwiched between two men, which would have been quite likely to happen on a stage coach.

Ellie wriggled more comfortably into her corner and put her notebook on the seat. It was an effort to concentrate on date production and wheat yields, especially when she could *smell* Blake. It had to be him—that elusive scent of starched linen, an astringent cologne and warm, clean man. Mr Wilton was too far away for it to be him setting her nostrils quivering every time the two of them shifted, leaning across to pass papers or stooping to rescue fallen sheets from the carriage floor.

It was very provocative, that intimate trace that he left in the air. And just because the threat of a man touching her made her anxious, it did not mean she did not wish that was not the case. Blake was beautiful to look at—strong and male, the perfect model for both fantasy and fiction... Perfect, that was, when there had been not the slightest danger of getting close enough to speak to him, let alone scent him.

Ellie wrenched her concentration back to the book. Goodness, but the production of dates was dull. She flipped through the pages. Perhaps water management would be a more riveting subject for the tiresome Oscar to explore. He might even fall into an irrigation canal.

The thought cheered her, and she picked up her notebook and began to scribble not notes but an entire scene.

'Bushey,' Blake said. 'We are changing horses here. Would you like to get down for a few minutes?'

Ellie almost refused. Oscar was now vividly describing the experience of being hauled out of a muddy irrigation canal, and the scene was giving her great pleasure to write.

Then it occurred to her that this might be a tactful way of suggesting that she might wish to find the privy. 'Thank you. I would like to stretch my legs.'

Polly looked grateful for the decision, and Mr Wilton helped both of them to descend from the carriage, then turned away, as tactful as his brother, as the two of them went towards the inn.

When they returned Blake himself got out to help them in. 'You look pleased about something, Cousin Eleanor.'

'We were admiring the facilities. A most superior stopping place—thank you.'

'Thank Jon. He sorts everything out.'

Mr Wilton glanced up from his papers and

acknowledged the compliment with a tilt of his head. 'Just doing my job, Miss Lytton.'

'So what does an earl's confidential secretary *do*, exactly?' she asked as the groom closed the doors and swung up behind as the carriage rolled out of the inn yard.

'I deal with Lord Hainford's correspondence, keep his appointments diary, monitor all the newspapers for him, organise journeys, settle his accounts, ensure that reports from all his properties and investments are received regularly, scanned, and that any matters requiring his decision are brought to his attention. I make notes on topics he might wish to speak on in the Lords. That kind of thing.'

'It looks like a great deal more than that.' Ellie could see a stack of notebooks, bristling with markers. 'Cousin Blake makes you work exceedingly hard.'

'And he makes *me* work exceedingly hard in return,' Blake countered dryly. 'Did you imagine that earls sat around all day, reading?'

'No. I imagined that they spent most of their time enjoying themselves,' she admitted, surprised into frankness.

'I do—when I am allowed to escape.' He cast her a sardonic glance. 'I do all the things you imagine, Cousin Eleanor. All the things that put that judgmental expression on your face. Clubs, sporting events, my tailor, hatter and bootmaker. Social events, the opera, the theatre, gaming. A positive whirl of dissipation.'

Mr Wilton snorted. 'Are you attempting to paint yourself as an idle rake to Miss Lytton? Should I not mention the House of Lords, your charity boards, investors' meetings?'

'It will do no good, Jon. My new cousin considers me to be an idle rake already. I have no need to paint myself as one.'

'I am quite prepared to believe that you work as hard at your duties and responsibilities as you do at your pleasure, Cousin Blake. It is merely that I imagine you have to consider no one else while pursuing those occupations.'

'I am selfish, in other words?' Those dark brows were rising dangerously.

How had she allowed herself to be tempted into saying what she thought? She should be meek and mild and quiet—so quiet that he forgot she was there, if possible. An apology and a rapid return to the details of the North African date harvest was called for.

'If the cap fits, my lord,' Ellie retorted, chin up, ignoring common sense. 'How pleasant not to be responsible for a single soul.'

Mr Wilton opened his mouth, presumably in order to enumerate his lordship's friends, staff, tenants and charitable beneficiaries.

Blake silenced him with an abrupt gesture of his hand. 'It is,' he agreed, with a charming smile that did nothing to disguise the layers of ice beneath.

Stop it, she told herself. *He will put you off at the next inn if you keep provoking him.*

She was not even quite sure why she was doing it, other than the fact that it was curiously stimulating, almost exciting—which was inexplicable. Rationally, yes, he had been thoughtless in ignoring Francis's plea for his time and attention. And, yes, he had behaved outrageously—stripping off like that, provoking that unpleasant Crosse man to the point of violence. But she could not pretend that she was devastated at Francis's death, that she had loved her stepbrother, and Blake had done all she might have asked afterwards.

Just as he would have done whoever Francis's relatives had been.

He did not help for your sake, whispered an inner voice—the one she always assumed was her common sense. *He thinks you are plain, argumentative and of no interest. Which is true. He is helping because his conscience as a gentleman tells him to—and because it happens not to be desperately inconvenient for him. Just because you have been daydreaming about him, and just because you want to put him in your novel, that*

does not mean he has the slightest interest in you.
You should try and be a nicer person. Ladylike.

After that mental douche of cold water she
picked up her notebook. Perhaps she should start
by being nicer to Oscar. Perhaps he might be
treated to a marvellous banquet tonight. What
would there be to eat…?

One of the travel books she had read contained
several accounts of food, so she put together all
the dishes that particularly appealed. Roast kid,
couscous—which sounded delicious—exotic fish,
pungent cheeses, flatbreads. Pomegranate juice,
sherbets, honey cakes…

Her pencil flew over the pages.

They stopped for the night at Aynho, a
Northamptonshire village Ellie had never heard
of. It was built of golden stone and had an exceedingly fine inn, the George, which Mr Wilton had
selected for them.

She was ushered to the room she would share
with Polly and found it large, clean and comfortable. A bath had been ordered and would arrive
directly, she was told, and dinner would be served
in the private parlour at seven. Would Miss Lytton
care for a cup of tea?

'We both would,' she said gratefully. 'I could
become very accustomed to this,' she remarked

to Polly as the inn's maid hurried out after setting a very large bathtub behind a screen.

'Me too, miss.'

Polly was soon answering the door to another maid with the tea tray. She set it on a side table and they both sat and gazed happily at dainty sandwiches and fingers of cake.

'But we must not. I do hope I will be able to continue to employ you, Polly, and that you will want to stay with me, but I have no idea what we are going to find in Lancashire or how far I can make my money stretch. The house may be half a ruin, for all I know.'

'We'll manage,' Polly said stoutly, around a mouthful of cress sandwich. 'It's in the country— we can have a garden and grow vegetables, keep chickens and a pig, perhaps.'

'Of course,' Ellie said.

It was her duty to give a clear, confident lead to anyone in her employ, she knew that, but it was very tempting to wail that the only useful thing she knew how to do was to write children's books and she had not the slightest idea how to look after chickens. Pigs she refused even to think about.

I am an educated, intelligent woman. There are books on everything. I will learn how to do all this, she told herself firmly, choosing a second cake for courage.

The hot water arrived and she persuaded Polly

to take one end of the big tub while she took the other. It was a squash, with both of them having to fold in with their knees under their chins, but she could not see why her maid should have to make do with a washbasin and cloth while she wallowed in hot water.

Fashionable ladies would faint with horror at such familiarity, she was certain, but she was not a fashionable lady, after all.

'May I ask a question, miss?' Polly was pink in the face from the contortions necessary to wash between her toes.

'Of course, although I won't promise to answer it.'

'Why don't you like his lordship? I think he's ever so lovely.'

'Polly!'

'Well, he is,' the girl said stubbornly. 'He's good-looking and rich and he's got nice manners and he's taking us all this way in style. That Mr Wilton's nice too.'

'Lord Hainford could have prevented Sir Francis's death,' Ellie said coldly, and Polly, snubbed, bit her lip and carried on rinsing the soap off her arms in silence.

And I should forgive him. It is the right thing to do. He has made amends as best he can, so why is it so difficult? It was an accident, just as he said.

She would be in close proximity with Lord

Hainford for at least another three days. She really must learn to be easy with him, she told herself.

It was not until they were sitting around the table in the private parlour, Ellie and the two men—Polly was taking her supper in the kitchens—that she realised what it was that made her react to Blake as she did. This was not about Francis, nor about Blake's character.

She could forgive him for ignoring Francis that night—for failing to suppress her stepbrother's expensive obsession with him. Francis had had a thick skin and it would probably have needed physical violence to turn him away from his admiration. And he had been infuriatingly self-centred and tactless—it would not have occurred to him that interrupting the game with a demand to discuss his own affairs was unmannerly and deserved a snub.

She could forgive and she could understand. That was not the problem. It was not Blake. It was her.

She was frightened of him in a way that went far beyond the straightforward fear of what a man might do to a lone woman without protectors. There *was* that, of course. There was always that whenever a man came close enough to touch, whenever she was cornered with a man between her and the door. That was her secret fear. and understanding why she felt like that was no help at all in conquering it.

But she *desired* this man—found him deeply attractive—and had done so from the moment she had seen him. It was irrational to feel like that, she knew. Even if she was not crippled by her anxieties she was crippled in fact—and plain with it—and he would never spare her a glance under normal circumstances. For men like him women like her did not exist. They were not servants and they were not eligible girls or members of the society in which he existed. Spinsters, those to be pitied for their failure to attract a man, were invisible.

Before she had met him it had been safe to keep Blake in her daydreams. But now, for him, for a few days, she *did* exist. She was a constant presence day and night, from breakfast to dinner. What if he could tell how she felt? What if her pitiful desire showed in her eyes?

And it *was* pitiful—because she was determined to manage her own life, to live a full and independent existence, earn money. *Be happy.* This wretched attraction was a weakness she must fight to overcome. It was merely physical, after all—like hunger or thirst.

'You look very determined, Eleanor,' Blake remarked. 'Claret?' He lifted the bottle and tipped it towards her glass, holding it poised as he waited for her answer.

He had called her by her first name without even the fictitious *Cousin*.

'Yes.' The agreement was startled out of her and he poured the wine before she could collect her wits and refuse it. 'Yes, I *am* looking determined. I was thinking about pigs.'

Mr Wilton blinked at her over the rim of his wine glass. 'Pigs, Miss Lytton? Not present company, I trust?'

'Raising pigs. Or *a* pig. And chickens. I should have thought of it before and bought books on the subject before I left London. But Lancaster is certain to have a circulating library.'

'Forgive my curiosity, Eleanor,' Blake drawled, 'but why should you need to know about raising livestock?'

'To eat. Eggs and ham and bacon and lard. I must learn about vegetables as well.'

When both men continued to look at her as though she was speaking Greek—which she supposed they would probably comprehend rather better than talk of chicken-keeping—she explained. 'I must make my resources stretch as far as possible. Polly suggested a vegetable garden and poultry.'

'Eleanor, you are a gentlewoman—'

'Who has not, my lord, made you free with her name.'

'What is the harm? I make you free with mine,

and Jonathan, I am sure, will do likewise. We have been thrown together for several days in close company—can we not behave like the cousins we pretend to be? I promise you may "my lord" me from the moment you step out of the carriage at your new front gate, and I will be lavish with the "Miss Lyttons."'

'Has anyone ever told you that you have an excessive amount of sheer gall, my... Blake?'

'I am certain that they frequently think it, Eleanor, although they are usually polite enough to call it something else.'

'Charm, presumably,' she said, and took an unwise sip of the wine. *'Oh.'*

'It is not to your taste?'

'It is like warm red velvet and cherries and the heart of a fire!' She took another sip. She had meant to leave it strictly alone, but this was ambrosia.

'Are you a poet, Eleanor?'

'No, a—'

She'd almost said *a writer*, but bit her tongue. He might ask her what she wrote, and she could imagine his face when she admitted to the ghastly Oscar and his equally smug sister. As for her desire to write a novel—that would be a dangerous admission indeed. She could just picture the scene: her, after a glass of this wickedly wonderful wine, blurting out that Blake was the hero of her desert romance. He would either laugh himself sick or he be utterly furious. Neither was very appealing, although she thought she would probably prefer fury to mockery.

'A mere amateur at poetry,' she prevaricated. Which was true. Her attempts at verse were strictly limited to the moon-June-swoon level of doggerel. 'But words are dangerously tempting, are they not?'

'All temptation should be dangerous,' Blake said. 'Otherwise it is merely self-indulgence. May I carve you some of this beef?'

'Self-indulgences can be dangerous, surely?' Jonathan passed her the plate and followed it with a dish of peas. 'In fact most of them are—even if it's merely over-indulgence in sweet things. Before one knows it one is entrapped in corsets, like poor Prinny, or all one's teeth go black and fall out.'

'Not a danger for any of us around this table,' Blake remarked, carving more beef and then passing the potatoes to Ellie.

She wondered if that was a snide remark about her skinniness. Her mother had been used to saying, with something like despair, that she would surely grow some curves with womanhood—and she had indeed begun to just before Mama had died. But they'd seemed to disappear in the general misery afterwards, when she'd so often forgotten to eat properly. At least that had made it easier to be inconspicuous…

'Some bread sauce and gravy?' Jonathan passed the two dishes, one glossy with butter, the other rich and brown. 'And will you take more vegetables, Eleanor?'

'Thank you, no. I have only a small appetite.'

They devoted themselves to their food for a while. The beef was good, and the two men clearly close enough friends not to feel the need to talk of nothing simply to fill a silence that felt companionable to Ellie. They were attentive to her needs, but when their conversational sallies were met by monosyllabic replies they seemed comfortable with her reticence.

'Where is our next destination?' she asked, when Blake began to carve more beef.

'Cannock, I hope. It is a village north of Birmingham and about another seventy miles from here.'

'A long day, then. At what hour do you wish to take breakfast?'

'Would seven be too early for you, Eleanor?'

'Not at all.' She was usually up by six on most mornings, hoping to get at least an hour to write before the house came to life. 'But I will retire now, if you will excuse me?'

'No dessert? This apple pie looks good, and there is thick cream.'

'Delicious, I am sure. But, no, thank you.'

Besides anything else, her life was not going to hold much in the way of roast beef and thick cream in the future, so best not to get used to them now.

The men stood as she did, and Blake walked across the parlour to open her bedchamber door, which was uncomfortable. She heard his footsteps retreat back to the table as she turned the key and then lifted a small chair and wedged it under the door handle.

'Isn't the lock sound, miss?' Polly was shaking out their nightgowns.

'I expect so. But it is best not to take risks in strange buildings, I think.'

And not just strange ones. She had followed the same routine every night at home, rising in time to move the chair and unlock the door before Polly came to her room—another reason to rise at six. She had forgotten that the maid would be on her side of the door while they were travelling.

'This seems very cosy. Did you have a good supper?'

Chapter Five

Blake listened to the low murmur of female voices from beyond the closed door as he settled back into his chair and reached for the cream jug to anoint the slice of pie that Jonathan had served him.

'Eleanor doesn't eat enough to keep a bird alive—no wonder she's a beanpole,' he said, keeping his voice down.

'We make her nervous—which isn't surprising.' Jon finished his wine before tackling the pudding. 'That might be what it is.'

'She is bold enough when we are at a safe distance,' Blake mused.

'Probably she has had some unpleasant encounters with wandering hands in the past, or it is simply a maidenly aversion to masculinity,' Jon suggested.

'She damn nearly heaved me over her doorstep when I was there that first morning—although I suppose I was obviously in no state to offer her that sort of insult.'

The memory of Eleanor's hasty retreat when it had become obvious that he could bandage his own wound, and her violent recoil when she had fallen against him and her hand had inadvertently touched his bare chest, seemed to confirm Jon's opinion.

His body, hurting though it had been, had responded inexplicably to that touch, to that cool hand spread over his bare skin, and he had been glad when she had bolted from the room and left him to compose himself.

How laughable to be aroused by that—like some callow youth desperate for the touch of a woman…any woman. How very strange to recall the urge to wrap his arms around her, to hold her close. It hadn't been sexual—more an instinct for comfort. He must have been in shock, because she was a most prickly female and he was *not* in need of…comfort.

That was definitely not something he was going to confide in Jonathan. He would never hear the last of it.

'This is a decent claret. Let's have another bottle.'

The next day was a repeat of the first. Ellie alternately read and wrote and gazed out of the window. Polly relaxed enough to put the dressing case down on the seat between herself and Jonathan and get out her tatting, and Blake and Jonathan worked, dozed and read.

No one teased anyone else, there were no hostile gibes—it was all remarkably comfortable, Blake thought. Positively domestic. He shook out the pages of the newspaper they had picked up at a stop in Birmingham and laughed at himself.

By noon the next day they were drawing to a halt in front of the Golden Crown inn in the middle of Stoke-on-Trent to take a light luncheon.

He watched Eleanor, worried again about how little she ate. Her lips, closing around the smooth, tight skin of a plum, were soft and pink and—

He jerked his gaze upwards and found those wide hazel eyes were focused on his face.

'Have some more.' He passed the bowl across. 'They are very good.'

'Thank you, no. I have had enough.'

In that steady gaze he could read discomfiture at his close attention and something else—something he could not identify. Or could he?

Blake found he was shifting uncomfortably in his chair, grateful for the all-concealing snowy expanse of tablecloth falling to his lap.

What? I am aroused by this woman? Damn it, celibacy—even for a few weeks—is really very bad for me indeed...

Jonathan cleared his throat and Blake jumped. So did Eleanor, who then gave herself an almost imperceptible little shake.

You too?

He almost said it out loud, then made a business of helping himself to fruit instead.

Well, why not?

Women had urges too, and those who said they did not had obviously had very little to do with women between the sheets. Just because a woman was on the shelf it did not mean that she was sexless. And Eleanor had too much dignity and reserve to make those kind of longings plain. If he had not lost himself in those rather lovely expressive eyes just now…

But it would be sensible to be wary. This business of chaperonage worked both ways—protecting men against scheming females just as much as it protected innocent girls from predatory men. That would be revenge for her stepbrother's death indeed: entrapping the man she blamed for it into matrimony.

She would be delighted finally to arrive somewhere and be able to stop jolting around and living out of valises, Ellie concluded when they started off again.

She stared out of the windows as a succession of smoking chimneys, grimy streets and bulbous bottle kilns gave way to open fields. On the other hand, this was more comfortable than the stage-coach would have been, and much safer, and she was in no hurry to discover what awaited her in Lancashire.

Yesterday had been extraordinary. What had she seen in Blake's eyes? Surely not desire? For *her*? There had been heat, and almost a question, rapidly followed by him diverting those penetrating grey eyes to a close study of a dish of apples.

If she was not a victim of her own torrid imagination then she ought to be wary. *Very* wary. And yet she could not feel threatened by him, and that was most strange. But then he had been at a safe distance, and she'd had her Dutch courage in the shape of a glass of wine.

The crack and the lurch came some twenty minutes after they had left the town, just as the coach turned a sharp corner going uphill.

For a second she thought the wheel had simply slipped into a rut, but then the lurch became a slide and the carriage tipped. There was a shout from the coachman, Polly's piercing shriek, hands reaching for her—and then the world turned upside down as the whole vehicle fell over and all went black.

'Stop screaming!' Blake rasped, and the girl wedged against his side subsided into terrified gulps. Where the hell was Eleanor? Her silence was worse than the maid's panic. 'Polly? *Polly*, listen to me. I can't turn over—something is on my back. Can you look up? Can you see the door?'

'Yes…yes, my lord.'

'Are you injured? Can you move? Climb out?'

'It hurts…' The whimper turned into a determined sniff. 'Not anything broken, I don't think. I can try. It's Mr Wilton, my lord, over your back. He's unconscious and his head's bleeding.' She sniffed again and her voice wavered. 'Not…not *spurting*, my lord. I'll try and wriggle past him.'

Blake braced himself against the pain the wriggling inflicted on him—the foot against his cheekbone, the pressure on his right shoulder that already felt as though it was on fire, the strain on his half-healed bullet wound.

Then Polly called, 'I'm out, my lord.'

There were voices—she was talking to someone. Help would come. He made himself think—which was difficult with Jonathan's dead weight pressing down on him.

Not dead, remember, he reassured himself. *He's bleeding, but not badly.*

They must have slid down almost twenty feet of steep bank, he reckoned. But Eleanor…

She had been on his left side. Then he realised that the soft, yielding surface he was pressed down into was Eleanor's body, and they were lying as close as lovers, as *intimately* as lovers, his pelvis wedged into the cradle of her thighs, his chest against her breasts.

Thank God—she's breathing, he thought, his nose pressed into a mass of springing, lavender-scented hair. *She smells delicious...she's alive.*

'Eleanor, hang on—help is coming.'

For a moment he thought she was unconscious, and then—so suddenly that he jerked his head, banging it hard against something wooden—she heaved under him like a trapped, netted deer.

'Get off me! *Get off, get off, get off...!*'

She sounded like a woman in a nightmare, fighting for her life, desperate, frantic.

'Eleanor, it is me—Blake. I can't move off you. I am sorry, but we're trapped—just for a little while. Eleanor, lie still until help comes.'

He kept talking—repetition, reassurance, nonsense. She kept struggling. And then suddenly, with a sob that might have been sheer exhaustion, she lay still.

'I can't,' she whispered. 'Can't fight...'

'You don't have to, Eleanor,' he said, and found he was whispering too. 'Don't try and fight. Help will be here soon.'

Would it? It was very quiet outside. What if Polly had got out and then collapsed? Or Frederick, his coachman, was too badly injured to go for help? What if the horses were dead or had bolted?

Stop it. This is a well-travelled road. Someone will find us soon.

He scrabbled with his fingertips, found wood and braced himself, lifting his weight half an inch off Eleanor's body.

'I'll make certain you get out safely,' he promised.

Beneath him he could feel her vibrating like a taut wire, and he remembered a leveret he had found when he was a boy, lying still as death in its form in a wheat field. It had stared at him with the huge, mad eyes that hares had, but it hadn't moved. Only when he'd lain his hand on it he'd been able to feel its heart pounding, feel the shivering vibration that racked it.

He had snatched his hand away, backed into the wheat until he had no longer been able to see it. But he could not stop touching Ellie, and before much longer he was not going to be able to support himself away from her body either.

'Blake?' The voice in his ear was puzzled. 'What the hell happened?'

'Jon!' The relief that he was well enough to speak was almost physical. 'We went over the bank. Polly scrambled out and I heard her speaking to someone, but that was perhaps half an hour ago. Eleanor is trapped beneath me and I can't move.'

'Not surprising with me on top. Hold on. The

damn writing case has landed on my gut. Sorry—
this is taking an age. I've been out of it for a bit—
must have banged my head.'

There was a heave, a loud and violent curse,
and then most of the weight shifted off Blake's
back.

'I've broken my confounded arm. If I can
just— Sorry.' His booted foot ground into Blake's
cheek. 'Damn difficult with one hand. There—
the door's open.'

More scrabbling, more curses and then light
flooded in.

'Right, can you get out now?'

Warily Blake felt around, got a handhold and
levered himself up and away from Ellie. The
coach was on its side and she was against the
window which, thankfully, had been open, so the
glass had not broken.

He got one arm through the open door above
him, heaved and was out. Jon looked appalling,
his face pale under a mass of blood from the cut
to his head and his left hand supporting his right
arm, but he seemed alert and otherwise uninjured.
Blake pulled him close, looked at his eyes. The
pupils were normal, thank God.

'Are you hurt, Blake?' Jonathan was looking
him over with as much concern.

'No, just bruises and scrapes. I've had a lot
worse in Gentleman Jackson's after a round of

sparring. I just hope and pray Eleanor is all right.'
There was total silence from inside the coach. He
climbed up and leaned in. 'Eleanor?'

She lay where he had left her, on her back, her
eyes wide, her freckles standing out against her
dead white face. 'Yes. I think so.'

Her voice was a mere whisper.

'Move your arms and legs,' he ordered, suddenly convinced that he must have broken her
spine, crushing her like that. And what had it
done to her crippled leg?

Obediently she moved her hands and feet, then
sat up. 'Nothing is broken.'

'Then take my hands.' He lay down flat and
reached in. 'Try and stand as I pull.' Behind him
he could hear horses, raised voices. 'Help is here.'

There was the merest hesitation before she
reached up. He took her wrists and pulled, his
bruised body screaming in protest, and she came
up, using her legs without any sign of pain, out of
the door until she could slide onto solid ground.

Blake got to her just as she folded neatly and
quietly into a dead faint.

She hurt all over. That was the first thing she
was conscious of. Then it all came back—even
before she opened her eyes. The terrifying lurch
and slide, the impact, the falling bodies and the
blow to the head that had stunned her. And then

coming back to herself in the gloom to find a man's body plastered to hers—intimately, heavily, his hands on her shoulders, his face against her cheek, his breath hot on her face, his...*maleness* all too evident.

Ellie's eyes flew open. It was daylight. Above her was a ceiling, beneath her a comfortable bed. And someone was in the room with her. She sat up too fast, and almost whimpered at the pain from her bruises. Blake was sitting on a chair in the far corner of the room.

'Eleanor?' His face was marked, scraped and discoloured.

That was who had been on top of her. *Blake.* She had fought him, beaten at him, struggled as he'd lain helpless. Injured. Goodness knew what she had said to him.

'I am so sorry. So sorry I hit you. I panicked.'

'No. Don't apologise.' He got to his feet, then sat down abruptly. 'I shouldn't be in your room, but I needed to make sure you were all right. In the carriage, when you were trapped beneath me, you panicked—and it was not because of the accident...it was because a man was pinning you down. I am sorry, it must have been terrifying, and there was nothing I could do until Jonathan managed to get out.'

She shook her head. 'It is no matter.'

'But it is. It put you in fear. Who was it, Eleanor? Who made someone as brave as you feel like that?'

She winced at the word. He thought her *brave*? How little he knew. All she had done was to pick herself up and somehow limp on.

'No one.'

Blake made a gesture—the abrupt, impatient gesture of a man used to getting his own way, to getting answers when he asked. She saw him catch himself doing it, saw the care with which he clasped those long fingers together and sat back in the chair, consciously making himself unthreatening.

'You flinch when a man touches you,' he said, his voice neutral, as though he was describing the view from the window. 'You move in a room so that you always have an escape route. You lock your door at night even when you share the room with your maid and you are in a private area. You reacted in terror to the feel of a man's body pressed to yours—overpowering you, it must have seemed. Who was it?'

Probably spontaneous combustion by blushing was impossible, but it did not feel so just at that moment. Ellie tried to get the memory his body against hers as they lay pressed together in the carriage out of her mind.

'*No one*. I am simply unused to being with men, that is all. I do not want to talk about this.'

She could hear him getting to his feet, walking towards the door, but she kept her burning face turned away.

'Of course. But I should say that both Jonathan and I would consider ourselves something less than men if we ever forced our attentions on an unwilling woman.' His voice was as cool, as clinical, as it had been throughout his little interrogation.

Oh.

'Of course.' She sat up again—again too fast. 'I would not for a moment think… My reaction—I cannot always control it. I am sorry. It is like… like running away from a spider, even though one knows they are harmless.'

His faint smile in response was lop-sided, and now she could see him without the light behind him the scraped, bruised side of his face was clearly visible.

'Are you badly hurt? And Polly? Mr Wilton?'

'Polly is fine—just bruised and shocked. I am black and blue and dented more by Jon's big feet than the original accident. He has a broken arm and, unlike your spider, he only has four limbs, of which he can write legibly with only one. One cannot help but think that a conscientious secretary would have broken the left arm…'

He was gone and the door was closed before

Ellie realised that he was joking, and that Jonathan could not be in a dangerous state.

How near she had come to telling Blake about that shameful, shaming night. *She* had done nothing to be ashamed of—she knew that—but all the knowing in the world did not stop the emotions. Her only fault, she had told herself over and over, was to have started to develop womanly curves in the months leading up to her mother's death. It had never occurred to her to try and disguise them other than by continuing to dress modestly, as befitted a gentleman's daughter.

She *knew* she hadn't *flaunted* herself, hadn't *teased and tempted*, hadn't *asked for it*—all the foul things her stepfather had thrown at her as she'd struggled. Why did knowing that not make it possible to ignore those words?

Along with the key and the barricades and the knife, her only other weapon had been to lose those curves. She had always been tall, always slender, never pretty. Now, by eating very little, she had become thin, her features plain. Hunger was a small price to pay for becoming unattractive to any potential predator.

Ellie sat up and threw back the covers. It was time she got up, reviewed the damage—the bangs and bruises.

The door was unlocked. She took a painful limping step towards it, then made herself turn back towards the dressing table. There were no predators here. She was safe with these men. Jonathan was a decent man and Blake... Blake made her feel safe in ways she could not begin to understand.

Her face, with a scratch down her nose, a bruise on her chin and dark circles under her eyes, returned her stare in the glass. The only things that were in danger were her own foolish daydreams.

'I am perfectly able to travel.' Jonathan's voice was raised well above his usual discreet tones.

For a man dosed with laudanum and recovering from the doctor's manhandling as he set his arm, Jonathan sounded a lot livelier than Blake felt. He winced at the effect on his thudding headache. A night's sleep in the inn at Stoke had done little to soothe it.

'You stay here while I take Eleanor to Lancashire. You need to rest—you heard the doctor.'

'Why have you got to take her in such a rush? She will come to no harm here for a while.'

'Because she is a lady, and she should not be with two men unrelated to her like this.'

'She's been with us for long enough to ruin a Mother Superior in the eyes of Society.'

'And do *you* want to end up married to her?'

Jonathan, who had been lying on his back on the sofa in the private sitting room, opened his eyes and turned his head to fix Blake with a hard stare. 'No.'

'No more do I. Plain spinsters are not for either of us, if I've anything to say to it.'

Plain and deeply wary of men, poor creature.

Why was he so vehement about it—as though he was trying to persuade himself, not his brother?

'She goes to Lancashire and you rest. When I get back we will go home. I had better get you a valet for while I'm away—you can't even hitch up your breeches by yourself in that state.'

Jon opened his mouth to argue—he always argued, the stubborn devil—and then his gaze switched to the door. 'Er... Blake—'

He turned and found Eleanor standing on the threshold of her room, her bruised and scratched hands folded demurely in the rusty black skirts of her disaster of a gown.

Oh, hell. How much of that had she heard?

Chapter Six

If Eleanor had overheard his remark about plain spinsters she gave no sign of it. Her expression was neutral, her tone simply matter-of-fact.

Blake expelled the breath he had been holding. Damn it, he didn't want to hurt her feelings—simply wanted not to have her anywhere around, muddling his feelings. After he had made that disastrous proposal to Felicity he had sworn to keep his dealings with women simple. Mistresses who knew what they were doing and had very clear expectations from him, and eventually a suitable marriage to an eligible lady—one who would not expect emotions to come into the equation.

Felicity had been his for the asking—or so he had assumed—since they were children. And he had taken her for granted—never bothered to explore his own feelings, let alone hers. He had lost his love before she was his, and since then it had been easier—safer—simply not to feel, not to allow his happiness to depend on anyone else. Except for Jon, of course, but he was his brother, and that was different.

But to accept responsibility for anyone else's happiness, to put them at risk of his own inability to care enough… He forced his thoughts to a juddering halt, back to the present.

Eleanor inclined her head and went to Jonathan's side, her expression concerned. Blake heard her murmured questions about whether he needed more laudanum, or a drink, perhaps. A shabby ministering angel. Which made him think…

'I must go out and find Jonathan a temporary valet. May I take Polly with me? She can help with some shopping, replace the things that were damaged in the accident.'

'Yes, of course.' Eleanor scarcely glanced up. 'She says she is quite well this morning, but please make sure she does not overtire herself.'

Blake left to find the maid, contemplating the wreck of his comfortable life just at the moment, largely thanks to the Lyttons. A scandal at the club—not that he could blame *that* on Lytton… that had been his own damned fault—a heap of boring sensitive work around the death and the inquest and the funeral, and then, to crown it all, he had allowed himself to be cozened into this trip up the length of the confounded country.

He knew why he had not simply loaned Eleanor his carriage and provided her with an escort. It had not been a quixotic act of gallantry on the spur of the moment. It had been because of his well-submerged conscience—not nagging him about this woman or about Lytton's death, exactly, but reminding him that he was capable of letting people down and that included women too.

Love was dangerous, because love meant loss, which meant pain, and the people you loved let you down sooner or later, or you blundered and hurt them… And why was he even *thinking* about love, of all things? He was done with that. This was all about the duty he owed as a gentleman to a lady in distress.

'My lord?' Polly stood in the middle of the corridor, where she had apparently come to a dead halt as he strode down it, unseeing. 'Were you looking for me?'

Now his infuriatingly tender conscience was prompting him to *more* insanity. 'Yes.' *Be tactful.* 'How are you? Should you be resting?'

'I'm just a bit bruised, my lord, thank you for asking. I'm keeping moving—stops it all stiffening up, like.'

'In that case I need you to come out shopping with me. There are clothes that need replacing after the accident. Miss Lytton said she could spare you if you felt up to it. Things for you too, of course.'

The maid grinned, the wide smile startling on her solemn little face. 'Ooh, thank you. I'll go and fetch my cloak, my lord.'

Finally Ellie had finished the chapter about the date harvest, had extricated Oscar from the drainage ditch, and was sketching out a plan for the next few chapters. The desert was too tempting by far, with its images of white-robed horsemen riding across the sand dunes. She would send Oscar by boat along the coast to Egypt. There was a great deal to write about Egypt without once mentioning date palms. All the romance of the pyramids and temples, the River Nile, pictures of tall pharaohs striding out, bare-chested, long-legged, black-haired...

Oh, stop it, Ellie. Make a note of the idea and get on with Oscar.

'I'm back, Miss Lytton.' Polly came in, laden with parcels, followed by one of the inn servants, his arms full of more. 'I'll just put these in your room, miss.'

Ten minutes later she was back.

'His lordship bought me a new dress, Miss Lytton, even though I told him I could mend the rips in the one I was wearing. A whole new outfit.' She lowered her voice. 'And he told me to buy *everything*, right down to… Well, he said *all the layers*, so as not to mention underthings, you know.'

'That was very good of him,' Ellie said absently, half her mind still on Oscar. Polly had undergone an unpleasant experience the day before, so it was only right that Blake had made her a gift.

'I've unpacked your things, miss.'

'Mine?' Ellie put down her pen. 'What things?'

'On the bed. They're ever so nice—the best we could find in the town. Not London standard, of course…'

Her voice trailed away as Ellie went past her into the bedchamber. A gown lay on the bed. A plain walking dress in golden-brown wool with a matching spencer in a darker brown beside it. And *all the layers*, just as Blake had told Polly. A heap of white lawn and cotton, even stockings.

A man had paid for her *underwear. That man* had paid.

Sitting next to the petticoats were gloves and a bonnet—a decent, plain pale straw with a golden-brown satin ribbon. It was a respectable, modest object whose very decency only served to highlight the outrageous fact that a man had bought it.

'I am in *mourning*, Polly. That—' she gestured rather wildly at the walking dress '—is brown. Not even dark brown.'

'His lordship said not to buy black, Miss Lytton. And that purple wouldn't suit you.'

'Did he, indeed?'

She snatched up the gown, almost whimpering with pleasure as her fingers closed on soft, fine cloth, then set her jaw and marched out into the sitting room, ignoring the jarring to her leg.

'Where is he?'

'You called?' Blake opened the door and leaned one shoulder against the frame. 'Good, I thought that colour would go with your hair. Suits your freckles too.'

'My—my freckles have nothing to do with it.' Trust him to tease her with one of her most prominent faults. 'I am in mourning. My brother has just died. This is brown. Golden-brown.'

'Your *step*brother,' Blake corrected her. 'And no one up here knows about it. I, on the other hand, have a reputation to uphold. I can't be seen with you in that frightful old black thing. It makes you look like a moulting crow in a thunderstorm.'

He was teasing her. She could tell he was trying not to laugh, and his eyes were crinkling at the corners and his mouth.

Oh, his mouth...

'Moulting crow? *Crow?*' She let anger sweep over the desire.

'It is simply the black gown,' he said, with

an unruffled calm that seemed uncanny given that an infuriated woman was shaking her fist, a gown clutched in it, under his nose. 'I did not mean that *you* look like a crow... Without the black dress...'

There was a glint in his eye that told her it was not simply her own mind that had seen a second meaning to that last comment. No doubt he found it highly amusing to tease her about her skinny body.

But she was a lady, however much she felt like shrieking like a fishwife, and she simply could not respond to that jibe. 'I cannot help the gown. I had to re-dye it. I cannot afford to buy a new set of mourning for every occasion like some Society lady.'

Now he had her discussing her impoverished state, blast him.

'I know you cannot. That is why I have bought this.'

For a moment it seemed almost reasonable. *For a moment.* 'I should not allow a man unrelated to me to buy me clothing—and certainly not intimate clothing. It isn't decent.'

'I thought it all exceedingly decent—positively Quakerish—but Polly insisted that was what you would want.'

He still lounged there against the door...all six foot something of gorgeous, infuriating male.

How would he like it if she went and bought him a pair of drawers? If he wore any, that was…

'*Now* what are you blushing about?'

'What do you think?' She fought back the image of Blake clad in nothing but a pair of white cotton drawers, sliding off one hipbone on an irresistible downward course. Oh, her *wretched* imagination. 'You went into the shop and actually argued with Polly over my… No, I do not want to even think about it.'

'Good—don't think, then. Just wear it.'

Something in his expression told her that he would be thinking about *exactly* what she was wearing—all the way down to the skin. The man must be some kind of insatiable libertine if he could become excited thinking about underwear on *her* angular body.

My plain spinster's body.

Oh, yes, she had heard him talking to Jonathan—the entire conversation—even if she had pretended she had not. She had too much pride to fling his hateful, hurtful, but perfectly accurate words back at him.

And yet he had been kind when he had talked to her in the bedchamber, even though that kindness had consisted of cool questions and simple assurances.

There might be heat in that grey gaze, and he

might be finding amusement in teasing her, but he would not act on that heat, she was certain.

That belief did not stop her wanting to throttle him with one of those fine cotton stockings now folded neatly on her bed.

'Thank you. I will, of course, return everything afterwards.'

'Do not be ridiculous, Miss Lytton.' The heat had gone, leaving nothing but a man confronting an irritating female. 'What would *I* do with a pile of female clothing?'

Ellie looked down at the brown gown in her hand and then at the black skirts of her dress. He was right. It was horrible. She knew he was not buying her favours, such as they were, and that it was only her foolish pride stopping her accepting it.

'Thank you, my lord. I will accept the garments with thanks. Thank you also for buying things for Polly.'

Try as she might to sound grateful, it came out sounding like a sulky child being forced to thank someone for an unwanted gift. Blake did not deserve that.

'I am sorry—that was ungracious,' she said, before she had the opportunity to lose her nerve. 'It is a delightful gown and I fully understand your motives in giving it to me.'

Her smile wavered as Blake looked at her, his

face expressionless. Was he going to hurl her apology back at her or simply snub her with a lift of those dark brows? Neither, it seemed.

'I stand rebuked by your courtesy, Miss Lytton.'

There was no heat now, and no teasing—just a warm smile that turned her insides to liquid toffee. Presumably that ability was something rakes acquired along with an unfair allowance of charm.

'And I am in awe that you understand my motives. It is usually more than I can do.'

'I have no wish to rebuke you. I would simply wish to exist on easy terms with you, my lord.'

I have agreed to spend another day, at least, in a carriage with this man. Easy terms is not what I want. And I fear what I do want.

'I am back to being *my lord*, am I?'

His smile did not reach his lips, only his eyes, and it seemed all the warmer, all the more personal for that.

She found she was returning that smile even as she kept her lips primmed up—which was probably what was amusing him. It was so easy to *like* this man. At least it was until she recalled his outrageous behaviour at his club, his neglect of Francis, his cutting words about her own lack of charms.

'Very proper, Eleanor. You may "my lord" me all you want when you are wearing my gift.' He ran the flat of his hand across the folds of the gown that was still in her arms.

My gift. That possessive gesture. *Oh, my soul, this man is dangerous.*

He would not take advantage of her, she was sure of that, but this intimacy combined with his teasing charm and good looks and wicked informality was like strong spirits to someone with no head for alcohol. Blake probably had no idea that her experience of men, other than family members, was virtually nil. He was used to ladies who played him at his own game, who flirted, fenced with him, setting wits against wits. What he doubtless thought was light teasing was as heady as a caress, a kiss, to her.

'Are you never serious, my lord?' she said, exasperated with herself for letting him affect her so.

'Serious?' The smile was wry now, almost bitter. 'Oh, yes, Eleanor. All the time.'

Blake didn't add anything else, and she had the uncomfortable feeling that she had opened a door onto something he had not intended to reveal—and yet he had given nothing away. The man was composed of layers, or perhaps boxes full of secrets, one inside the other.

'If you will excuse me I will go and see if Jonathan needs anything,' Ellie said briskly. 'Did you find a temporary valet for him?'

'Apparently the landlord's nephew acts as a body servant to the gentlemen staying here, so he has undertaken to assist him tomorrow and to drop by regularly throughout the day to make certain there is nothing he needs. Whether he is capable of ensuring he stays on the couch and rests is another matter.'

Despite a sense of lingering unease, she could not help but smile at the mental picture of a confrontation between Jonathan, being stubbornly conscientious, and a dogged valet, paid and under orders from the Earl to make him rest.

Ellie took the gown back to the bedchamber to find Polly had put away all the rest of the new clothing. She had obviously had no doubt about who was going to win that particular argument.

'I said half past eight.' Blake stood with one foot on the step of the carriage, his gloved fingers beating a silent tattoo on the door's glossy paintwork.

'It *is* half past,' Ellie said. 'Listen—there's the church clock now.'

'So where is Polly? Why isn't she here?' His brows snapped together into a frown, and then he glanced up at the windows of their suite. 'Is she frightened of the carriage after the accident?'

'She will be but a moment. If you would just give me a hand to get in—'

Blake held out his hand to assist her into the carriage, but stayed outside when she sat. 'I am endeavouring not to make you feel uncomfortable in a confined space.'

'I have every confidence that you are not a rapist, my lord.'

It was worth the embarrassment of using that word to see his mouth open in shock, just for a second, before he collected himself.

'I am aware that sometimes I cannot control a reflexive shrinking when I find myself very close to a man but, as I said, that is like a fear of spiders and it is quite irrational to react like that with everyone—especially when I know I can trust them.'

If she was in the company of more men then it would be easier to learn to discriminate between them, to overcome the reflex, of course. But if she was more used to men in general then probably she would not find herself so lacking in composure around this one.

As she had hoped, the distraction was enough for him to forget about Polly for the moment and climb into the carriage beside her. The maid soon came hurrying out and the driver set off as the door banged shut.

'There is the world of difference between violent assault and the possibility that I might, shall we say…take liberties,' Blake said. He seemed to be eyeing her with a wary curiosity, ignoring Polly.

'And there is all the difference in the world between cold-blooded murder and what I might do with my penknife if you try to,' she returned sweetly, provoking an answering grin. 'And if by "liberties" you mean you might flirt, or try and put me to the blush, then I would suggest that you are even more weary of this journey than I am.'

Blake put his head back and laughed—a full-bodied, utterly male peal of laughter that left him rubbing his hand across eyes that watered. 'You, my dear Eleanor, are a breath of fresh air. If I edge towards overstepping the mark you have merely to sharpen a pencil in a meaningful manner and I will be as good as gold.'

'I know you are only teasing, of course.'

Somehow Ellie managed to keep her own face straight. Rolling about the carriage hooting with laughter—his was exceedingly infectious—would definitely be unseemly, and her words were as much a reminder to her as a comment aimed at him.

'Really? What makes you so certain?' That wicked spark was back and those mobile tempting lips were curving into a smile that somehow produced the hint of a dimple in his right cheek.

Plain spinsters.

Ellie almost said it, just to watch him squirm, and then bit her lip before she could embarrass herself. 'Feminine intuition,' she said, and buried her head in her book.

Two hours later and Ellie was cross-eyed with reading and her leg ached from sitting for so long. The sun was shining and the view, although of barren hillsides, was wild and intriguing.

'I would like to stretch my legs. Do we have time to stop for a while?'

Blake looked out of the window at the open spaces without any more cover than scattered bushes within yards of the road. 'I don't think—'

'That was not a euphemism,' she said primly. 'I really do want to stretch my legs.'

'It is very rough country.' He still looked embarrassed.

'Are you worried about my limp? The bone did not set correctly—there is no diseased hip joint, or anything like that. I limp, but it isn't painful.' Her leg ached in damp weather, and limping was tiring, but that was not relevant now.

'Are you certain?'

For a moment Ellie thought he was going to be male and stubborn and over-protective, but then Blake shrugged and rapped on the roof to signal the driver.

'We could walk over to that slight rise. I think there may be a view,' he said, and climbed down.

Polly looked so appalled at the thought that she might enjoy a walk across rough ground that they left her in the carriage.

'I like this,' Ellie said a few minutes later as she perched on a fallen tree and looked around. 'The air is wonderfully clean after London. Listen— there's a curlew calling, so wild and free.'

Blake pointed to the small hill. 'From there we should get a good view of the valley. Coming?'

I am enjoying this, Ellie thought as she followed Blake. He was not making any reference to her limp, but he kept his pace slow enough for her to keep up and did not insist on making small talk. She could look at the view, listen to the birdsong and admire the frankly very decorative view of his broad shoulders, narrow hips and long legs as he walked just in front of her.

They climbed a stile into a pasture, and he held out his hand to assist her over—but that, she thought, was simply what he would have done for any lady he was out walking with.

'Here.' Blake stopped in the middle of the field. 'Yes, I thought so—with the sun on those slopes the colours are vivid. There are times when I wish I could paint.'

'Blake?'

'Hmm?' He was shading his eyes and staring out towards the horizon. 'I think that's a buzzard...'

'*Blake*. There's a bull in that corner of the field.'

It was black, short-legged, massive in the shoulder, wide in the chest and had an unpleasant spread of horns. And it was beginning to paw at the turf.

'No need to worry—they are fine by themselves, with nothing to protect.' He did not look round.

'But his heifers are in the opposite corner, down in that dip, and we are in the middle and he really does *not* look at all happy. Blake! *Run!*'

He looked round, swore, then reached for her. '*Ough*.'

Blake tossed her over his shoulder and began to sprint. Behind them was the pounding of cloven hooves and the snorting of an enraged beast getting up to speed. All she could see was the tussocky ground below and Blake's booted legs running. If he tripped the bull would go right over them...

'Hold tight.' Blake tossed her upwards and she twisted, grabbing instinctively as her hands found a splintery wooden rail, and then she was over it and Blake had a foot on the stile behind her, almost safe.

'Behind you!' she screamed.

He didn't spare the fraction of a second needed to look. He could probably feel the bull's breath, it was so close. Blake vaulted the stile and landed virtually on top of her. They both fell, Ellie underneath.

Chapter Seven

He had lain like this before, over this woman, and surprise at how feminine she felt against his body hit him again. Only this time he was not half-stunned, shocked and disorientated—this time he knew exactly who and where he was. His blood was pumping, and they had just escaped a dangerous beast. He had reacted on instinct—had slung Eleanor over his shoulder like a Viking marauder with a captive, and run with every ounce of strength in his body.

And, hell, it had felt good.

She stared up at him, her undistinguished, sensible face white under its drift of freckles, her bonnet gone, her appalling hair escaping from its rigorous constraints, her hazel eyes wide. Her lips were parted, and under the softness of the pretty walking dress he had given her her breasts were heaving with her panting breaths.

Instinct made him roll onto his back, taking her with him so that she lay along his body, his hands light on her shoulders. From there she could knee him in the groin—right in the iron-hard erection that surely she must be aware of. Or she could roll free and leave him lying there, abandoned. Or...

Eleanor blinked, then touched the very tip of her tongue to her lower lip. She was studying him as though she had never seen anything quite like him before and was interested in examining this strange life form more closely. His legs bracketed her hips, positioning her just at the point of greatest torment for him, and he forced himself to lie still—so still that he could feel his own heartbeat and hers too, because small, delectable breasts were squashed to his chest.

Frankly, Blake thought hazily, the Spanish Inquisition might have made good use of her, because just at that moment he was willing to confess to anything—every embarrassing peccadillo, every deep, dark secret—if only she would stay where she was, directing her warm breath into his face. He could smell the wild mint leaf she had plucked as they walked.

Eleanor sighed softly and her long, light lashes drooped. And Blake curled one palm around the back of her head, pulled down her head and kissed her.

She tasted of the mint, faintly of tea, and very

much of woman—of Eleanor. She gasped as their lips met and he took advantage, sliding his tongue between her lips, urging her to open to him. He could feel her surprise at the intrusion shivering through her, could almost read her thoughts. *Bite? Flee?* And then she relaxed, let him in, let him explore, and began to kiss him back.

She was unsure, unskilled, had almost certainly never been kissed before, and Blake thought it was the most erotic kiss he had ever had—innocent, generous, curious.

When he was certain that she was willing he rolled again, without breaking the kiss, and came over her, taking some of the weight on his elbows so he could control the kiss. He felt her arms come around his shoulders as she angled her mouth under his, the better to explore.

This had to stop, and soon—he knew that. He was aroused to the point of pain, and he did not dare touch her in any other way but this. If he got his hands on her body he knew what would happen, and she was an innocent—not some bawdy country lass to be tumbled by her swain in the long grass.

Blake pushed up and off her, onto the turf, to sit with his knees up and his forehead on them while he waited for his body to calm down.

Eleanor made a small sound and he jerked his head up, terrified that it had been a sob. But she was lying on her back still, looking up at the sky, her mouth a little swollen and red from his kisses and—thanks be to whoever the patron saint of careless males was—smiling just a little.

'Do you think we have our hats?' she asked. 'Or perhaps the bull has eaten them.'

'Yours is there. Goodness knows where mine is,' Blake said, after a quick survey of the flattened grass around them. The bull was staring at them through the rungs of the stile, presumably thinking that he managed matters better with his heifers.

'I thought you were truly wonderful,' Eleanor said seriously as she sat up.

'Ah, well, I wouldn't say that exactly.'

She was an inexperienced virgin, after all. That had been her first kiss…

'Picking me up and running like that. I know I am skinny, but I am quite tall. I must weigh quite a lot.'

'Not at all. And in the heat of the moment one gets extra strength.' Blake shrugged, trying for modesty and attempting not to feel ludicrously cast down by the fact that she had not mentioned the kiss. He deserved a boxed ear, at the very least, but he had expected *some* reaction.

'And I believe that danger is also an aphrodisiac?' Eleanor said seriously, making a question out of it and pronouncing *aphrodisiac* as calmly as she might have said *potato*. 'Hence that kiss.'

'That kiss,' Blake said firmly, 'had nothing to do with danger. We wanted to kiss—that is all.'

'Oh, really, my lord. I am plain, and not the kind of woman that men *want* to kiss except in the course of attacking me or out of relief at not being gored by a bull. I am quite well aware of that.'

She stood up and began to brush down her skirts. Then, when he made no move to stand, picked up her bonnet and shook the grass off it.

'It was very…interesting.'

Interesting?

'Eleanor, you are perfectly kissable.' He got to his feet. At least this conversation was having a dampening effect on his visible arousal.

'But I am—'

'Being a conventional beauty is not a prerequisite for being kissable,' he said, thinking that he sounded a pompous ass. The bull stared at him, drooling slightly. It had ludicrously long eyelashes for something so male.

'Oh. You are being kind, but thank you. What will you do now?'

'What?'

Visions of marriage proposals, of what any respectable woman's expectations might be after that little episode, of *doing the right thing*, flashed through his mind.

What the hell have I done? What does she ex-

pect? Look what happens when you let down your guard—you hurt someone else.

She was looking at him as though he was having trouble understanding plain English. 'Do you want to walk any more or should we go back?'

'Go back.'

Blake looked round for his hat, saw it was in the field, trampled, and sought for some kind of mental balance in the conversation.

He had just kissed Eleanor after a life-and-death flight from an enraged bull. He had been rolling about in the grass with her, damn it. She was completely inexperienced. And all she had to say about it was that it was *interesting*. The woman was extraordinary and, as for himself, he could not recall when another female had confused him quite so thoroughly. But at least she did not appear to be alarmed or expecting anything else.

She handed him her bonnet, took hold of her escaping hair in both hands and screwed it into a knot, then snatched back the bonnet and jammed it on her head before it could get free again. 'Bother it. My hair has a life of its own.'

'Cut it,' Blake suggested as they began to walk back in the direction of the carriage.

'I do cut it,' she said. 'The ends…to trim it.'

'No, I mean cut it really short—it would make little curls then. Rather charming. Very fashionable.'

Charming little curls? Whatever is coming over me?

The sideways look Eleanor gave him was wary, as though she thought he was teasing. Or had lost his mind, more likely. 'It would be easier to look after, I suppose,' she said doubtfully. 'Look, there is the carriage.'

She began to hurry, her limp suddenly more pronounced.

No doubt she will be delighted to get back to Polly, Blake thought grimly as he lengthened his stride and opened the carriage door for her with a word of thanks for their patient driver.

'What is it?' she asked after a few minutes. 'Have I got grass stains on my gown?' She fussed with her skirts.

'No. It is fine.' Blake resisted the temptation to brush away a single crushed daisy. What *was* this feeling she provoked in him? Whatever it was, it had prompted him to buy her nice clothes to give her pleasure, not because she was so shabby. Well, that too, he admitted.

And why was she so easy around him, come to that? He supposed the latter was easier to answer. Eleanor, the innocent, divided men into potential rapists and gentlemen. He, it seemed, was a gentleman from whom she was quite safe—except for *interesting* experimental kisses.

As for her...he supposed it was the novelty of

a gentlewoman who was not setting her cap at him, who was not pretending to be in love with him, who had no expectations of him. He felt relaxed around Eleanor—dangerously so. Well, he thought ruefully, relaxed in most areas of his body. It was almost as though her plainness made her no threat, although he supposed it was that plainness which meant she had no expectations.

She looked at him, head on one side, intelligent, brisk, puzzled, obviously wondering what was wrong with him. He wondered himself, and then he realised. Last month he had known exactly who he was and what he was doing—and he had been doing only what he'd wanted to. His responsibilities had been only those he chose to take on.

Now here he was, miles from London, with a battered brother and a ridiculously kissable, thoroughly awkward female for whom he had, madly, made himself responsible.

That was what was wrong with him. Insanity.

Blake seemed to be giving himself a brisk mental shake. At least his grey eyes were focussed and he had lost the slightly dazed look he had been wearing since he'd climbed back into the carriage.

Ellie wondered briefly about concussion, although she hadn't seen him hit his head. Or shock? But a big, strong, capable man like him

would not go into shock after a confrontation with
a bull—especially when he had come out on top
in the encounter.

Perhaps he was simply preoccupied with concerns about Jonathan and about being dragged
away from London for so long. She watched the
big, long-fingered hand that rested on his crossed
knee. It made her think the things she should
not—the pressure of his lips on hers, the taste of
him, the surprising pleasure of that shockingly
demanding tongue in her mouth, the feel of that
long body on her, under her, over her again.

So very different from that nightmare in her
bedchamber. *This* was what it should be like between a man and a woman.

It had been a moment of madness on his part,
of course, she knew that.

You are perfectly kissable.

His eyes had been closed. Any woman under
him like that would have been...*kissable*. Even
so, she thought it would be hours before her pulse
recovered its even rhythm. She would write about
it—capture those sensations, the feel and the taste
and the scent of him while they were still vivid.
Lay them up like lavender, to bring out on long
dark nights and recall one perfect spring moment
when she had been...*kissable*.

She was almost at the end of this strange diver-
sion from reality. By tomorrow night she would be

in her new home in Lancashire and Blake would be out of her life for ever. She should be glad. He had disturbed her equilibrium quite enough as it was. What her future life held was vegetable plots, chickens, Oscar's travels and perhaps a novel. And a pig.

It would definitely *not* hold handsome earls with grey eyes and broad shoulders and wicked mouths and dark shadows behind their smiles, and she had better get used to the fact.

'Is this it?' Blake let down the window as the coachman turned on to a rutted track. 'I suppose it must be. The man back in that village seemed to know what he was talking about. And the directions were clear enough. What a wilderness.'

'It is just...farmland, I suppose.'

She was not used to the countryside, but this was not exactly a howling moor or a rocky hillside. It was, in fact, rolling green fields broken up by stone walls, straggling hedges and clumps of windblown trees. By the look of them the wind blew a lot of the time, and from one direction— the sea, she supposed.

'It is very green.' *And muddy.*

'Plentiful rain,' Blake said. 'That's the Forest of Bowland over there.' He waved a hand in the direction of the lowering hills that had previously been on their right and were now behind them.

'They are part of the Pennines. Too high for much of the rain to get over, so it dumps itself on this side. The damp is good for cotton spinning—and ducks, I suppose.'

'Oh, excellent...' Ellie said weakly.

Still, if it was pouring with rain she couldn't be expected to dig vegetable plots and would have to stay inside and write. Her spirits had been plunging with every mile north today, and now all she wanted was to get into a big, warm goosedown bed and pull the covers over her head, or sit and write by a roaring fire, drinking chocolate and never having to emerge.

'Good for slugs and snails too,' Polly said helpfully. 'But ducks eat those. Perhaps we had better get some as well as the chickens, Miss Lytton.'

'Why not?' *What next? Sheep?* Please, no—then she would have to get a spinning wheel.

'That must be the house.'

She dropped the glass on her side of the carriage and leaned out. A solid farmhouse sat squarely on the rise of the hill, farm buildings straggling around it. It was built of a pinkish-grey stone, had a stone-tiled roof—and looked about two hundred years old.

'At least the roof seems to be intact.'

They drove into the yard and stopped. There was a wait while the groom got down and opened the door, and Ellie saw he was trying to pick his way through the mud to preserve the shine on his gleaming boots. He was unsuccessful.

'There's stepping stones, of sorts, to the front door, Miss Lytton,' he volunteered. 'I'd take my hand if I were you, miss.'

'Let me.' Blake eased past her and down onto a flat stone just as a man came round the corner of a farm building, a black and white dog slinking at his heels, belly to the ground. 'Good afternoon!'

'Aye.' The man wore boots and gaiters, old breeches and a vast frieze coat. He made no effort to remove the hat from his straggling brown hair.

'This is Carndale Farm?'

'Aye.'

Ellie could tell Blake was becoming irritated, but he kept his voice pleasant. 'And you are…?'

'Ebenezer Grimshaw. He who farms this,' he added, in a tone that suggested that the information had cost him actual money to part with.

'Right. Well, I am Lord Hainford and this is Miss Lytton, who owns the farm. Your landlady, in fact.'

'Aye. Yon lawyer wrote and said as you'd be coming up. Got a key, have you?' He jerked his head towards the farmhouse. 'Don't have nothing to do with the dwelling. Don't rent that. Just the shippons and the byres. You mind your feet… that's reet clarty underfoot.'

He turned and stamped off through the mud.

'Helpful,' Blake remarked. 'Could you make that out through the whiskers and the accent? He rents the farm buildings, but not the house. And I suspect he was warning us about the mud.'

'Kind of him.' Ellie looked down. 'Rather more than mud, I suspect. I do have the key.' She produced it from her reticule, where it had been shedding rust, and handed it to Blake. 'I would be obliged if you would get the door open and evict any chickens, or sheep, or whatever else is inside.'

She had to joke or she would simply burst into tears. And she would not allow that to happen.

It began to drizzle, and fine rain was blown into her face as she stood in the carriage doorway, watching Blake negotiate his way to the front door. There was a handkerchief in her reticule. She pulled it free, shook out the rust flakes and blew her nose defiantly.

I will not cry.

The farmer, Mr Grimshaw, trudged back around the corner. 'The back yard's not in with mine, missus, nor the sheds out there neither,' he said when he was standing in front of her. 'And there's wood chopped in the back porch. Happen some of it'll be dry.'

He turned round and walked away again before she could respond.

The front door opened with an eldritch shriek suitable to a Gothic novel and Blake vanished inside, into the gloom. Ellie sat back on the deep, luxurious upholstery with an instinct to cling to the vanishing threads of comfort and waited for him to reappear.

How long since the place had been lived in? A year, Rampion had said. It looked more like ten. It was bone-cold, thick with dust and cobwebs, and the furniture belonged to some distant decade of the past century. Blake walked through the ground floor—a sitting room, a big kitchen, various other rooms he could not judge the use of—then went upstairs. Four bedchambers and a staircase that must lead to the attics.

What the devil was that lawyer doing, sending Eleanor all that way to this? It was impossible.

He went out, re-crossed the mud to where she sat in the carriage, her hands neatly folded on her reticule, her pale oval face perfectly composed. Her nose was pink at the tip and her hair, rebelliously escaping from under her bonnet, was the only sign that something more than a meek spinster lurked inside the simple clothing. She had resumed her blacks.

'It is impossible,' he said bluntly.

She winced. 'It is my home now.'

'It is miles from anywhere. Cold, filthy.'

'There are logs, apparently. We have brought food and oil lamps and candles. Bedding.'

'I am not leaving you here with a man we know nothing about lurking in the cattle sheds and no way to get to a village, let alone Lancaster.'

'There is no option. This—' she jabbed a finger at the muddy ground '—is all I have.'

'Then sell it. Let me drive you into Lancaster, find you respectable lodgings.' She opened her mouth to protest but he pushed on, overriding her words. 'I will lend you the money. Then you can find a lawyer, sell this place, buy a little cottage in some small town.'

'But—'

'Eleanor, if you insist on getting out of this carriage and going in there I am going to stay here, on your doorstep, until you see reason. I cannot and will not leave a woman in a place like this. Damn it, Eleanor, I do not *care* what you want, or what your stubborn self-reliance is telling you. I am going to stop you turning into some drudge in a rural slum and that is final.'

'I do not care what you want, Felicity. I do not care what nonsense you are spouting. This is a perfectly suitable marriage for both of us and it has been arranged since we were children. You knew I would marry you—I fail to see why I had to rush to do so the moment I inherited. If we do not go through with it, then what is to become of you, a woman who broke off a perfectly good betrothal?'

He had said all that to the girl who had been his betrothed since they were children—the pretty, sweet, gentle girl of impeccable breeding who had told him she did not want to marry him because he did not love her and had neglected her.

Not because she didn't like him, but because she didn't *love* him. Because he didn't love *her*. Of course he had not allowed her to have her own way. And look how *that* had turned out. Because he *had* loved her, and he had told her so, and she had refused to believe him.

He had been wrong then and a woman had died. It seemed he was going to be wrong again, but he refused to leave *this* woman here.

Chapter Eight

'Fine,' Eleanor said. 'You can stay on the doorstep until you rust and get rheumatism. See if I care.'

She got down from the coach, as angry as he was, and glared at him.

'Mr Grimshaw!'

The man appeared again—suspiciously quickly, in Blake's opinion. Presumably he was lurking, listening to their edifying discussion.

'Thank you. I apologise for shouting like that. Do you have any farm hands who would be willing to help me take my luggage inside and fetch in the firewood and some water?'

'Aye, I have that.' He turned and bellowed, 'Seth! Greg! Get out here!'

A big man and a skinny lad came round the edge of the barn, knuckling their foreheads and sending sideways glances at Blake, Eleanor and the carriage.

'Help this lady in with her traps. This is Miss Lytton, the owner. You mind and call her ma'am, now.'

'You will do no such thing. Miss Lytton is not staying.'

The lad who had lifted down the bags stood fumbling with them, then dropped one in the mud.

'Clumsy lummock.' The farmer cuffed him. 'You this lady's brother? Or her betrothed? Or what—?'

'He is none of those things,' Eleanor cut in. 'He kindly gave me a ride here and has now been seized with an inappropriate desire to order my life, it seems.'

'I am Lord Hainford and—'

'I don't care iffen you're the Lord Chief Justice. Yon's the lady's house and she wants to go into it and that's the end of the matter. Get on, now!' he roared at the two hands, who broke into a shambling run towards the house with the first load of baggage.

Blake contemplated brute force. There were two large men and a lad against himself and his coachman and groom. Very good odds. Then he saw Eleanor's face. That was what she expected— that he would brawl in the mud to get his own way.

'Miss Lytton. You cannot expect me to leave

you in this isolated place with only a slip of a maid and three men of whom we know nothing.'

'Now, you look here, your lordship.' Grimshaw clenched weatherbeaten fists. 'I'm a sidesman of our chapel and I'll have the minister here iffen I have any more from you about my good name.'

'Thank you, Mr Grimshaw. I look forward to meeting the minister and I appreciate your help. Perhaps if I could just have a word with his lordship in private?'

The farmer nodded, gave Blake a look strongly reminiscent of the bull, and plodded off to supervise the unloading of the bags and boxes of supplies.

'Eleanor, you are not going to be stupidly independent and insist—?'

'Miss Lytton to you, my lord. And, yes, I *am* going to insist. This is my home, my property— and, grateful as I am for transport to this point, I think our association is now at an end. I fail to understand why you should wish to involve yourself in my affairs when you have made it clear from the beginning that you have found this an imposition. Unless you wish to add kidnapping to your roster of outrageous behaviour?' she flung at him, as if trying to provoke a response, an answer. 'Perhaps you could strip off here and now—that would certainly divert Mr Grimshaw while you toss me into the carriage and drove off.'

He could do it—snatch her, that was, not strip. The three of them could get Eleanor and the maid into the carriage and drive off. But where would *that* get him? He knew *what* it would get him—a furious female who was in the right. And he, who had no rights at all, would be entirely, and legally, in the wrong. A kidnapper.

Chivalry would allow him to fell Grimshaw if the fellow insulted or threatened her, but the farmer was apparently fully on her side and respectful in his gruff way. And, as for anything else, Blake wasn't her brother or her guardian or her legal advisor, and most certainly not her betrothed.

Miss Lytton was an unusual creature in English society: a woman of property, old enough to order her own life. The fact that her property was a filthy rural slum in the middle of what to southern eyes resembled a howling wilderness was neither here nor there.

He had tried to bully a woman into doing the right thing before and that had been fatal. *Never again.* A gentleman knew when to apologise. A gentleman knew how to withdraw gracefully.

'Are all your belongings and the supplies in the house now, Miss Lytton?'

She glanced round, then narrowed her eyes at him suspiciously. 'They are.'

'Is there any way in which I may be of further use to you?'

'There is not, my lord.'

'In that case I will bid you good day and wish you every happiness in your new…home.'

He bowed, got into the carriage with as much dignity as a routed earl in full retreat could muster and knocked on the roof. The coach lumbered out of the yard, and as it went he caught a glimpse of Eleanor standing in the mud and the rain, flanked by Polly and her rustic assistants.

And that, Blake thought savagely, *will teach me never to strip naked in White's again.*

Temper and affronted pride got Blake as far as Lancaster and an inn where, try as he might, he could find nothing to criticise and no outlet for his foul mood.

A bath, a decent meal and a bottle of surprisingly good claret improved his mood to the point where anxiety won out over the humiliation of having his will so comprehensively flouted. The port after dinner was not as good as the claret, which meant that he was regrettably clear-headed as he sat staring into the fire and brooding.

He had handled that confrontation with Eleanor about as badly as was possible. He knew she was strong-minded, opinionated, stubborn and intelligent. He should have tried reasoned argument—should have discussed the alternatives, not laid down the law and demanded that she submit to his will. Once she'd had her hackles up and her back to the wall she had been as fiercely determined not to yield as a chained bear facing a pack of dogs in the baiting ring.

In the morning, after Eleanor had had a night to sleep on it, to discover the discomforts of the place, he would go back and apologise and try talking it through with her.

Even as he decided that he felt uneasy. There were just the two of them, young women, miles from anywhere, hundreds of miles from anyone they knew, and he had left them with strangers—men he knew nothing about. And Eleanor was uneasy around men. How would she be feeling now that she'd had time to get over her annoyance with him?

Leaving her to sleep on it seemed less and less possible, because if nothing else *he* was not going to be able to sleep. And if anything happened to that infuriating creature he would not be able to live with himself.

It had at least stopped raining by the time Blake rode into the front yard of Carndale Farm. There was a faint glimmer of light from behind the drawn curtains of the front room, but rather than pound on the door Blake led his hired horse through the mud and round to the back. There was light from the kitchen as well, he saw as he tied the animal up under the lean-to shed. No one had covered that window, and he looked in and saw Polly sitting at the table, her hands cupped around a mug, her whole body sagging with weariness.

Why was she not in her bed? He couldn't imagine that Eleanor was the kind of mistress who would keep an exhausted servant from her rest.

He knocked on the door, and when he heard the chair scrape back stepped into the light from the window so Polly could see him.

'My lord?' She blinked up at him.

'I was worried about you both,' he said. 'May I come in?'

'Yes, of course. Sorry, my lord.' She opened the door wide, then closed it behind him and stood swaying slightly.

'You are exhausted. Why aren't you in your bed? Surely Miss Lytton isn't making you stay up?'

'No. Oh, no, she said to go up a good hour ago, it must have been. I heard the church clock strike eleven, I think, but it was faint. I might be wrong. But she won't go to her bed, my lord, and I don't like to leave her. She worked just as hard as I did.

We got the beds made up, and the worst of the dirt out of those two bedchambers and in here. And we dusted off some of it in the front room and lit the fires. That Mr Grimshaw and his men carried the wood in, and he brought in a great load of sheepskins.'

She gestured to one in front of the kitchen range.

'Anyway, Miss Lytton's sitting on a pile of them in front of the fire, just staring at it. I can't go off to bed and leave her there, can I, my lord? I'd never sleep easy.'

'You can now I am here. Off you go, Polly, and I'll persuade Miss Lytton to go to bed as well. Don't you sit up waiting for her. She can perfectly well manage and you've done enough for one day.'

As he'd hoped, Polly was used to the man of the house laying down the law about everything, and now Blake was there she was happy enough to leave the responsibility in his hands. He watched her trudge upstairs and then let himself into the front room.

There was a good blaze in the wide stone fireplace and a pile of logs by the side. Grimshaw and his men had at least done that job well. The heat was still superficial, though, barely touching the bone-deep cold of a house that had stood empty throughout a long winter and a wet, miserable summer.

Eleanor was sitting on a pile of sheepskins with blankets around her shoulders and her hair loose and curling wildly on her shoulders. She did not look round as he closed the door with a soft click.

'Do go to bed, Polly, please.'

'She has,' Blake said, and saw her stiffen, although she did not turn from the leaping flames. 'I was worried about you so I came back.'

'Blake?' She did finally look round, and he thought her like something from a fairy tale—silhouetted against the fire, enthroned on her pile of sheepskins, her hair unbound and undisciplined, the glimmer of her pale oval face almost invisible against the light.

'You must be exhausted.' He shivered despite his caped greatcoat, but he unbuttoned it, tossed it onto a settle and went to hunker down beside her. 'Are you frightened to go to bed, is that it? Did Grimshaw—?'

'Oh, no, he couldn't have been kinder, in that abrupt, growly way he has. And Mrs Grimshaw came and brought us a can of milk and some bread and eggs. I am just...' Her voice trailed away and she hunched her shoulders under the blankets.

'So tired that you have gone beyond sleep, even?'

He had been that way himself before now, after an all-day, all-night orgy of card-playing, but that hadn't been accompanied by anxiety and an argument and having to struggle to make a dirty, cold house habitable.

'Mmm,' she agreed.

'Go to bed,' he said. 'I'll sleep down here in front of the fire. Stand guard.'

'What against?' she asked, and lifted her head to look him in the eye. 'Ghosts? I don't think this house has any.'

'Against whatever it is stopping you sleeping,' Blake said. When she did not respond, except to give a little shake of her head, he shifted onto the sheepskins beside her, put his arm around her shoulders and pulled her in close. 'I'll carry you up.'

'Cold up there,' she mumbled, almost limp against his shoulder. 'I put the warming pan in Polly's bed.'

Of course you did, Blake thought with exasperated admiration. Most mistresses wouldn't even have thought of it—would assume that the servants would heat themselves a brick on the range.

'All right,' he said. 'Sleep here.' He laid her down, then slid his arm out.

Eleanor was asleep as soon as her head touched the soft curling wool, he realised. He heaped the skins up to make a barrier between her back and the draught from the door, then quietly mended the fire and banked it down with some turves that had been stacked on the hearth—presumably for just that purpose.

He couldn't leave now, he realised, because unless he woke one of the two women to lock up behind him he could not secure the house. He could spend the night in the lean-to, of course, but he didn't feel quite *that* chivalrous.

Blake went out to see to the horse, then came back in through the kitchen, dealt with that fire and blew out the lamp. Then he went into the front room and eyed the available furniture. It was all bare wood—two settles and an uncompromising upright chair with arms. And it was cold.

He pulled off his boots, took off his coat, waistcoat and neckcloth, and eased down behind Eleanor. He pulled the sheepskins over both of them, pillowed his head on his bent arm and closed his eyes. The skins smelt of lanolin and sheep, the room of woodsmoke and dust…and Eleanor of woman and good plain soap.

He pushed away the sheepskins until he could curl his body around her, wriggled his cold feet into the skins and closed his eyes, expecting to find that he was also too tired, too full of churning thoughts to be able to sleep. Oblivion came almost on a breath.

She was warm, and the bed smelt of sheep and—and *Blake?* The realisation of why she was warm came with the awareness of an arm lying heavily across her waist and the large, solid body she was held against.

Ellie blinked into the dawn light and the weight over her waist lifted away. The pressure of the body—Blake's body—left her back.

'You are awake.' He was still so close that his breath tickled warmly on the nape of her neck. 'Sorry, I didn't mean to crowd you.' He sounded sleepy, comfortable.

'Blake. *My lord.* You are in my bed.'

Now that the immediate shock of finding herself in bed with a man had left her, she found she had to force herself to pretend outrage. It was really rather lovely to feel that warm, big, male body curved around hers, protecting her. More than lovely.

'It was the only warm, comfortable place and we are both clothed. And nobody knows.'

'*I* know,' Ellie pointed out, making no attempt to move. 'And so do you.'

'I won't tell if you don't,' Blake said, the words caressing her nape in warm breath.

This was real. She could not pretend it was a dream. Because if it had been then he would be kissing her, not making foolish quips, and she would be beautiful, and one part of her mind would not be shrieking, *Man! Danger!* while the other part said, *Trust him...this is Blake.*

She heard him draw breath to speak, felt him inhale because he was so close. Then his breath caught and his lips pressed against her skin, exploring, tasting.

'*Blake*...' Her heart was pounding with fear and excitement and emotions she had no name for.

He mumbled something—*Hush,* perhaps—as his mouth moved to the skin beneath her ear. Ellie wriggled to give him better access, and then froze as his weight came down over her.

She was no longer dizzy with fear and excitement from their escape from the bull, and this was no field under the open sky. This was a bed and she was trapped and...

She gave a sudden heave and his arm shifted and came down over her ribcage.

Blake rolled away abruptly. 'Hell. I'm sorry. Half awake and... No excuse.' He ran his hands through his hair and frowned down at her. 'Eleanor, you are far too thin. You aren't eating properly—you are skin and bone.'

Nothing could have jerked her back to reality out of the tangling feelings of fear and desire more effectively. Of *course* she was in no danger from Blake. Even if he was the kind of man who would force himself on a woman he quite obviously didn't want when he was fully awake and not giddy from danger or fuddled by sleep.

She sat up and twisted to glare down at him. 'How could you say such a thing?'

'Because it is true. Between your ribs and your hipbone I have probably got bruises on my forearm.' He lay there, sprawled on the sheepskins like a Barbarian warrior king, his shirt open at the neck to reveal a glimpse of dark hair. 'Some people are naturally slender, but you are half-starved, Eleanor. And all the time we've been together I have never seen you eat a decent amount.'

'I have a poor appetite. And it is none of your business.'

All the time we've been together...

'No, it is not. But I am worried about you. Yesterday I was wrong to hector you, to demand that you come away. I should have tried persuasion. I came back to apologise, to make certain you were safe. Not to make love to you. And for that I have to apologise even more.'

She wondered just how often this man felt the need to apologise for anything. How often the words to do so actually passed his lips. Not often, she'd wager. Was it pride that kept his thoughts locked up so tightly? What about all that she glimpsed when she saw that shadowy, inner Blake—a man keeping his secrets close out of an arrogant refusal to allow anyone close?

'Thank you. Apology accepted for leaving me and for...for what just occurred. I quite understand. You were only half awake. So was I, or it would never have happened. And thank you for your concern. But will you now, *please*, go away?'

Before I fall on you, kiss you, beg you to make love to me, skinny creature that I am. Before I lose all pride. Because just now I am angry enough not to be afraid.

When Blake did not move she said, 'I promise you that Grimshaw is a perfectly decent man, that this house is sound, and that once it warms up we will be exceedingly comfortable.'

'Last night—'

'Last night I was blue-devilled. Too tired and too cold to look forward and be positive. Now I have slept well, I am warm and I will be fine.'

She stood up and gathered a blanket over her sensible flannel nightgown and wrapper—to find herself wearing them, and not some exquisite wisps of silk and satin was yet another clear indicator that this was not a fantasy.

'I will put a kettle on the kitchen fire. I have no doubt you would prefer to start your journey back after a cup of coffee.'

It was a physical wrench, turning and walking away—a tug as though he had taken hold of her arm to hold her. But of course Blake had done no such thing—would do no such thing. Not when he was fully awake.

Ellie went through into the kitchen, chilly despite the fire in the range that had been burning all night beneath its turves. She pushed them back with the poker and put on more fuel, filled the old iron kettle from the pump in the corner. The kettle looked as though it had come new with the house. She hoisted it over the fire and went upstairs to dress. She did not want to face Blake again, but if she had to then it would be armoured behind as many layers of clothing as possible.

Chapter Nine

'It's raining again, miss.'

Marjorie, the youngest Grimshaw daughter, who came in three times a week to do the cleaning and help with the laundry, paused in the doorway to impart the good news, then went on down the passageway to the kitchen, a basket of ironing on her hip.

'Amazing,' Ellie muttered, chewing the end of her pen as she scanned her accounts. 'What a novelty. Raining this morning *and* this afternoon. And presumably this evening and all night. Just like yesterday, and the week before, and the week before that. The minister will be preaching on the subject of Noah soon—although if anyone expects me to help herd sheep into an ark they can think again. Stupid animals.'

The accounts did not look any better the more she pored over them.

At first she had been so optimistic. Dear little

Oscar's North African adventures had, to her considerable surprise, pleased Messrs Broderick & Alleyn—presumably because she had refrained from having him captured by corsairs—and was even now being printed for the delectation of young people thirsting for information on date-harvesting, camels, and the uses of papyrus for paper-making. Even better was the money for the book that was now sitting in Hodgkin's Bank in Lancaster, along with Mr Grimshaw's quarterly rent.

A significant part of that flowed back into the Grimshaw coffers, in the form of Marjorie's wages and payment for eggs, milk and a weekly ride into Lancaster for marketing, of course, but that was perfectly affordable.

And they were comfortable enough. After a month of hard work the house was clean, and mostly warm now that constant fires had had time to sink their heat into the thick walls. She and Polly had a bedchamber each, and the other upstairs rooms were closed off. Downstairs she used the parlour as a sitting room and study, and Polly reigned in the kitchen.

When—*if*—it stopped raining Polly had plans for a kitchen garden and a hen coop, but that would only put some food in their stomachs. It would not help with the main problem.

She mended her pen and tried to think of the

positives. The rain kept her inside and usefully occupied in writing a novel of passion and romance, with a grey-eyed desert lord on a black stallion…a hero who kissed like a dream… It was a rational use of her North African research, Ellie told herself, and was considerably more warming than her latest project for Broderick & Alleyn—a juvenile history of Scotland that was dragging along because it took so much longer for her to obtain the books she needed for research, being so far from the London libraries and bookshops.

When she finished the novel she hoped to sell it to the Minerva Press, and was trying to think up a suitable *nom de plume*. But she had to complete it first, and get it accepted. Goodness knew when—*if*—that would produce some money.

And she was well. Not cold, moderately comfortable, doing productive work. Putting on weight…

She grimaced at the thought, running a finger over the rather tight seams of her bodice. Much as it had smarted, she had taken Blake's criticism—or perhaps *concern* was a kinder description—to heart. She had no need to peck at her food to keep her womanly curves at bay. There was no potentially dangerous man in the house, and outside it no one saw her without the layers of clothing the weather forced on everyone this year—the year they were calling Eighteen Hundred and Froze to Death.

Even so, it had been difficult at first to abandon the discipline of always being hungry and to get used to the feeling of sometimes being full up without feeling apprehensive.

So she was well, busy, plumper... *Lonely.* The answer to that was to work harder. But, although she was tired by eleven in the evening, there was nothing to fill the long, sleepless hours at night as she lay listening to the soft hiss of rain, the soughing of the wind and thought about a strong male body curled protectively around hers.

How was he? Where was he? Was he happy? She feared not, although why she could not say.

Ellie gave herself a brisk mental shake and looked again at the accounts book. Blake was no longer any concern of hers and she had other things to worry about. Good health, hard work and even all the success in the world with one as yet unwritten novel would not help with the problem of the state of the roof.

She had called in a builder to investigate a wet patch Polly had discovered, and he had found a dozen more. The roof itself would stand for a hundred years, he assured her. The problem was it would leak like a sieve while it did so. Some of the heavy stone slates had slipped, their pegs had rotted, and it all needed stripping off and re-fixing.

When it stopped raining, of course.

Then there was the stream that provided their water supply. Despite the rain, the thing was becoming a trickle—and that, Grimshaw had informed her, was because Farmer Bond over on the next farm was diverting water for his new stockyard. Apparently he was perfectly entitled to do because the spring rose on *his* land. At least, so had said the lawyer she had asked to advise her.

Now she had no stream and a fat lawyer's bill for unwelcome advice. Grimshaw had said the only thing to do was to sink a well. And then he'd told her what that was likely to cost. As it was, he was having to take his stock over to the far side of the land he rented from her to water them. The lawyer had said that according to the terms of his lease she was supposed to provide him with an adequate water supply, and if she did not he could legitimately ask for a reduction in rent. So far he hadn't asked for one, but Ellie was braced for the shock when he did.

The lawyer had also helpfully pointed out that either she had to raise money for the well and the roof or accept a lower rent and the loss of income—which would further delay the roof and the well—or find someone to buy a farm where there was little water despite constant rain. Except, of course, in the attics, and soon in the rooms below as well. And with the farm went her rents…

The figures tumbled over and over in her head, getting in the way of her writing, getting in the way of her attempts to plan. If she spent the money from the publishers on the roof or the well—it wouldn't do both—then there went her tiny nest egg…

The knocker was rapped sharply. *Strange.* Ellie put down her pen. The Grimshaws and the farm workers would go to the kitchen door, so did pedlars. It sounded again. Polly was probably up to her elbows in bread dough.

Ellie took off her writing apron and went to the front door, opened it and found a bedraggled young gentleman on the step and a pony trap standing in the muddy yard.

'Excuse me, ma'am, but I've lost my way. I was hoping for directions to Lancaster.' He took off his hat politely and stood there with the rain soaking his hair.

He seemed eminently respectable—and very, very wet. 'You had best come in out of the rain and have a cup of tea before you go on. It will take you another hour, and you will catch your death if you don't warm up a little. Lead the pony around to the back, where you will find a shed to shelter the trap. Then come in through the kitchen door.'

'I am very much obliged to you, ma'am.' He

resumed his hat, somewhat pointlessly, and did as she'd said.

Ellie went through to warn Polly to put the kettle on while she went upstairs for a stack of towels. Ridiculous how much she was looking forward to an hour's conversation with a total stranger when what she *needed* was a pixie or an elf, or whatever the local supernatural life forms were, to come and guide her to a crock of gold. That or the arrival of a financial wizard.

The young man introduced himself as James Harkness, on his way to conduct some business in Lancaster. Polly took his dripping coat and hat to put in front of the fire and promised to find him an oilskin for his shoulders before he ventured out again.

He proved good company, regaling them with tales of his encounters on the road north. He accepted a second cup of tea and a slice of cake with expressions of gratitude.

'This is a fine old house, ma'am. It looks sturdy and warm.'

'Sturdy enough except for the roof,' Ellie said grimly, and reached for another slice of cake. The seams in her good brown gown would have to be let out soon. 'Which is in dire need of work.'

'I am sorry to hear that, ma'am. It will be a big job on a place this size, I should imagine.'

'Big enough.' Ellie made herself smile, even

if it was somewhat lopsided. 'We will sort it out in time.'

They sent the damp young man on his way with an oilskin and careful directions, and she went back to her desk. If she could only forget Blake's words the day they had arrived.

Stupidly independent...

'*You can stay on the doorstep until you rust and get rheumatism. See if I care,*' she had retorted.

But despite her hostility he *had* cared. He had come back to make certain she was all right.

It was a good thing he did not know about the roof or the water supply.

She wanted Blake, wanted his practical good business sense. Wanted his advice. Wanted *him*.

That is just too bad, Ellie. You are stupidly independent, remember? And plain, and of no interest to his lordship whatsoever. So get on and manage. Lord Hainford is no more likely to materialise here than that mythical financial wizard with his pointed hat.

Mr James Harkness, private enquiry agent, sat on the other side of Blake's desk and produced his notebook. 'It is not good, my lord. There's a water dispute that will reduce the rents and the land value, and the roof is an expensive job. The place is clean, tidy, but it reeks of just making do and I have never been so cold and wet in my life. The locals say it has been the worst summer anyone can recall, just like it has been everywhere this year, and that there'll be famers heading for ruin. I imagine a farm like hers will be impossible to sell for anything like what it is worth.'

'How did Miss Lytton seem to you?' Blake kept his voice studiously neutral. He had given Harkness the impression that Ellie was a distant relative and he wanted to keep it like that—although the man would find out soon enough if his interest was aroused.

'Tired,' the other man said after a moment's frowning thought. 'Tired and worried and... *dogged.* The lady has courage—I will say that for her. The local people say she is always pleasant, pays up on time, is a good neighbour. But you can see they wonder what on earth a southern lady is doing on a remote Lancashire farm with just the one maid.'

She is up there because some idiot was too tied up in a game of cards to stop her even more idiotic stepbrother ruining her, Blake thought. *And then said idiot put her back up to such an extent that she dug her heels in and now her pride won't let her yield. And the same idiot hasn't learned from the past...hasn't worked out how to deal with an intelligent woman without driving her to disaster.*

He had sworn not to become emotionally involved with a woman again, and yet here he was once more with his instincts and his intentions all awry. Very well—he would throw his money and influence at the problem. He could do it at a distance…there was no need for him to become involved.

'Right, get back up there and go and see her lawyer. You will pretend to be the agent for someone. Let me think… I know—some newly rich manufacturer from Manchester who is buying up land while prices are depressed because of the agricultural crisis. Anonymous, of course. Assure her that her tenant is safe, because she will worry about that, and pay top price. Don't haggle.'

A month later Blake tossed the deeds for Ellie's farm across the desk to Jonathan. 'It worked. I imagine her lawyer could hardly believe his luck, finding a Manchester manufacturer desperate to own land and willing to pay the first price he mentioned. And Harkness says it is still raining—just like it is down here, only colder.'

'What will she do now, do you think?'

'I have no idea. Buy an annuity and a nice cottage somewhere, one hopes. I— Yes, Turner?'

The butler came in and closed the door. 'A Miss Lytton, my lord. Asking to speak with you. *Demanding*, to be more accurate. A most…determined lady. Should I tell her you are not at home?'

'Eleanor Lytton? Here?'

'Yes—here.'

The door behind Turner opened and Eleanor stalked in. Blake and Jonathan got to their feet. Blake only hoped he was not looking as ridiculously amazed as his brother was.

'I want my farm back, Lord Hainford.'

'Thank you, Turner. That will be all. Eleanor, will you sit down?'

'Do not *Eleanor* me.' She took hold of the back of the chair but did not sit. 'You bought my farm under false pretences.'

She looked dreadful, he thought, although she *had* gained weight and in the process developed a figure he most certainly did not remember...

He dragged his eyes away from her bosom, which was frankly heaving with suppressed emotion, and looked at her face. There were shadows under her eyes, her skin was even paler than before, and beneath the anger she seemed desperately tired.

'I paid a very fair price. The sale is perfectly legal,' he said. There seemed no point in denying it. 'How did you know I was the buyer?'

'I was so grateful at first that I didn't think.' She came around the chair and sank into it.

Blake sat too—warily, ready to jump up and catch her if, as seemed likely, she fainted. Anger appeared to be the only thing keeping her going.

'Then the morning after it had all gone through I realised it just did not add up—that either it was a miracle or something strange was going on. I thought perhaps there was coal or iron or something under the land, and in that case I wanted it. So I bribed a chambermaid to let me into that nice Mr Harkness's bedchamber at the inn while he was eating his breakfast and I went through his papers.'

'You searched his room—?'

'Of course I did. When I saw your name I knew it was too much to hope that he would take the money back—not if he was working for you. So I came straight down here.'

'Why?'

'To give it back myself.' She opened her reticule and produced a bank draft. 'Here it is. Now, give me the deeds.'

'No. *Why*, Eleanor?'

'I do not take charity.'

When he shook his head she picked up the bank draft, walked across to the fireplace and tossed it into the flames.

Jonathan leapt to his feet with an oath and seized the poker—but too late. He threw it into the grate with a muttered curse and stalked back to his seat.

'I will simply write another,' Blake said.

'And I will not take it. I cannot be beholden to

you.' She swallowed, but kept her head up, staring at a point over his left shoulder.

Her hazel eyes swam with tears that she would not let fall, and he realised suddenly that this was not anger, but the stubborn defiance of a woman at her wits' end.

'Why not?' he asked, holding up a hand to silence Jonathan. 'Why not let me help? You blame me for Francis's death, for letting him ruin you. All I am doing is making amends as best I can. I might have paid over the odds for that land now, but eventually I will get my investment back and you need the money at once—not in some indefinite future.'

'No...' she whispered, and closed her eyes on those betraying tears.

Her lips were parted, just a fraction, and suddenly he was back in that meadow, with her body warm and eager beneath his, those lips fresh and sweet and open to him. Back on that heap of sheepskins, with her defenceless and trusting, asleep in his arms, turning drowsily to meet his questing mouth.

Blake blinked and there she was, sitting opposite him. Drab and plain and, despite the new curves, a beanpole. And as fierce and proud as a defeated queen.

'All right,' he heard himself saying. 'If you won't take my money then take me. Marry me.'

'*What?*' Jonathan's chair went over with a crash as he shot to his feet.

'*Marry* you?' Eleanor's eyes were wide open now. 'Me?'

'Why not?'

The room seemed to swim around him and he wondered if he was coming down with something. Certainly words seemed to be issuing from his lips without any conscious thought behind them.

'You are from a good family, perfectly eligible, and I really ought to get married—should have done it sooner. Yes?'

Jonathan was staring at him as though he had gone mad. He probably had. That was it—not a fever but insanity. Or he was drunk. Or this was a dream.

He had just asked a plain, penniless spinster to marry him.

Chapter Ten

Ellie blinked and swallowed salt. Blake had just asked her to marry him. *Lord Hainford* was asking her to be his countess. But it could not be true, of course. She was so tired, so worried, so *miserable* that she had made herself ill and now she was hallucinating in the grip of a fever. Or she was dreaming.

But if this was a fantasy, she might as well enjoy it until she woke up.

'Yes,' she said as his face blurred and she felt herself slide from the chair.

Where was she? Somewhere warm. Somewhere that was not damp and that did not smell of woodsmoke. Somewhere exceedingly comfortable, with deep feather beds. *Oh, yes.* She was going to be a countess. That explained it.

Ellie sat up in bed with a muffled yelp and

clutched at her swimming head. That had been a dream, not real—so where was she now?

There was a bell-pull right next to the bed and she tugged on it. It would not bring Polly. She was still up in Lancashire, keeping an eye on the farm. Unless that was all part of the dream as well…

'Good morning, Miss Lytton.' Not Polly, but a tall, dark-haired maid in neat blue, with a crisp white apron. She was holding a tray. 'I was just coming up to see if you were awake yet and to bring you some chocolate. Would you like breakfast in bed? Or I can lay the table over there if you would rather get up, miss.'

'Where am I?'

'London, Miss Lytton. The best guest bedchamber in Lord Hainford's townhouse in Berkeley Square. No wonder you are confused, miss, after that faint. And it's so lovely and quiet here at the back you'd never believe you were in town, would you?'

So this was real and perhaps…

Oh, no, she had *not* agreed to marry the man, had she?

Impossible—he would never have asked her in the first place. How embarrassing it would have been if she had said something before she'd realised it was a dream and she hadn't been quite well.

The maid put the tray on the bedside table and

went to pull back the curtains. 'It's a beautiful morning, Miss Lytton. There is actually a little bit of sunshine.'

'It is not raining?' Ellie struggled up against a mountain of pillows and blinked at the watery glow. 'No, it isn't.'

More unreality—although the maid seemed solid and rational, and the chocolate, such a luxury, slid over her tongue like warm velvet. But she must get up, have breakfast, confront Blake and make him give her the deeds back.

'I will get up and wash and then have breakfast,' she decided.

'I'll run the bath then, miss.'

The maid went out through what must be the dressing room door and almost immediately there was the sound of running water.

A bathroom?

She would marry the Prince Regent himself for a bathroom with hot water, Ellie thought wildly, and put a hand to her forehead. No, she wasn't feverish.

She was still attempting to separate reality and memory from dreams and fantasy as she made her way downstairs to the study where they'd told her Blake awaited her.

He was alone when she entered. He stood looking out of the window, one arm bent and resting on the window frame, so that his whole lean, elegant form was silhouetted against the light. He turned when he heard the door close and came to move one of the chairs before the fireplace slightly for her.

'How do you feel this morning, Eleanor?'

'Much better, thank you.' She sat, and he took the chair opposite, leaned forward, forearms on his knees, eyes focused on her face. 'I apologise for fainting,' she added.

'I suppose you came tearing down here without stopping to eat properly. What was it? The Mail?' When she merely nodded he sat back with a grunt of annoyance. 'You have made yourself ill. Look at you.'

That was satisfactorily un-lover-like.

'I was…upset.'

'Yes,' Blake said drily. 'I gathered that. Now we must consider carefully. I had intended getting a special licence and marrying you immediately, but with you looking so unwell I think it would be best to postpone it for a few weeks, so I will just get an ordinary one. There is no need to advertise our business by having banns read—'

She made an inarticulate sound and he stopped.

'What is it?'

'A marriage licence?'

'Yes. Don't you remember? Yesterday afternoon you agreed to marry me.'

'No, I couldn't have. It was a dream. A hallucination. I am not well—you said so yourself.'

'Eleanor, if you are the one hallucinating, how is it that I am the one certain that we agreed to marry?' He was smiling at her as the logic of that sank in. '*I* am in perfectly good health.'

'But why would you *want* to marry me?' Was this some kind of cruel joke to punish her for involving him in her problems? But *he* had involved himself—all she had done was try and get rid of him after that first demand that he take her to Lancashire. And he was smiling in a way that made her want to slide forward from the chair into his arms and...

'Why shouldn't I? I need to marry sooner or later, and sooner is probably better. You are of perfectly good family, and we know each other a little now. You are intelligent, capable, and you are in a difficult situation that would be resolved by marriage. A situation *I* helped put you in.' When she still simply stared at him he added, his face suddenly expressionless, 'And I have absolutely no commitments to anyone else, if that is worrying you.'

There it goes again. That door slamming shut. There is no one, and I believe him. So what is he hiding?

'I am plain. I limp,' she said.

And why is there no one else?

'I am used to my own company, and stubborn and argumentative when I am out of it. I have no dowry as I have just lost my farm to a confidence trickster. I have never had a come-out and have no idea how to go on at the level of Society I imagine you live in.'

'Yes, I know all that.' He did not even attempt to counter the *plain*. 'But do you actively dislike me? When I am not stripping off in White's or trying to assist you, I mean?'

'I frequently want to throw things at you.'

'But in the intervals between?'

The smile was back and she wondered if it was a weapon, or perhaps a mask. He reached out and took her hand, turned it over and began to trace a pattern round and round on the inside of her wrist—a delicate, barely-there touch that seemed to go straight to something deep inside her.

'When we kiss, for example? I seem to recall you found that...interesting.'

'I found that very... It was not at all unpleasant.' Ellie found that her eyes were closed, and every inch of her body, of her concentration, was focused on the drift of Blake's fingertips over her wrist.

'It could be *not unpleasant* every day if you marry me.' There was the faintest thread of laughter in his voice. 'You slept in my arms— you trusted me then. Wouldn't you like to be a countess? Think of the good you could do…the charities you could support or found. Or the artists you could sponsor if you wanted a *salon.*'

Ellie opened her eyes. With them closed, and only his deep, warmly persuasive voice to focus on, she could almost believe it was possible.

'I have responsibilities. The Grimshaws have been good to me and there are problems with the water supply. I cannot just walk away from that. I thought I was selling to someone who would deal with the problems—not someone who was tricking me in order to give me charity.'

Blake did not blink at the accusation. 'I will have my legal people sort it out. I would have done so anyway. And if the stream is a lost cause I will have a well sunk. Say *yes,* Eleanor, and stay down here. I really would find attempting to court you over such a distance exceedingly wearing, you know.' When she looked up at him, indignant, he said, 'But I *will* do it if I have to.'

'I need to think.'

She drew back her hand and he let it go.

'Very well. I will be at home all morning.'

'I mean I need *time* to think,' she began.

But he shook his head and went out, leaving Ellie to stare at the door.

I cannot marry him.

Then… *Why can't I marry him?*

He is infuriating, stubborn, and refuses to be

serious...except when he is. He is cunning and de-
termined and manipulative. He does not love me
and he certainly cannot desire me...except when
he literally falls on top of me or is half asleep. He
will probably stray as soon as we were married.
I will be an embarrassment in Society, although
that is his problem, not mine. But I desire him. I
like him when he isn't being infuriating. I am tired
of being poor and anxious. I would do my very
best to be a good wife in return for all the things
he would be giving me.

But one other anxiety nagged at her. Blake
was eminently eligible. Titled, wealthy, handsome, personable, intelligent. So why was he not
already married or betrothed? Why had he waited
for *her*, of all unlikely brides?

Because I am not at all the kind of woman he
might be expected to want? Because he is in no
danger of ever falling in love with me?

Without asking him directly—something she
was not willing to do—there was no way of answering that question. All she could do was ex-
amine her own feelings.

It was pride and the anticipation of certain
heartbreak that had made her say *no*. But *would*
her heart break? Blake had made no promises of
love or eternal devotion, so he would not be betraying her when he strayed. She had lived without love, without anyone to care for her feelings,

for so long that this would be nothing new. Provided she did nothing idiotic like fall in love with him, she was safe.

What could she bring *him*? Loyalty, a determination to be a good wife, the intention to be a good mother if she was so blessed. It did not add up to very much—and certainly nothing that another woman could not offer.

But he had asked *her*, not another woman. So what should she say?

'Have you completely lost your mind?' Jon paced down the length of the study, then back, his hair standing on end from where he had dragged his hand through it. The other arm was still weak, although he constantly forgot his sling. 'You really mean to go through with this marriage to Miss Lytton?'

'Yes.'

Yes, he would marry her. *Yes*, he probably had lost his mind.

'She is a baronet's daughter,' Blake said, studying his fingernails.

'That is the one positive—although you know you can do better. Considerably better. She has no money—except the inflated amount you are attempting to give her in exchange for that farm— no connections of any use whatsoever, and she is a plain, lame beanpole.'

'And intelligent, loyal, courageous,' Blake added. He lifted his gaze to skewer Jon's. 'And might I remind you that you are speaking of the lady I have asked to be my wife?'

Jon stopped pacing, but with more courage than sense did not back down.

'I thought you liked her,' Blake said mildly. Jon was only defending what he saw as his brother's best interests, he reminded himself.

'I do. She is all you say. But… We can buy her off—it isn't too late.'

'Buy her off—?' Blake began, half out of his chair.

But Jon was pacing again, his back to Blake. 'I know you have not had the best of experiences with marriage proposals, but there is no need to go from one extreme to the other.'

'What exactly do you mean by that?' Blake was on his feet now and round the desk, and when Jon turned they were face to face.

'Oh, hell… All right—if you must make me spell it out. You were betrothed to the perfect young lady. She was well-bred, well-dowered, beautiful, and I strongly suspect that you loved her. It did not work out, and ended in tragedy, so now you have gone to the opposite end of the scale—presumably in reaction.'

'*"Did not work out"* is one hell of a euphemism for *drove the girl to her death*, is it not? And five years is quite a long time for a reaction to set in, don't you think?' Blake enquired evenly. 'Normally reactions are much faster. Like this.'

He balled his right fist and hit Jon squarely on the chin—just as the door opened and Eleanor walked in.

She leapt back so that Jon crashed to the floor at her feet, then fell to her knees beside him. 'Jonathan, are you all right? Blake, what on *earth* do you think you are doing?'

'Yes, I'm fine,' Jon said, his voice muffled as he worked his jaw with one hand. 'I do apologise, Eleanor, we were…er…sparring.'

'Poppycock! Blake punched you. What exactly is going on?' The question was quite plainly directed at Blake. 'And shame on you,' she added, looking daggers at him. 'Hitting a man with only one good arm to defend himself.'

Jon got to his feet and held out his hand to help Eleanor to hers. 'I was exceedingly tactless and provoking and I deserved all I got. I will leave you to discuss things.'

The door closed behind him, leaving Eleanor on the inside, brows raised.

She probably had too many questions to articulate, Blake thought bitterly, flexing his smarting hand as he stooped to pick up a fallen chair.

'Please, sit down.' He waited until she was settled, then went back to his own chair behind the desk. It felt like a retreat. 'Jon reminded me that I do not have a very successful history of betrothals. I felt that it was inappropriate of him to bring that up now, but he would not let the matter drop.' He shrugged. 'I lost my temper.'

'Were you going to tell me about the other unsatisfactory betrothals?' she enquired politely, as though the matter was of only the faintest interest to her. Perhaps it was.

'Only one.' And that was bad enough. He was going to have to tell Eleanor something, however difficult it was. 'I was promised to a young lady I had known all her life. One of those cold-bloodedly *suitable* matches thought up by our respective fathers when we were both minors. Her family were our closest neighbours.' He shrugged. 'I had no strong feelings one way or the other.' *Or so I thought.* 'But I liked Felicity, and we had always got on well. It was, as my father had ensured, very advantageous on both sides.'

He was all too conscious of the steady gaze of a pair of clear hazel eyes and made himself meet it—made himself stick to the story he had decided to tell and not get sidetracked into the emotions, the damnably complicated feelings, the sickening realisation of what he had done to Felicity and to himself and how it had left him. *Shattered.*

'I went to university, went on the Town and enjoyed myself. I didn't really think much about marriage until my father died. Then I found myself with the title, and Felicity's father enquired—somewhat impatiently—when I was going to get on with it.'

'At which point you discovered that she did not want to marry you.'

'How did you guess that?'

'You had neglected her, taken her for granted, and then you turned up and demanded that she marry you, at your convenience.' Eleanor shrugged. 'Why on earth *would* she want to marry you?'

'That just about sums it up. She said she did not want to marry me and I put my foot down. Bullied her, I suppose. I told her that she was breaking a long-standing agreement, pointed out that the gossip would be harmful to her, that she would have the reputation of a jilt. I kissed her with rather too much enthusiasm. Nothing I am at all proud of now, believe me, but at the time I thought it was for the best. Best for *her.*'

I told her everything except the truth. But of course I did not know what that was until it was too late...until she was gone.

'And?'

'She ran away with another man. A poet, of all things. I suppose he seemed more sensitive than I.'

It would not have been difficult.

'There was one hell of a fuss. And that was the end of my marriage before it began.'

Do not ask me any more.

But of course this was Eleanor, so she did.

'What happened to her?'

'Her caring poet left her when he discovered that Felicity's father was not going to release her dowry. They had fled to Rome. She caught one of the summer fevers that plague the place and... died.'

Alone and in poverty and betrayed. And that was all he was going to say about Felicity. He could hardly bear to think about what had happened—he certainly was not going to talk about it.

Leaving aside his own pig-headed stupidity in failing to see what had been under his nose, and failing to do anything as unmanly as actually analyse his own emotions, he had thought that Felicity had no choice other than to marry him, and that by forcing the issue he had been doing the right thing. And he had been wrong. She'd had plenty of choices—only he had panicked her so that she had failed to see them. And he... He had been left staring into the empty space that had once contained the woman he'd realised he had loved all along.

Now the very different woman on the other side of his desk watched him through clear hazel eyes that were apparently unclouded by any emotions at all—except distress for Felicity and extreme irritation with him.

Unlike Felicity, Eleanor had very few options. They boiled down to genteel poverty if she was lucky, and real hardship if she was not. Or marriage to him. And by giving Eleanor that choice he might, somehow, make up for taking Felicity's choice away from her. Whether it did or not, or if anything ever could, he knew he could not walk away from Eleanor. Not and live with his conscience. And *that*, damn it, was increasingly difficult to keep locked away.

'And you think that, having heard that, I will still marry you?' It did not, somehow, sound like an aggressive question, more a puzzled one—as though she really did want to understand.

'I am hoping that you can overlook my past, overlook the unfortunate beginning to our relationship and say *yes*.'

'Because that will soothe your conscience?'

The woman had been born with a scalpel instead of a tongue. He would swear it. Fortunately she thought it was only his conscience in question here. He had not revealed that he had *loved* Felicity—still did—and that whatever he could offer a wife in terms of position and comfort he could not give her his heart.

'Because I am never going to be at a loss for

a stimulating exchange of views with you in the house,' Blake said, throwing away all attempts at diplomacy.

'Then, yes. How could I refuse such a flattering proposal?'

For a moment the sarcasm stopped him hearing exactly what she had said, and then it hit him. *She has surrendered!*

For a moment he was not certain whether the emotion tangling inside him was shock, relief or horror. Perhaps all three. It took him a second to realise that Eleanor was still speaking.

'I assume you have calculated how much damage marriage to me will do to your political ambitions and your social life? If not, I am sure Jonathan will soon point them out to you. I would only ask that you do not…that you are not…'

For the first time Eleanor lost her composure. Blake glanced down at her hands, twisting a handkerchief into a knot in her lap, and realised that her composure had been lost some time ago, and what he had been looking at was a desperate mask of serenity.

'I would ask that you do not flaunt your mistresses…that you leave me that much dignity,' she said, all in a rush, and went crimson.

'If you give me the same assurance about your lovers, ma'am.' She looked shocked. 'I take my promises seriously, Eleanor,' he said, dropping the mocking tone. 'While we agree that our marriage is real then you will have my fidelity—not only the appearance of it.'

'And you will have mine—which is an easy promise for me to make.'

Blake felt a flare of irritation at her self-deprecation. He had stopped noticing the details of Eleanor's appearance, he realised. Stopped assessing the details of her figure or profile or hair. She had become familiar, had become something of *his*—and as his she should accept that she was perfectly adequate just as she was, he told himself, realising that *that* was at the core of his anger with Jon's criticisms.

A small stirring of discomfort warned him that perhaps he was being a trifle arrogant. He pushed it aside. How to convince her? You could not tell a woman that she was *perfectly adequate*.

'So you say now—before you are tempted.' He smiled to show it was a joke and she narrowed her eyes at him, whether in threat or speculation he was not certain. 'But I am certainly not going to discuss infidelity on the day we become betrothed. I am delighted that you consent, Eleanor.'

Chapter Eleven

Eleanor watched Blake open a drawer and take out a red morocco leather box. He pressed the catch and she blinked as the light caught the sullen red glow of a large ruby. It was difficult to take her eyes off it when he took it from its case and came round the desk to stand in front of her.

'This is a symbol of our betrothal, if you care to accept it. If you prefer a different stone, another style, of course we can choose something else.'

Was this the ring he would have given his lost betrothed? What had been her name? Felicity—that was it. Surely he would not have a ring of this magnificence just lying around on the off-chance that a lady might come along and take his fancy.

She could hardly ask.

She looked down at the stone in his hand, the dance of light deep in its heart reflecting Blake's pulse beat, or perhaps the slightest tremor of his nerves.

'It is a beautiful stone.' But for her? This was a stone for a lady of status, of power, and she would simply be Ellie…pretending.

But once married she must pretend successfully that she was a countess—because that, surely, was her side of this unequal bargain. Blake was giving her status, security, wealth and the opportunity to pursue what interested her, what she thought worthwhile. In return she must act the part of a woman to whom that rank came naturally, so that she could support him politically, socially and on his estates.

Jewels and gowns would be part of the mask she must construct to hide the real Ellie behind.

She held out her left hand, palm down. 'I think it is an exquisite ring and I would not dream of asking for anything else.' He slid it onto her finger and she instinctively closed her hand into a fist to support its weight. 'My goodness, I am not used to wearing such a gem.'

On her other hand Mama's little pearl ring seemed to fade like the moon in the light of the sun.

'You will soon become accustomed. There are family jewels as well, of course—those that pass from countess to countess. We can match them against the family portraits one day so you can trace them back. It is an interesting exercise, and will distract you from worrying that the Pencarrow nose will manifest itself in the children.'

Children.

She had not really considered children as a reality—which was ridiculous. Of *course* Blake wanted children. That was the primary aim of dynastic marriages. She had resigned herself to not marrying, which meant not having children, and had told herself that it did not hurt, that many women did not have families and that she would become accustomed.

Have I become accustomed, or have I simply pushed that hurt away like all the others?

'I will send them to Rundell, Bridge & Rundell for cleaning,' Blake said.

She was still staring down at the ring, and he must suppose that her attention was all on the precious gem, because he did not appear to find her lack of response unusual.

'You can select what you like from them and the ones you do not favour can go back into the vaults.'

Ellie pulled herself together, looked up and found a smile from somewhere.

Blake smiled back. 'Some of them are fairly frightful, I have to admit.' For a moment she thought he was referring to the painted noses, then he added, 'We can look at getting those reset, I suppose.'

The thought of disliking antique family jewels and simply relegating them to a vault was startling, and certainly suppressed her almost hysterical desire to laugh about the family nose. Neither her father nor her stepfather had been anything other than comfortably off, yet neither had showered a bride with family jewels. But it would seem gauche to express surprise.

'I look forward to seeing them. I have read about some family gems with long and fascinating histories. Are there any with curses or legends? There's the Luck of Edenhall, isn't there?'

'That is a glass goblet. For magic, we Pencarrows have Great-Aunt Matilda's garnet set, which probably dooms the wearer to extreme melancholy, it is so ugly, and a diamond parure which turns other ladies green with envy, so I am told.'

Ellie felt herself relax almost to the point of laughing. Here was Blake back again—the amusing, unserious Blake, the one she hoped she was marrying rather than the dark one, bowed down under a weight of heavy memories.

'We must definitely get the diamonds cleaned for the wedding—you will want the entire set, I imagine,' he said, and the urge to laugh fled.

'The wedding? Where do you want it to be?'

She had a sudden mental picture of herself limping down the length of the endless nave of some fashionable London church while the congregation either tittered into their handkerchiefs or shed tears over Hainford's disastrous choice of bride.

'I have no family. Friends, of course, but nowhere near the number of people you would want to invite.'

'There's the Hainford family chapel,' Blake suggested. 'Mind you, that would mean kicking all the house guests out before we could have a honeymoon there.'

Oh, what the...?

Ellie got a grip on her language.

Countess, remember? I limp, I am always going to limp, and they had better get used to it.

'St George's Hanover Square?' she said recklessly. 'You can invite everyone. Give Jonathan something to do organising it, instead of disapproving of me.'

And I will find a wedding dress that will give them something other than the fact that I am lame to think about.

Jonathan—subdued, clearly embarrassed, and with an equally clear bruise on his chin—had been put to work on the wedding plans. Six weeks, Blake had pronounced, for reasons best known to himself.

St George's Hanover Square was organised for the ceremony and the townhouse readied for the reception, wedding breakfast and the first night before they travelled to Hainford Hall for a prolonged stay.

But first Blake had summoned a distant cousin to act as chaperon and installed her, Ellie and Polly in a small but highly respectable hotel in Albemarle Street. Miss Paston was in her forties, very quiet and retiring, and had been helping 'Cousin Margaret'—otherwise known as the Viscountess of Crampton—with her children. She seemed pleasant enough, if rather vague, but Ellie suspected that was a barrier she put up between herself and the realities of life as a poor relation.

That might have been me, she thought with a shiver. *The eternal companion, always in the shadows, growing older and quieter as the years rolled past. And instead I am to marry an earl.*

Ellie had accepted a new bank draft for Carndale Farm and went to call on Mr Rampion. She would have taken Polly and gone in a hack, but Miss Paston had been appalled and had sent a note round to 'Dear Cousin Blake', who had provided a carriage and footman. Future countesses did *not* travel by hackney carriage.

Mr Rampion, invigorated by the prospect of detailed negotiations over settlements, took the draft, gave Ellie an advance against it and details of her new bank account, and saw her out to the carriage with considerable ceremony.

Ellie clutched her reticule with its fat purse and bank details and sat staring rather blankly at the beautifully buttoned upholstery of the carriage seat opposite her.

'Where to now, Miss Lytton?' The footman was still holding the carriage door.

'Oh. Where…? Brook Street, please.'

She gave the direction and sat back. She was never going to be a beauty, and she was always going to be…different. Well, she would be 'different' in the best way she could manage, and Lady Verity Standing, the most eccentric female of her acquaintance, was the very woman to ask how to go about it.

Verity was the sister of the Duke of Severingham, now in her thirties, ridiculously wealthy, stubbornly single, the despair of her family and one of Ellie's circle of writing friends. It was well known that the love of her life had died of a fever over ten years before. What was *not* so well known was that her beloved had been a woman.

Ellie, who had long ago come to the conclusion that one took love as it came and was lucky if it *did* come, saw no reason to be shocked by this— was only saddened for Verity.

Now she sent Patrick the footman to knock at the smart black front door and kept her fingers crossed that her friend would be at home—because if anyone could create a silk purse out of a sow's ear, then Verity was the woman to do it.

'You are never going to be a beauty...' Verity walked around her, eying her as a gardener would an overgrown yew bush that might, just *might* be transformed by some creative topiary into something to grace an earl's garden.

It was exceedingly refreshing not to have to deal with someone determined to flatter. 'No,' Ellie agreed.

'But you could be an Original,' Verity pronounced.

Given that she dyed her already red hair an even more flamboyant shade, always wore black and took a small scarlet parrot which clashed nastily with her hair everywhere, she certainly knew what she was talking about.

'That is what I was hoping for,' Ellie said, in competition with the parrot's mutterings.

'Do you want to do away with your limp?' Verity cast herself into a deep armchair and pulled the bell-cord. 'Tea, please, Hopkins—and something indulgently sticky.'

'I would if I could, but there is nothing to be done. One leg is shorter than the other,' Ellie pointed out as the butler left the room.

'But not by much. If you had your shoes made

specially you would have more of a sway.' Verity wafted one hand back and forth. 'I know just the man. Now, then…' She put her head on one side. 'That hair.'

'Not red,' Ellie said hastily. 'Blake said I ought to cut it short.'

'Did he, indeed? What an intelligent man—I do congratulate you. Now—a list.' She picked up a notebook from the litter of books next to her chair. 'Hair, shoes, gown, all the ghastly details of surviving the *ton*… Who is going to give you away? I would offer to do it myself, but your poor Blake does not want the scandal of his bride being given away in marriage by her Sapphic friend. I know—Podge can do it.'

'Who?'

'Podge—Percival, my brother. He's a terrible old bore, but he will rally round, and there's nothing like a duke at a wedding to set the tone—unless it is a *royal* duke, in which case the tone goes downhill rapidly. There. Now, how long do we have?'

'Six weeks,' Ellie said, not sure whether she was excited or petrified. A duke to give her away, a transformation at the hands of one of the most eccentric women in London…

'We will do your Blake proud. You *are* madly in love with him, I assume?'

'I…'

In love with Blake? Am I?

She desired him, dreamt about him, liked him—most of the time. But *love?*

'No. And it would be a very bad thing if I was,' she said truthfully. Then, 'Why am I doing this insane thing?'

'Because you were on the verge of being poverty-stricken, stuck in a rain-soaked Lancashire farmhouse with drips coming through the ceiling and miles from a decent library?' Verity suggested.

'If it had been anyone but Blake who had asked I would have still said *no*,' Ellie said, thinking it through. 'I do not wish to take charity. But because it *was* Blake I thought maybe I could give something back to him. And I do think he needs *something*. Perhaps something I can give him. He has dozens of friends, a half-brother who adores him, and yet he has such darkness inside…'

Verity sat up sharply, sending the parrot off in squawking flight and making Hopkins start and almost drop the tea tray. He put it down with a reproachful look at his employer and left.

Ellie took a small, wicked-looking pastry and bit into it. 'Oh, bliss—do try one.'

Verity waved the plate away. 'Darkness? Ellie, darling, do be very certain that it is a dark space that you can bring light into and not a black emptiness that will suck *you* in too.'

* * *

Ellie was still brooding on Verity's Gothic pronouncement five weeks later. She had not seen a great deal of Blake, other than during his punctilious calls to enquire after her heath, report on the progress of the preparations and to take her for drives in the park when it stopped raining.

She was still in mourning, so she was able to retreat into anonymous blacks and wear a veil, which meant that while London might be buzzing with the news that the eligible Earl of Hainford was betrothed to an unknown, no one could fault her for remaining quietly out of sight.

It did increase the speculation about exactly who she was, beyond the bland information offered by various genealogical reference books. The dreadful accident that had claimed her stepbrother's life and its connection to what had been shocking goings-on at White's might have been a problem, until even the most assiduous gossip had finally had to accept that Sir Francis Lytton had simply been standing in the wrong place at the wrong time.

Verity, recounting all of this, had added that the general consensus was that the tragedy had brought the stepsister and Hainford together, and that, everyone agreed, was a *good* thing if he finally got around to marrying—especially after the scandal of his early betrothal. What a foolish,

wicked girl that Felicity Broughton had been, the
gossips said, happily dredging up the old scandal.
To throw away wealth, position and ultimately her
life—and all for a poet, too.

Three days before the wedding Blake took Ellie
driving at ten o'clock in the morning—much earlier than usual, at a time when the fashionable
crowd was delicately sipping its hot chocolate or
still slumbering behind tightly drawn curtains.

'How are you?' he asked, almost abruptly, as
they turned through the gates into Green Park,
leaving Blake's tiger to perch on a bench and wait
patiently for their return.

'Well, thank you.'

*Wishing you would find me 'kissable' again.
Or is that just a thing that you say to all the girls
you tumble in the long grass?*

'And you?'

'Also well. Suffering from Jonathan's efforts
to create the perfect wedding, when he ought to
know that no social occasion can *ever* be perfect.
I have had to endure discussion about the precise
shade of my neckcloth, the number of horses for
the carriage, and which carriage, whether there
can possibly be sufficient champagne for the number of guests and exactly how much to tip the bell-
ringers.' He negotiated a sharp turn and added,
'And that was just this morning.'

'I do not believe you,' Ellie said, laughing. 'And

what about me? I have to *shop* endlessly. And have pins stuck in me, and endure my bridesmaids squabbling genteelly about headdresses, ribbons and prayer books.'

As her bridesmaids had been selected from amongst her bookish friends, who normally took little notice of what they wore, it was taking all Verity's best efforts to turn them out looking like Society ladies.

And then there was the little matter of learning to walk in the new shoes Verity's cordwainer had made for her. It hurt, changing the whole way she had adapted to cope with her slightly shortened leg, and she was not going to wear them every day—she was certain of that. But just for that walk down the aisle, when all Blake's friends, family and acquaintances saw her properly for the first time, she was determined not to give them something else to criticise.

The gossip and comments about marrying a plain nonentity would be quite enough for Blake to have to put up with, without adding her lameness to the list. Once they were used to her, then she would be her normal self again.

Verity's *modiste* had stalked around her, clicking her tongue and muttering about enhancements. But Ellie drew the line at padding. She was doing her best to eat well, but sooner or later— much sooner than later—she was going to be skin to skin with Blake and he would know what had been false and what was true. Honesty was something else she owed him.

Whether she was receiving honesty from Blake in return was something Ellie wondered about in the early hours while she lay awake and told herself that there was nothing to worry about. That there was *everything* to worry about—

'What is wrong?' Blake asked, and she realised that she had fallen abruptly silent. 'It is not like you to brood.'

'How do you know it is not?' Ellie said, far more lightly than she felt. 'I could spend most of my time brooding for all you are aware.'

She usually spent most of her time writing, and that involved a great deal of brooding, although she had hardly touched either of her manuscripts since Blake's proposal. She must finish the latest and final account of Oscar's educational travels, because she had an undertaking with her publisher, but as for the Minerva Press romance...

No, countesses did not write faintly shocking novels. She might not know much about the *haut ton*, but she was pretty certain of that. The manuscript and all her notes were securely locked away in the bottom of her trunk. Besides, she had her grey-eyed, black-haired dashing hero in reality— there was no longer any need for her to weave fantasies about him.

Blake was still looking at her with that small vertical line between his brows and she realised that he could not see her expression clearly because of her black veil.

She tossed it back and smiled at him. 'I am teasing. It is simply that there is a lot to do, and Verity is tutoring me intensively about Society and how to go on, which is making me dizzy. I promise you, I woke up last night from a nightmare in which I had to plan the seating for a dinner with a rural dean who was the son of a marquess, the well-born but scandalous mistress of a royal duke, the Archbishop of Canterbury and the Prime Minister. It was a miracle that my screams did not wake Polly.'

'You have my promise that I will never invite the Archbishop to dinner,' Blake said solemnly, and then they were both laughing, and she slipped her hand into the crook of his elbow and everything was all right.

Under her fingers his muscles flexed, making small adjustments that must be communicating themselves to the horses, although she could see no movement in his hand. It was very arousing to touch the subtle strength, to sense his awareness of the animals. Would he be as aware of a woman when he was making love to her?

She thought about that kiss in the field, about waking with the weight of his arm—*this* arm—

over her, about the heavy-lidded appraisal whenever she caught him looking at her mouth.

Yes, he would be aware of his bed partner, of her pleasure.

Ellie shivered, unsure whether it was with anticipation or alarm. What if he did not want her when they finally got to bed? What if he found her skinny body too unattractive, or missed the beautiful faces of the women who had been his mistresses? Men could not disguise a lack of arousal—she knew that.

And what about her? She had somehow avoided thinking beyond kisses, but the wedding night was very much more than kissing, and she was not certain that she would be able to hide her fears and her shrinking from Blake. Women could feign arousal—she knew that too—but *wanting* Blake was not the problem…

Chapter Twelve

'Cold? I can stop and find the lap rug.' Blake craned round to look over his shoulder, reining in as he did so.

He must have noticed that tiny shiver.

Ellie looked about her. They were in the lee of a large clump of shrubbery, screened from the open part of the park. It was ridiculous to feel emboldened by there being no one else within sight, because no one would overhear them unless they shouted. Even so…

'I am not cold.'

Blake stayed where he was, half turned on the seat, then he thrust the whip into its holder and wrapped the reins around it.

'Stand.'

The well-trained horses flicked their ears at the sound of his voice, but stayed still as he stripped off his gloves—almost, it seemed to her, a signal that he would wait, would listen to what she had to say.

'I am afraid.'

'Afraid?'

He looked appalled—as well he might. What had come over her, blurting it out like that?

'Ellie, I should have thought. You do not have a mother or married sister to advise you, to make you feel comfortable about what will happen. Do not worry, please.' He lifted a hand and laid it gently against her cheek. 'I won't… We will take it very slowly. Nothing will happen—not until you want it to.'

'No, no, that isn't it, Blake!'

Oh, Lord, now she must be crimson with embarrassment. What on earth had made her think that this rush of honesty would be a good thing?

'I have absolutely no fears about *that*,' she lied.

She couldn't bring herself to say that she was aching for him, and neither could she find the words to tell him what had happened—the fear, the horror of that night when she had broken her leg and her stepfather had died.

'I am afraid that I won't…please you. That night, in front of the fire, you said that I'd bruised your arm because I was so bony.'

'I am an idiot,' Blake said. 'I was worried about you—you *were* thin. Worried that you would make yourself ill. I meant to joke, perhaps to encourage you to eat more. I would not have hurt you for the world, Eleanor.'

Honesty, she reminded herself. *I should tell him.*

Tell him how she had made herself thin because she had started to become afraid of her stepfather. It had begun when she'd started to develop a figure, so she had tried to make those treacherous curves go away.

She looked at the horses, the trees, her gloved hands. Anywhere but into those concerned grey eyes.

'I was not well after my accident,' she prevaricated. 'I lost my appetite and it was hard to get into the habit of eating again.'

'Poor darling,' Blake said.

He ran his fingers down the curve of her cheek until his thumb met her mouth. He lingered there, rubbing gently across the swell of her lower lip, until she raised her eyes and met his gaze.

'You are very feminine, Eleanor. Lush curves are not everything—or anything, come to that. So long as you are not frightened of me then it will all be well, you will see. I promise,' he added, his voice husky.

Without her conscious volition her lips moved against his thumb, in the whisper of a kiss, and then he slipped it into her mouth, rubbing across the sensitive inner flesh and she gasped, her tongue flickering out to meet the blunt thrust of Blake's thumb.

'Eleanor...'

A question, a statement, or a demand? She did not know, but she swayed towards him and Blake took her into his arms, brought his head down and kissed her. Hot, open-mouthed, urgent.

This should scare her, she knew. This was not how a gentleman was supposed to kiss his fiancée—not how any man was supposed to kiss a virgin. This was a quite blatant statement of desire as his tongue replaced his thumb in a way that left her in no doubt what that penetration symbolised. He tasted as she remembered from that kiss in the field, on the sheepskins, but the intent behind this kiss was different. She could tell that even in her ignorance. This was, after all, only her third kiss.

And then Ellie lost the ability to analyse, to treat this as a new experience to be carefully considered, to savour. All there was, as she leaned into Blake's embrace, was heat and desire and the unexpected delight of creating pleasure with another person. He was not simply kissing her... they were kissing each other. When she pressed into his mouth with her tongue he growled, deep in his chest. When he pulled back a little and nibbled at her lower lip she followed, took her turn, learning the exact pressure on the firm flesh that made him groan, made her heart beat faster at the masculine, primitive power of his response.

The horses moved, jerking the curricle and breaking their kiss. They fell apart, both of them panting a little. Blake's mouth looked swollen, sensual.

I did that. I kissed him back and I was not afraid. Perhaps I can do this after all.

'Do you doubt,' Blake asked, his voice husky, 'that I desire you?'

Why? Blake asked himself as he worked to get both his reactions and the horses under control. He had just kissed an inexperienced young woman in the middle of Green Park and he was as hard as teak, aching to drag her down from her seat and into the shelter of that shrubbery and make love to her until they were both screaming. He had kissed Felicity like that and she had recoiled in horror, but Eleanor had kissed him back.

She blinked at him as though bemused, her mouth pink and swollen, her eyes wide, her pale skin flushed. Even a passionate kiss had not rendered her beautiful, simply rather sweet... endearing. Vulnerable. He had always demanded beauty in his lovers. No, he realised, not *demanded*, just expected. He was eligible, handsome, desired, so he could ignore the plain and the awkward.

Arrogant bastard, he thought, looking at himself from the outside. It didn't happen often that he was forced to see himself as someone else might, and it was not pleasant. Was that how Eleanor had seen him when they'd first met? As some privileged, top-lofty aristocrat cutting a swathe through Society, taking what he wanted and ignoring the side-effects?

Felicity had been beautiful. Exquisite. It had been one of the things he had loved her for.

Blake winced, and the pair backed edgily.

He always tried very hard not to use that word when he thought of Felicity—the woman he had loved without realising it, the woman he had alienated with his neglect, assuming she would still be there when he got around to snapping his fingers for her.

She would not have been beautiful as she lay dying, racked by fever in some second-rate Roman boarding house. He had destroyed that along with everything else.

Yet this woman—her undistinguished face now returning to its normal pallor, worsened by the deadening effect of mourning black on her complexion, her wildly curling hair once more making a bid to escape its cage of pins and the confines of her bonnet—he desired her.

He licked his lips, tasting her. Marmalade and black tea, innocence and desire. Eleanor's eyes were fixed on his lips, and he knew that if she echoed that lick, if he so much as glimpsed the pink tip of her tongue, then he would not be responsible for his actions.

He hauled his attention back to the horses, and it did feel like a physical effort. 'Walk on.'

'No, I do not doubt your desire,' she said, prim as a Sunday School teacher.

Had she licked her lips? He flicked the reins, sending the pair into a fast trot.

'I gather from my researches that almost any female may arouse male desire, as it appears to be quite separate from actual emotions.'

'Your researches?' Blake glanced across at her then. What possible 'research' had she been doing into male desire?

'Theoretical,' Eleanor said in a soothing voice.

He suspected that she was laughing at him. Her voice certainly shook a little.

'One reads...talks to one's friends.'

Blake found his shoulders relaxing. He hadn't realised that the thought of Eleanor encountering male desire would make him react so strongly. 'I see. Book research—like your textbook on Mediterranean agriculture?'

'That had very little in it about male desire,' she said. 'Rather more about date-harvesting and Nilotic irrigation.'

He was on the point of asking just why those topics should be of the slightest interest to her when Eleanor spoke again.

'I have a confession to make.'

'A confession?' he said flatly. *Days before the wedding and* now *she makes a confession?*

'Tell me.'

That had not been well-timed, Ellie realised. Talking about a confession immediately after that kiss and a discussion on male desire would be open to misinterpretation. No wonder Blake was bristling like a dog catching the scent of a rat.

'I had best show you, I think. Will you take me back to the hotel, please?'

Collecting the tiger at the gate did nothing to aid their conversation, but it was only a short distance to Bailey's Hotel. Long enough to bring back that tell-tale furrow between Blake's brows, she noticed.

Miss Paston was surprised to see her back from her drive so soon, and decidedly flustered to find that Ellie was accompanied by Blake. 'My lord. Er... Cousin. Good morning.' She went pink when he bent to kiss her cheek as well as shaking her hand.

'I just want to show Lord Hainford something, Antonia.'

Ellie took down the works of Mrs Bundock from the shelf where she had arrayed them, in the hope that they would stimulate her to finish the Scottish book as soon as possible, and put them down on the table.

'I wrote these. *I* am Mrs Bundock.'

'Bundock?' He picked up *Oscar and Miranda Discover London*. 'Who on earth is Oscar?'

'An insufferable little prig,' Ellie confessed. 'I have just finished a book about his visit to the North African coast—hence the date palms and the Nile—and I must confess to an almost irresistible urge to have had him seized by Barbary corsairs. As it was I had to cheer myself up by letting him fall into an irrigation ditch.'

Blake moved on to *The Young Traveller in Switzerland*. 'I would be tempted to drop him down a crevasse in a glacier. And do Messrs Broderick & Alleyn know the identity of Mrs Bundock? Your real name, I mean?'

'Yes, of course. I had to deal with them direct, because I did not think Francis would be very reliable over the money. Do you think it might be a problem?'

It had never occurred to her that it would be, her only fear had been that Blake would disapprove of her writing at all and would try and prevent her from honouring her contract.

'I should imagine that dear Oscar's adventures from the pen of Countess Hainford might sell even better than this edition, don't you think? Publishers are businessmen—they will not miss such an opportunity for publicity. We can only be grateful that you have not written a torrid novel,' he added absently as he scanned the titles.

Ellie could feel herself turning pink, then pale. *Thank heavens.* 'I had better have a word with them.'

'Jonathan will have a word. More than one, if necessary.'

'But I am still working on a book for them. I have an agreement.'

'Jonathan can deal with that also.'

'I do not like letting people down, Blake. Writing for them kept me afloat financially, and they have always dealt with me in a most straightforward manner.'

The look he gave her was considering, but he was not frowning, she was thankful to see. Starting their marriage with a flaming row about Oscar, of all things, was not a good omen.

'If we have their guarantee of discretion, then, yes, very well. Why did you not tell me about your writing before now, Eleanor?'

Miss Paston had effaced herself—presumably going to her bedchamber. Ellie sat down at the table and thought about why she had kept her writing a secret from Blake. The real reason, she supposed, was her novel, with him portrayed as the dashing desert lord. Keeping that a secret had somehow encompassed the juvenile travel books—as though once he knew she wrote the words *sensation novelist* would be emblazoned across her forehead.

He hitched one hip on the edge of the table and slapped his gloves against his thigh while he waited. It was not impatient—more an unconscious gesture, she thought, her eyes fixed on the hard muscles under the close-fitting buckskin breeches. Polly had confided that Francis had got into a bath wearing his new buckskins in an effort to mould them to his form as tightly as his idol Hainford's.

'I got into the habit of being secretive,' she said at last. 'I kept it from Francis because of the money. And I hardly have a wide social circle. Besides, it is not as though I have written a *roman à clef* to set Society by the ears, guessing who each character is based upon. Oscar is modelled on our curate, who is a pompous soul.'

'No, I suppose it cannot do any harm—even if it does come out—and I agree it does not do to break contracts. Is that why you so often have inky fingers? I had thought you merely a clumsy penwoman.'

'I forget everything when I write,' she confessed. 'I suspect I wave my pen about when I am holding conversations in my head. I certainly chew the end—which is disastrous when I pick it up wrongly. It is very hard to get ink off the tongue, you know.'

Blake snorted with laughter. 'I couldn't taste any. Put out your tongue and let me see how black it is.'

When she did he leaned in closely, pretending to inspect it, then snatched a kiss. 'When I gamble away all my money you can write that scandalous Society novel and save our fortunes.'

'If you gamble to that extent I will leave you, my lord. I give you fair warning.'

The laughter ebbed from his eyes, leaving them bleak, even though he kept his tone light when he said, 'No, do not leave me, Eleanor.'

'I will not,' she promised. 'I keep my vows too.'

I could never leave you to that hurt. Somehow we will fight it together—whatever it is.

This is my wedding day.

Her head felt so light she thought it might bob off her shoulders and fly away like one of those exciting hot air balloons, hardly tethered by the weight of the diamond earrings.

Ellie opened her eyes and looked in the mirror to find herself confronting a woman even more different from the one she had seen after last night's ruthless haircut.

This Eleanor was still no beauty, of course. Rice powder could only do so much to subdue all those freckles, and nothing could shorten her nose or make her face anything but an undistinguished oval. But with her hair shorn into a myriad of tiny curls that actually looked as though they were meant to be a coiffure, rather than a nest for an unknown species of bird, she realised that she *did* have cheekbones. And her nose did not look even longer, as she had feared it would, and the tips of her earlobes showed, so that the lovely earrings were on display.

'Now the gown.' Verity and the modiste and her maid lifted it and lowered it over her head. 'Stand still. No, do not look until it is laced up. There—*now.*'

It was the palest almond silk, with a hint of warm creamy brown in the layer of net in the overskirt, and it was rippled through with gold embroidery. White or pink would have taken all the colour from her face, but this warmed it... made her eyes sparkle deep hazel.

'Oh,' Ellie said as Verity smudged something from a little stick on her eyebrows, darkening them a trifle. 'I *have* got a figure.'

It must be the corset and the seaming of the gown, but even so...

'Told you so. Bite your lips—suck them. I don't want to paint them,' Verity ordered. 'The necklace and the veil next.'

The necklace was more diamonds—they should take everyone's eyes off her face, Ellie thought, blinking at their magnificence. Then the veil went on, secured by a matching diamond tiara. Finally she slid her feet into the shoes, wincing at the sudden strain the correction made on her hip.

Just for today, she promised herself. *And at Court, if Blake arranges for me to be presented.*

He had said he would, but that seemed so improbable that she could not really believe it.

She walked slowly up and down, accustoming herself to the painful pull on muscles that had adjusted to the shortening of her leg after the break. 'I still limp.'

'You sway elegantly,' Verity said, prowling behind her to tweak at her skirts. 'Time to go.'

'Yes. Of course. I do not want to be late.'

'Of course you do. It does men good to be kept waiting. Kept wondering. Veil down, now.'

Chapter Thirteen

Blake stood and studied the dark wood panelling behind the altar and willed himself not to fidget. Eleanor was late—the church clock had chimed the hour at least ten minutes ago—but looking at the time would only betray his anxiety. The whispering and speculation was bad enough without presenting the congregation with a picture of a nervous bridegroom. Beside him Jonathan stood silent and still, exuding competence and the aura of a man who knew exactly where the wedding ring was.

He had put up a spirited resistance to the request that he be best man until Blake had snapped that it would prove a welcome distraction for the gossips, and that speculation about exactly why his secretary looked so much like him would give the busybodies something to think about other than Eleanor.

'Most of them know already,' Jon had pointed out.

'Yes, but it really irritates Great-Aunt Hermione.'

'Oh, well, in that case I would be honoured,' Jon had said with a grin.

Now he nudged Blake with his elbow.

'Eleanor has arrived.'

Despite his resolution, Blake turned as though he was a trout on a line and looked down the aisle. There was a flurry of movement in the porch— probably inevitable when the Duke of Severingham was involved, because the man was probably the greatest fusspot in London. But he appreciated the gesture from Lady Verity in securing him to support Eleanor.

He had no idea what to expect when he saw his bride. She had told him she was leaving off mourning, which had been a relief he had tried to keep off his face. Marrying a woman in dowdy crow-black draperies really *would* have given the newspapers column inches of comment.

But this—this slender figure in a subtle shimmer of almost-colour coming towards him—this he had not expected. Then he realised something.

'Jon, that's not Eleanor—she is not limping,' he said in an urgent undertone.

'She is…slightly. She must have done something—her shoes, perhaps,' Jon whispered back.

It was not a long aisle in St George's, a relatively modern church, so Blake had little time to collect himself, but he thought he looked adequately solemn and composed when his bride reached his side and they faced the altar rail together.

Blake had studied the marriage service, in order to be prepared, but now it might have been chanted in Latin for all he knew. He must have made the appropriate responses in the right places, because Jon's elbow did not come into play again, and he was aware of Eleanor's voice making her responses, clearly but quietly.

And finally, 'Man and wife.'

There was silence, as though the congregation was holding its collective breath. Then Blake turned, took the edge of the filmy cream veil, lifted it back to drape it over the scintillating crescent of the diamond tiara and caught his own breath.

For a moment he did not recognise the woman looking at him, and then he realised that the big hazel eyes were those he had come to know well, and that the freckles were still there, hiding under their own veil of rice powder, and the curve of the jaw and the simple undistinguished oval of the face was Eleanor. But her hair... The unruly tangle of curls had gone, replaced with a softness cupping her head, baring her face and emphasising her neck.

Not beautiful, his wife, but unique, striking, characterful. He lifted both her hands in his, kissed her fingertips, then drew off the big ruby that she had put on her right hand and slid it over the wedding ring, trapping it.

'There,' he murmured. 'Mine.'

Brave girl, he added mentally, feeling the tremor in her hands, seeing the serene smile on her lips. *She must be a mass of nerves*, he thought, as he turned her to face the massed pews. All these people she did not know—all of them judging and commenting and pigeonholing her.

Eleanor held his arm firmly as they walked slowly down the aisle towards the double doors. Touching her like this, he could feel the effort she was making to walk straight.

What has she done? he wondered.

Demanding to know would not be tactful, but he was worried. Under the rice powder she was very pale, although perhaps that was simply nerves. He laid his right hand over hers as it rested on his arm and squeezed, trying to send messages of reassurance.

Blake felt the slightest recoil in her as they stepped out and she saw the crowds that always gathered around this most fashionable of churches when a wedding was in progress. He saw people scribbling in notebooks, getting every detail of the gown for the Court and Social columns. There was even an artist, frantically sketching.

The gown would appear in the pages of *La Belle Assemblée* or *Ackermann's Repository* next month: *'Wedding gown as worn by the Countess of Hainford'*, followed by a description of the fabrics, trimmings and accessories, presumably provided by the *modiste*.

It felt exceedingly intrusive, and he wondered if Eleanor would mind or whether she would be amused by the attention. He knew her well enough to guess that she would not be flattered. She knew all too well that this was nothing to do with her own taste or personality, but everything to do with her new rank and newsworthiness.

'Safe,' he said as they sat down in the open carriage and the door was closed. 'I felt rather like a hunted fox there for a moment.'

'Yes.' She gave a little shiver. 'A mob is a frightening thing, even in a good mood. Today the steps of a church...yesterday the steps of the guillotine.'

'How morbid we are,' he said, and she smiled. 'You look quite stunning, my dear. Elegant, striking—every inch a countess.'

'And every inch Ellie?' she said, with a laugh that had a slight edge to it.

'Every inch,' he agreed, letting her see his gaze

linger on the scooped neckline of her gown. 'Your dutiful application in eating cream cakes is fully appreciated,' he said as she blushed. 'But—*Ellie?* Is that what you prefer?'

'It is how I think of myself. But I like you calling me Eleanor. It reminds me that I am someone else now.'

'I hope you are no one else. I married Ellie as well as Eleanor, surely? Who did I kiss in that field…in Green Park?'

'Definitely Ellie.'

This time there was no shadow behind the laugh, only genuine amusement and a warmth that stirred his sensual imaginings.

'Any airs and graces had been very thoroughly shaken out of me.'

'I like your hair,' Blake said, following some inner train of thought he could not quite analyse. And, although he had never seen her with short hair before, he rather thought that this was Ellie too. Eleanor was a countess. Ellie was the girl with hazel eyes and the surprising *alter ego* of Mrs Bundock. Ellie was the woman who faced life on a rain-soaked, leaky farm with courage.

'You suggested it, and you were right. I like it too now—although my head feels so light it might float away.' She put up a hand to touch the newly shorn curls. 'It is a good thing it is weighted down with all these diamonds.'

'They suit you. You must keep them on.'

She frowned, puzzled. 'You mean I would normally take them off once we get to the house? I thought I would wear them while all our guests are there.'

'I mean later. Much later. When everything else comes off.'

He wished the guests to the devil now. Wished he had decided to leave early and travel out of London for their first night. But that might have implied that he wanted to limit the amount of time the guests had to observe his new countess.

'*Blake!*'

She was flushed and pink and delicious, and Blake, who had been telling himself that he must do his duty in the marital bed and not be hankering after one of his beautiful, sophisticated mistresses, had the startling revelation that he was unlikely to be doing any hankering at all.

He had always expected—demanded—beauty and assurance and luscious curves, also knowledgeable sensuality in a lover, and had expected that his wife would have all those attributes. Except, of course, the knowledge. And that would be something that he would have looked forward to imparting. He was *still* looking forward to that, he realised, smiling at Eleanor.

The tiny lines of strain had gone from around her eyes and mouth. Perhaps it had simply been apprehension and shyness—not, as he had feared, physical discomfort.

He would have asked, but the carriage was already drawing up at the Berkeley Square house, and footmen were running down the steps. Turner presided from the doorway with an expression that might have straightened a crooked red carpet at twelve paces and the groom was opening the carriage door.

He gave Eleanor his hand to help her descend from the carriage, then led her across the pavement and up the steps, pausing at the top. 'I promise this will be rather more comfortable than the field,' he said, before he bent and scooped her up in his arms to carry her across the threshold.

She made a surprised little sound in his ear, then tightened her arms around his neck.

'I am not going to drop you,' he said as he stepped into the hallway.

'I know,' she murmured in his ear. Then kissed it.

Blake almost dropped his bride.

The impulse to kiss Blake had come out of nowhere, emerging from the dizzying sensation of being swung up into his arms mixed with embarrassment at the sight of his butler beaming at them. His ear had been right by her mouth and the temptation to bite the lobe had been irresistible.

Appalled, and mystified as to why she should even *think* of such a thing, Ellie had kissed it, nuzzling surprisingly soft skin, inhaling the seductive scent of warm male and peppery cologne, smiling at the tickle of his hair on her face.

Blake jolted to a halt and drew a deep, shuddering breath before setting her on her feet. 'Wicked woman,' he breathed as he bent to kiss her cheek, now at a normal level. 'Welcome to your new home, Lady Hainford.'

There was applause, and she looked around to find that the hall was full of staff—footmen, maids, a male cook, a severe-looking dame who must be the housekeeper, a tweeny peeping out from behind the aprons of the kitchen maids... All these staff—and this was only the townhouse. Tomorrow they would set out for his Hampshire estate and their honeymoon.

Honey. Moon.

Ellie turned the words over in her mind, feeling as though she was prodding a coiled snake that might or might not be a viper. A honeymoon implied all kinds of unspoken things, including intimacy, togetherness, being the focus of each other's full attention for days, perhaps weeks. She had no confidence at all that she could stand up to such close scrutiny without disappointing Blake, and she had no idea at all how she would feel about *him* at such close quarters either.

But first there was the wedding breakfast to survive, and then their wedding night—the skeleton in the cupboard waiting to leap out at her.

She found she was splitting the day up into small, hopefully manageable, pieces, trying to look no further forward than the next challenge. And that was to stand with Blake and greet all the guests who would be streaming through that door very soon.

Stand and ignore the nagging pain in her legs and back and hips. Smile and look confident despite the fact that she was certain to forget every person she was introduced to. Remember the exact depth of her curtsey to a marquess or a duke.

I can do that, she told herself. Verity had drilled her over and over again.

Polly came, led her away, removed her veil, twitched at her skirts, powdered her freckles into submission, then took her back downstairs to stand by Blake.

'Here they come,' he said as the first arrivals walked through the door, and then, just as she was thinking that it was going to be manageable, 'Oh, good. I hoped some of them would make it.'

'Who?'

'The royal dukes,' he said, and before she could

turn and run went on, 'Two of them anyway. Sussex and Clarence.'

Ellie took a deep breath as two bulky gentlemen, both recognisable from endless scurrilous caricatures and prints, seemed to fill the hall. They were talking amiably to Blake, shaking hands after he had bowed, and then they turned to her. She willed her aching joints into the deepest curtsey she could manage, and by some miracle rose again without stumbling.

After that the day passed like a dream.

Ellie was jolted out of the trance in which she moved, smiling and talking—apparently coherently—by hearing Jonathan say, 'And that is the last of them—thank goodness.'

'What did you do?' Blake drawled. 'Use a pitchfork?'

'More or less. Stopped bringing up the champagne, which had the same effect. I will be off myself now. Turner is working his usual magic on the reception rooms, Polly is in her ladyship's chamber, and Jacques informs me that a light collation is being set out in *your* bedchamber. Unless there is anything else I will be away to my rooms, where I intend removing these bloody shoes, destroying this neckcloth and getting dead drunk before falling into bed.'

He bowed to Ellie.

'With apologies to your ladyship for my language.'

He was gone before either of them could thank him.

I can stop now, Ellie told herself. *I have done it.*

As far as she was aware she had made no ghastly errors, and everyone had been exceedingly civil to her. Even the royal dukes had made conversation, flirted with her rather too warmly, and been gracious to Blake on the superiority of the food.

All that was left of this part of the day was somehow to get upstairs. The special shoes were like instruments of torture now, racking her protesting joints and muscles as they were forced into positions they had not taken for years, and both sitting and standing were equally painful. All she wanted was to take them off—take *everything* off—and lie down.

But this was her wedding night. That was the next step.

No, do not think about steps. This time you cannot run away. This time you cannot even run.

'Jonathan is a miracle-worker,' she said. 'I'll… I will go up now, I think.'

'Of course. I will come and collect you for some supper in a while, shall I?'

Supper.

She supposed that was not a euphemism—not

after Jonathan had mentioned the *light collation*. No, the events that might require euphemisms would come afterwards.

She got out of the room, across the hall and to the foot of the stairs. Two footmen were stationed at attention and she smiled at them before she turned to tackle the steps.

One at a time.

'My lady!' Polly came at a run as Ellie finally made it through the bedchamber door and leaned back against it, quite incapable of another step.

'It is these *damnable* shoes. Take them—burn them. I never want to see them again and I do not *care* if I have to limp up to Her Majesty to be presented, or whether Blake refuses to take me to Court. I am never going to wear them again.'

Polly was on her knees, easing them off, and reached up to steady Ellie as she gasped in pain.

'Oh, now the pain is throwing everything out in the opposite direction. Help me to the bed, Polly. I will see what lying down does to ease it.'

Not a great deal, she discovered, when Polly had her stripped down to her chemise and into the sweeping velvet robe that she had been so delighted to find for her trousseau. Everything ached appallingly, and her joints felt as though someone was sticking sharp blades into them.

'Shall I fetch the laudanum?' Polly suggested.

'Polly, this is my wedding night! I cannot drug myself into a stupor with laudanum—whatever would Lord Hainford think?'

But the thought was appallingly tempting. Just enough to make everything into a hazy dream…

'Isabella takes it in *The Lord of the Dark Fortress*,' Polly said. 'I saw it at the theatre when Thomas from next door took me. She did it to escape the loathsome embraces of Count Horatio.'

'I am not attempting to escape "loathsome embraces",' Ellie said, with a laugh that verged shakily close to tears.

The exact opposite. Only, can I make myself believe that when it is actually about to happen?

'No, my lady. Should I brew some willow bark tea? That is good for headaches and the monthlies.'

'Yes, we will try that. And then a hot bath.'

Ellie lay back on the heaped pillows, closed her eyes and made herself think about all the good things. Her gorgeous gown, how kind the Duke had been, taking her down the aisle. Blake standing at the altar rail, so serious, so handsome. Her dream man. Her fantasy. *Hers*. His expression when he'd raised her veil and looked at her—looked at her as though she was just for one moment beautiful.

And the wedding breakfast had gone without a hitch, and no one seemed to have been whispering about what an awful *mésalliance* Hainford had made.

Now all she had to do was summon up the resilience to make it through the rest of the evening and the night without Blake realising there was anything wrong.

The hot bath helped—especially as it was a new fixed tub that she could actually lie down in. The practical benefits of marrying a rich man had not really come home to her before, beyond being showered in jewels, which was a worry, and having the burden of concern over Carndale Farm and her tenants removed. But hot baths like this—that was very definitely a benefit.

She sipped the tea, grimacing at its bitterness despite the honey Polly had stirred in, and dozed a little in the steam until she finally called the maid to help her out before she became as wrinkled as a prune.

'There.' Polly stood back and admired her efforts. 'Lady Verity's woman said that was the right nightgown, with the green velvet robe over the top and the matching slippers.'

She'd wanted to get dressed again, so that they could eat the light supper as though it were a normal meal, not a prelude to...*that*.

Now that the hot water and the tea had taken the edge off the pain there was room for nerves to come fluttering back.

Blake had liked how she looked in her wonderful gown, shimmering with diamonds, corseted and shaped and presented like a magnificent bouquet of hothouse flowers. Now, stripped of all that finery, she was a bunch of roadside wildflowers at best.

Then there was a tap at the door and the time to worry had run out.

Perhaps he will keep his eyes closed, she thought hopefully. *Perhaps he will not expect too much this first time.*

But *she* did, she realised. If she could only control her fears...

It would be her own fault if the whole thing passed in a blur of pain.

Chapter Fourteen

Polly opened the door and slipped out as Blake came in. He had changed too, Ellie saw, thinking that he looked every inch her exotic desert lord as he stood there in a long crimson robe, the open collar of his shirt just showing at the neck. Then he strode across the room, lifted her in his arms and took her across to the door in the far corner.

'We share a sitting room,' Blake said, shouldering the panels closed behind them. 'But I have the study, so you must treat this room as yours and tell me what changes you want made.'

Ellie looked round at the cream-painted room and the rose-pink drapery and thought it all looked perfect. It even distracted her for a vital second from the delicious awareness of being in Blake's arms, from the moment when he shifted his grip to set her on her feet.

The velvet nap of her robe slid against the silk

of his and she landed on her feet faster than he'd intended, judging by the sharp exclamation he made.

Ellie jolted, stumbled, seized the back of a chair for support and bit back a cry of pain. But not quickly enough to prevent Blake from hearing her.

'Eleanor? You are hurt? Damn me for a clumsy idiot. What is it? Your ankle?'

She turned, took a limping step towards the nearest chair and sat down. 'No, it was not your fault in the slightest—merely my leg. I am a little tired.'

'Tired?' He was on his knees in front of her now, examining her face. 'No, not tired. In pain. What have you done to yourself, Eleanor? *Tell me*. There was something... I should have questioned it when I saw that you were hardly limping as you came down the aisle. Whatever it was has made your leg worse now, because it did not pain you as much before. Tell me—or do I have to shake it out of you?'

'You *are* shaking me,' she said between chattering teeth.

He stopped, his hands cupping the points of her shoulders. 'I am sorry, Eleanor.' It sounded as though his own teeth were clenched, and he was not giving up on his questioning. 'How did you stop yourself limping?'

'I had a shoe built up to compensate for the shortening in my broken leg. But I did not realise how much strain it would put on all the joints and muscles that have become accustomed to being shorter. So now it is rather sore—that is all.'

'*All?* You were in pain. I should have realised. You have been in pain all day. Why not take the damned shoes off?' He threw his hands wide, as though to prevent himself from shaking her again.

'Because I did not want to give them something else to criticise,' she snapped. 'I thought at least I could walk down the aisle without limping, so they wouldn't say you had married a lame woman on top of everything else. They would find out soon enough, but at least not on your wedding day.'

'*Them? They?*'

'Your friends. Your acquaintances. Your *world.*'

'*Our* world now,' Blake said. 'Our acquaintances. And soon many of them will be your friends too. Eleanor, you have a limp. That does not matter. And if it concerns someone then they may go to hell with my compliments. What *does* matter is that you might have done any amount of damage to that leg. I will take you straight back to bed and call the doctor.'

He made to pick her up but Ellie batted his hands away. 'You cannot call the doctor out at this hour. Besides, what can he do? I have had a soak in a hot bath and some willow bark tea.'

'Of course I can call the doctor.' Blake looked as though he was one breath from completely losing his temper. 'I am *Hainford.*'

'That is the most arrogant thing I have ever heard!'

'It is fact. I am his highest-ranking patient, so of course he will come—even if it *is* only because my countess has been wantonly careless with her own wellbeing.'

'*Wantonly careless?* All I wanted was not to embarrass you, Blake. And I do not want to go back to my bed. I want to go to yours.'

I think.

'If you believe I am going to have sex with a woman who is in pain, who might have done goodness knows what damage, who—'

'I was rather hoping that you were going to make love to me, Blake—not *have sex.*'

Ellie did not even attempt to hide her hurt and the anger. It had been a long, exhausting, emotionally draining day and this was not how she had expected it to end.

'You must forgive me for being insecure and for trying the impossible—to be a perfect countess for you.'

And for hoping for your lovemaking to soothe my fears and drive away my nightmares.

'I never asked you for perfection.' He turned and stalked across the room, stood regarding a chest of drawers as though he would like to kick it, and then stalked back.

'You made it quite clear that a *plain spinster* like me was not up to your standards,' she flung back.

Blake stared at her, then she saw recollection sink in. 'You heard that?'

'Yes, I heard it. So I have been eating until I am queasy to try to put some flesh on my bones, and spending all my money on clothes and my hair and those damnable shoes because I did not want you to feel ashamed of me—for all those people to despise me and despise you for choosing me.'

She was going to cry in a moment, she thought, desperately whipping up her anger to try and stop that, the ultimate humiliation.

'As for you—frankly, I do not care what you think any longer, because you will obviously take any excuse not to go to bed with me. Which is a pity, because it is rather late for second thoughts.'

Although if I am still a virgin he can have this marriage dissolved. Does that happen any more?

'Any excuse? You are in *pain*, Eleanor. What sort of brute do you take me for?'

My brute. My darling brute, who would never intentionally hurt me.

'I do not take you for any such thing,' she managed. 'But you married me out of pity and I do not think I—'

'Pity? Eleanor, what nonsense is this?' Blake dropped to his knees again, took her by the shoulders. But this time he simply held her, his fingers warm and gentle.

'Then why did you marry me?' she flung back.

'Because I desire you! *Like* you! Because I thought we would get along together! I did *not* marry you so that you could cripple yourself trying to live up to standards that *I* certainly have not set for you. And there is no need to look at me like that. I was stupid and I made superficial judgements before I knew you properly. I did not *want* to like you, Eleanor. I felt guilty because of Francis, and thinking of you as anything other than an abrasive, difficult woman made it worse. And, before you point it out, I know that is absolutely no excuse.'

'It is not even logical,' she said with a shaky laugh, and leaned forward against the pressure of his hands so that her forehead rested on his. 'Are we having our first married row?'

'I believe we are.' He sat back on his heels and studied her face. 'Only we are not quite married yet.'

She could feel herself blushing, even though that was why she had been storming at him only moments before. 'I wish we were.'

If I can just get tonight over with, surely it will be better after that?

'Eleanor, tell me truthfully what you want. You can go back to your own bed and rest. You can come to my bed and we can sleep together and that is all that will happen. Or we can make love and I will do my level best not to hurt you. And we can have supper before or after—whichever you choose.'

She did not have to ask which he wanted. The heavy-lidded look, the visible thud of his pulse in his throat told her that. And she wanted it too— wanted him and wanted this fear to go away.

'I would like to make love in your bed,' she said without hesitation. 'I am really not hungry.'

Except for you.

Blake nodded, as though they had just had a lengthy, perfectly calm discussion, and then reached for the ties of her robe, his gaze intent as he unfastened it and pushed it back over her shoulders so she was sitting in a pool of green velvet, clad only in her nightgown.

'Would you like me to blow out the candles?' he asked as he pulled her gently to her feet.

Ellie shook her head. She wanted to see him, look at him. See that this was Blake, not any other man.

He held out his hand and she took it, let him lead her slowly through into his bedchamber. It was dominated by a bed that looked as though generations of his family had made love in it since the reign of Henry VIII. The thought of all those other nervous brides was strangely cheering.

'It will be easier to take all our clothes off before we get into bed,' Blake said, sounding practical. Perhaps he thought that would steady her nerves.

He untied the sash of his robe and shrugged it off, then pulled his shirt over his head—which was anything but steadying. Ellie managed not to gulp audibly as she fixed her gaze on the middle of his breastbone, stared at the swirls of dark hair that she remembered from that day he had come to the house, wounded. It was not so thick that she couldn't see his nipples or the planes of muscle.

She dragged her eyes upward to his shoulders, seeming broader without clothes, to the line of his collarbone, the dip at the base of his throat where that betraying pulse beat out its signal to her own heartbeat. She let her gaze flicker down for a second, saw the white line of the bullet scar.

Blake leaned in and she inhaled warm, clean skin, intangible maleness, something spicy. *Him.* There was a fleck of shaving soap just under the hard line of his chin and that was reassuring, reminding her that this was a fallible human being, not a creature of fantasy or of nightmare.

Her nightgown was up and off before her instinctive grab for it could make contact, and Blake picked her up and set her in the middle of the big bed. And then he just looked.

Ellie wanted to cover her breasts. She wanted to cover the intimate curls and she wanted to cover the dreadful scar on her thigh. There were simply not enough hands to do all three.

The ridiculousness of the thought made her smile, and Blake smiled back.

'That's better,' he said, reaching to trail his fingers down her ribcage, making her catch her breath.

It was the last place she had expected him to touch her.

'I was so worried about you that night in Lancashire. I thought you were fading away.'

He got up on the bed beside her and this time she could not help but look at him. How strange the male body was—and how magnificent. Somewhere at the back of her mind the fear stirred.

I want this, she told herself. *This is not what happened before.*

It nagged at her—the anxiety that she would be frozen because of what had happened with her stepfather.

It is nothing connected with this place, this man.

'You are all in proportion,' he said, and stroked

down over her breasts, then cupped them gently, one on each palm. 'Small, but perfect.'

'Truly?'

Ellie looked down, trying to comprehend the sight of her breasts in those big hands, her skin milk-white against his brown fingers. Her nipples had hardened into tiny aching points. Her body trusted him, responded to him, even as her mind struggled.

'Truly.'

His thumbs teased across each peak and she jumped as the sensation lanced straight down to the centre of her, where a pulse was beating, insistent and demanding.

Bake trailed his hands down over her hips to rest on her thighs. Ellie shifted, uncomfortable that he was so close to her scar.

'Does it hurt?'

She shook her head. 'It aches sometimes. And it is ugly.'

'Yes,' Blake agreed, serious. 'But that does not make *you* ugly. Look.'

He shifted so that his back was to her and she saw the ragged red line that ran diagonally from his right shoulder blade to just above his waist on the left-hand side. Unlike the white bullet scar, this had not healed cleanly.

'Mine is bigger than yours. I fell out of a tree when I was fourteen and a broken branch tore a track right across.' He moved back to face her. 'Life leaves scars on all of us. Some show…some do not.'

How does he know? Does he guess?

Perhaps he had not believed her evasion when he had asked her at the inn if she had been threatened or maltreated by a man.

To her surprise, even as she was worrying over that, he lay down on his back beside her. 'Do you want to touch me?'

'Anywhere?'

'Well, not *that*.' Blake gestured downwards. 'That is over-excited enough as it is, without any further encouragement.'

She had no idea if he had meant to make her giggle, but he did not seem offended when she did. It was very difficult to be afraid when you were laughing, or to be nervous of a man who could laugh at himself at a time like this.

Ellie shifted round and smoothed the palm of her hand over his chest, enjoying the sensation of the hair, at once crisp and soft. Under her fingers his nipples hardened, just as hers had—just as his had done before, that long-ago morning when he had come to her, bleeding. Blake made a soft sound, deep in his chest. She ran her palms down over his ribcage, over the bumps of his pelvic bones, to rest on the top of his thighs either side of…

That.

'I think you could make me come just by sitting there looking at me while I look at you,' Blake said, his voice husky.

Come.

That meant orgasm, and Verity had explained about those—and rather more about the male anatomy than Ellie had thought she wanted to know in theory. But she *did* know that Blake was aroused by her, even if that was only because she was female and in his bed.

'Kiss me?' he asked, and that meant almost climbing over him—which, she suspected, was what he wanted. His body was warm and strong and hard under her, and the feel of his chest hair on her breasts was exciting as his arms came around her and held her close.

Ellie realised that he had put her on top quite deliberately, so that his weight did not hurt her aching legs. But she was beginning to feel impatient. She wanted more than kisses, more than gentle caresses. She wanted Blake and she wanted to be done with this apprehension. She refused to call it fear, because *apprehension* simply had to be endured until it was proved to be needless.

She rolled away so that she was lying on her back next to him. 'It is all right, Blake. The willow bark tea is working, so you do not have to treat me like spun glass.'

It was rather more the effect *he* was having on her than the tea, if she was honest with herself.

He turned on his side, supported on his elbow. 'You *feel* like spun glass. You aren't skinny any more, Eleanor, but you are so slender—and I am so large and—'

'Mmm...' she murmured, not at all sure that was helpful.

Blake seemed to hear it as an appreciative, provocative sound. 'Hussy.'

He came over her, weight supported on his knees and elbows, and lowered himself slowly.

She kept her eyes open, reminded herself over and over, like a litany, that this was Blake. She breathed him in as she wriggled so that he fitted against her as instinct told her he should, and tried to listen to the messages her body was sending her. The aches and pains were still there, somewhere in the background, but the magic that was happening with the exchange of touch, of heat, of taste swept them away.

Blake nudged against her intimately and she tipped her pelvis by instinct—and then stopped as he slid inside, just a little, rocking back and forth, murmuring to her as he nuzzled her newly cropped curls, kissed his way down her neck.

He held her closer, lowered his body—and suddenly she couldn't see his face, and all she could feel was his weight and his strength, far greater than hers, holding her helpless.

And all at once—as though someone had opened a floodgate—the panic surged up and she was back in that bedchamber in London. The candlelight was flickering on the bulk of her stepfather, who was pushing her down into the mattress, his leg pushing hers apart, his hand over her mouth as she struggled.

No, no, no!

She freed a hand, reached out, groping frantically. It closed around the candlestick beside the bed. She swung it and felt the thud as it made contact. And then, just as had happened all those years ago, the body crushing down on her was gone.

Chapter Fifteen

'*Hell and damnation!*' Bake rolled out of range of the flailing hand and its lethal weapon. 'Eleanor, you only had to say stop—'

And then he saw her wide, sightless eyes, felt the tremor running through her stiff limbs and heard the same whispered, frantic words he had heard when she'd been trapped under him when the carriage crashed.

'Eleanor, it is me—Blake. You are all right. I'm here—no one else.'

He got off the bed and scooped up her velvet robe, swathed her nakedness in it and got back onto the bed, held her against his chest.

'Eleanor, sweetheart, you are safe. I promise.'

The candlestick fell from her hand onto the rumpled covers and she curled into his body with a little sob. 'Blake? I am so sorry. Did I hurt you?'

Her voice was muffled against his chest and

he felt dampness on his skin. She was weeping. He had made this brave woman weep when every disaster he had seen her weather before had been met with dry-eyed determination.

'No,' he said, ignoring the pain in his left shoulder where the solid base of the stick had thudded into the muscle. 'Tell me, Eleanor. And tell me the truth this time. Who was it?'

He thought she was not going to answer him, that she had fallen asleep huddled in his arms. Then she sniffed and pushed herself away until she could slide onto the bed beside him. She scrubbed at her eyes with the back of her hand. The very clumsiness of the gesture yanked at his heartstrings as she pulled the robe tight around her and straightened her spine. But she kept her gaze fixed on her clasped hands and did not look at him.

'My stepfather. But he didn't…didn't manage to…'

He saw her swallow.

'To do more than try. I hit him with a water carafe and screamed, and Jane—who was my maid then—came in. He dismissed her the next day, but I never let him be alone with me after that. I locked my door at night and put the dresser in front of it. I carried a knife.'

He stayed quiet, forced himself to stillness, knowing from her tension that there was more.

He had not listened to Felicity—had blundered in, talked over her, convinced that *he* had the answers, that *he* knew best. He was not going to make that mistake again.

'It is not that I am afraid of *you*, I swear,' she said, her voice low and vehement. She looked up—just a fleeting glance—then looked back down at her hands again. 'I want… I wanted you to make love to me. I enjoy it when you kiss me, when you hold me. I thought it would be all right…' Her voice died away, then lifted again. 'I am so sorry.'

'You have nothing to be sorry for. *Nothing*. It is a pity he is dead,' Blake said. 'There are some people for whom you feel dying once just is not enough.'

She moved abruptly.

'Eleanor—it wasn't…? He didn't try again and you…?'

'No, thank goodness, it was not me. At least I have no blood on my hands.'

She sounded a little stronger now, but Blake did not risk pulling her back against his chest.

'He cornered me in the drawing room one evening. I thought he had gone out, so I was careless. I ran from him and tripped—landed on the hearth and broke my leg…high up, near the joint. I was screaming with pain and the fear of him, and I was lying on my knife so I couldn't get to it. Then the servants rushed in. I don't know what it was that killed him—perhaps the thought that I was going to tell everyone, the thought that they would assume he had pushed me? But he had a stroke, there and then, and died two days later.'

The words were pouring out now, and he realised that she had never told anyone the truth about this before.

'Everyone supposed that I had tripped and he had been rushing to help me. I didn't tell them otherwise—there was no point. Then Francis found out that there wasn't much money to inherit and had to sell the house we were living in—it was not entailed, fortunately. We ended up in a rented house, and once my leg had more or less healed it saved money for me to become the housekeeper. With the limp, what else was there for me to do?'

'Did Francis ever—?' He had to hear it all now—get the whole festering mess out into the open so she could start to heal again.

'No. He never gave me the slightest cause to be uneasy. Although he did so all the time simply by looking like a younger version of his father,' she admitted. 'He liked *pretty* things—good clothes, beautiful women, handsome men.'

Blake felt as though she had hit him again. He had dismissed her with as much arrogance as had her stepbrother, simply because she was plain and drab. And he suspected that the *handsome men* she'd spoken of included him—that she had been forced to watch while Francis frittered away their money, aping what he had seen as the glamour of Blake's life.

'I should have told you.'

She had been watching him while he had been lost in those painful thoughts, wallowing in his own guilt, while she needed comfort and reassurance—not his confessions.

'You would not have wanted to marry me, I know. But that wasn't why— I honestly thought I would be able to…to overcome my apprehension or at least hide it.'

The idea that he might have taken her virginity while she struggled to hide her fear made him nauseous. And the realisation that he should have guessed—that her reaction after the carriage accident had been due to something far more serious, far deeper than simply a wariness about men—was no help either. Was he *really* the arrogant, selfish creature she had accused him of being all those weeks ago? Someone incapable of empathy and understanding other people while he strode through his privileged life, secure and superior?

Blake looked as he had done that morning he had arrived on her doorstep—bleeding, hiding pain and shock and what must have been churning emotions behind a façade of unsmiling control.

What was he thinking? Not that she had been *asking for it, flaunting herself, teasing*—all those ugly words her stepfather had thrown at her. His anger with the other man had been unfeigned, and he had been concerned about Francis and whether she had been forced to kill her stepfather in self-defence.

But he must be wondering whether he had married a woman crippled in mind as well as in body—one who would never be a proper wife to him, or a mother to his children. And he must have realised that she had kept this from him when she should have told him well before their wedding day.

What had Verity said about men when they were in a state of interrupted arousal? That it was actually painful for them? So he had to cope with that as well as whatever bruises she had inflicted with the candlestick—because she did not believe for a moment that she had not hurt him.

'I am sorry,' she said.

'*You* are sorry? What for?' Blake demanded. 'You are not to blame.'

'I should have told you.'

'Not the easiest thing to talk about, is it? And you thought you could conceal how you felt. I understand.'

His smile, which was probably meant to be reassuring, was a trifle skewed, a bit quizzical.

'And I hurt you. No!' she said when he shook his head and rolled his shoulder to demonstrate that it was all right. 'Verity said that when a man wants…um…and doesn't…it hurts.'

She was probably crimson now, on top of tear-stained.

'That is not a problem when one is distracted,' Blake said. 'And I think I can honestly say I was very thoroughly distracted by your story.'

This time his smile was unforced, intimate.

'I…could we try again, Blake?' He looked as though he might protest but Ellie hurried on. 'If you want to, I mean. I know you probably don't any more. But I think that now it will be all right.'

'Are you just being brave about this, Eleanor?'

Blake sounded severe, but a rapid downward glance reassured her that his body was more than willing, even if he had doubts.

'No. I think so long as I can move… It was when all your weight came down on me and I could not see your face that I panicked.'

'You are calling me fat?'

It was all right. If he could tease her, then it was going to be all right. 'Certainly not,' Ellie said demurely and, heart thudding, slipped off the robe and held out her arms to him.

Blake was gentle, but not hesitant, and she found some corner of her distracted mind was thankful for his experience and his self-confidence. If he had been tentative, had acted as though she had something to fear, then she was sure the panic would have come flooding back. But when he did come down over her he kept the whole weight of his upper body off hers, left her arms free to do as she wanted. And she found that what she wanted was to hold him, tug him down so she could wrap her arms around his shoulders and bury her face in the angle of his neck as he began to ease into her.

Ellie began to rock with him, found she could open to him. It felt as though it ought to hurt, because there was a lot of him to fit, but somehow, although it felt strange, it didn't. Blake surged, thrust, and there was a pinch, a yielding. He gasped out something she did not catch, and she was gasping too, holding his broad shoulders, lifting to meet his urgency.

She wanted something—something more, something just out of reach—and then she found it, and lost herself in the intensity of the sensation.

Blake went rigid, then thrust again.

'*Ellie...*'

And then there were lights behind her eyelids, and fire in her veins, and magic—it had to be magic—because just for an endless second they were one person, and a moment ago they had been two.

Eleanor slept with the utter abandon of the very young or the totally exhausted. Blake sat up against the pillows and watched her as she lay curled against his side, one hand under her cheek, one arm flung across his stomach, her fingertips tantalisingly close to his very obvious arousal.

He found that much as he wanted her again he wanted her to rest more. He inched his hand down and lifted hers up to his chest, into a less provocative and provoking position.

Those curls nestling around her head sharpened her features a little—made her look almost elfin, like some faery overlooked and left sleeping after a production of *A Midsummer Night's Dream*. She had washed off all that confounded rice powder and her freckles were once again on display for him to count—a labour as endless as counting the stars in the Milky Way. She had a few dusting across her breasts as well...

Yesterday had been shattering. First the wedding, then the reception, then Eleanor's appalling story, and finally the unexpectedly good experience of making love to his new wife. His expectations had been low, his level of anxiety about hurting or frightening a virgin high. He should have guessed from what he had already known of her that she would be not so much apprehensive as terrified.

Last night had been a revelation as much of his own lack of perception as of Eleanor's past. He suspected that married life was going to be one long series of revelations—not all of them enjoyable.

Against his side his wife stirred, wriggling closer, then stilled again, a slight smile on her lips.

'Dreaming of me?' he murmured, but she was sound asleep.

She had been so brave, and so responsive, and so passionate in the end. He'd had to go on instinct with her, desperate not to hurt her, and it seemed he had succeeded.

Lord, but he had been angry with her last night over those confounded shoes. And furious with himself for letting her think it mattered so much that she turned herself into a pattern-book countess. And under it all she had been steeling herself to endure what she had feared so much.

He had proposed to this woman on an impulse. She'd needed help, he'd been aware he really ought to marry, and Eleanor was intelligent and good company. He had thought they could have an amiably companionable marriage that would not involve deep feeling or the risk of hurt on either side.

Now he wondered if he had made a serious mistake. He had a wife now—one who expected more from him than a title and status. Eleanor *had* been in trouble, but she had been fiercely independent and her life had been her own. Now, as a married woman, a member of the *ton*, she had no independence, no free will.

It was in his power to make her very unhappy indeed if she became emotionally attached to him, because he had no emotional attachment to give her in return. So she must not be allowed to get attached—or to see the void, the lack in him which could only hurt her.

His stomach rumbled, which made her stir a little, jerking him out of his brooding. Blake grimaced, and glanced across at the clock. Seven—which went with the amount of light in the room. He hated having the curtains drawn right across, even in the depths of the winter. They'd had no supper last night, all thought of food having vanished in the heat of that row.

He would order a large breakfast and make certain she ate it all. Eggs and cream and hot chocolate—that was what she needed to build her up, he thought, looking at the way her ribs showed even with the weight she had put on recently.

A large breakfast and then the doctor to come and look at her—make certain she had done no damage to her hips and joints. She was his now, and he was going to look after her.

Eleanor stirred again, shifted, and climbed onto him as though he was a large bolster in the bed. Her head was on his stomach now. One hand was clenched and jammed against his armpit and the other draped across his ribs. Her breath tickled and he found himself smiling. Then he felt the flutter of eyelashes against the sensitive skin of his belly.

'Your stomach is rumbling,' she said, her voice muffled.

'I am hungry. My wife was cross with me, and then seduced me so I missed my supper.'

She gave a little snort and then kissed him, shifted, found his navel and kissed that too, then opened her eyes properly. 'Oh, my goodness. Is it always like that?'

Blake levered himself up on his elbows to look over her body. 'No. It is all your fault, and now you will have to help me subdue it before we can have any breakfast.'

'Are you sure?'

He nodded and reached down, pulled her up for a kiss, then tumbled her over. 'Do you remember what to do?'

'Of course—but I expect we will have to practice.'

She was laughing at him. He could see the

gilt flecks in her eyes sparkling as they always seemed to when she was amused. He recalled one young lady confiding in him that it was fatal for anyone with pretension to beauty to laugh because it made lines, and lines led to *wrinkles.* She had lowered her voice on the word, as though it was an obscenity, or perhaps a contagious disease. He hadn't thought anything of it, but now, looking down at Eleanor's smile, he thought how sad it was…that girl denying herself the expression of happiness.

Surely sex was safe enough? Keep her happy in bed and perhaps she would not notice the things he could not give her?

'Oh, yes. Practice is absolutely compulsory,' Blake said, and proceeded to demonstrate.

'Blake, you are making me feel like a Périgord goose being stuffed for *foie gras*,' Ellie protested as he refilled her cup with chocolate.

He glanced around the room, saw it was temporarily empty of staff, and smiled. 'I worry that you will blow away like thistledown at any moment.'

'You will just have to keep me pinned down,' she whispered, delighted when colour came up over his cheekbones. Making Blake blush was delicious. The fact that she could make a joke about being *pinned down* was almost as good.

'I have sent for Dr Murray,' he said as he handed her the strawberry conserve. 'I want him to make certain no damage was done yesterday by that shoe.'

He could have said, *make certain that* you *did no damage,* Ellie thought, biting back her immediate response that she did not need to see a doctor. She had to admit he would have been perfectly justified. The thought made her keep silent.

'He is very good,' Blake assured her. 'Young, trained in Edinburgh. A Scot. You will like him.'

Liking a doctor was a new concept. Her only encounter with the medical profession had been over her broken leg, when there had been numerous ham-fisted and agonising attempts to set it, and it had not left her feeling very kindly towards it.

'Yes, Blake,' she said obediently, and was rewarded by a very suspicious look.

Dr Murray turned up so soon after they had finished breakfast that Ellie suspected Blake had summoned him at some ungodly hour before she was dressed, and that even if it had been two in the morning, with the intelligence that the new countess had a mild head cold, the doctor would have hastened to Berkeley Square.

Her faint irritation with Blake vanished when she found Dr Murray was cheerful, sensitive and did not talk down to her—all novelties in her experience of the medical profession. He examined her dispassionately through her shift while chatting of the difference between London and Edinburgh, the weather, the latest ludicrous fashions—all interspersed with questions.

'How does it feel if I press this joint? Could you lean as far to the right as possible? Had you ever tried a raised shoe before?'

While she was behind the screen, dressing again, he said, 'There are two options. You can persist with the raised shoe and everything will gradually but painfully adjust, or you can go back to ordinary shoes and accept the limp. As it is, there will be soreness for some days, but you have done no damage.'

'If I learn to walk with the raised shoe then whenever I do not wear it—?'

'You will be worse off than you are now,' he finished for her. 'You will be reliant on the shoe.'

'In that case there is no question. I will go back to how I was before,' Ellie said as she came out from behind the screen. 'I could always walk with very little discomfort, whether I was barefoot or wearing shoes. Now, there is something else I want to ask you.'

She smiled inwardly as she sat down and gestured for the doctor to take a chair. He was bracing himself for a new bride's blushing enquiries about some intimate matter, she was certain.

'Is there any reason why I cannot learn to ride?'

Dr Murray had an open, freckled countenance which, she suspected, he had had to school into the proper impassivity for a medical man. She let her smile show, finding she liked him for all kinds of reasons—not least because he was as liberally freckled as she was and just as plain.

'No reason at all,' he said. 'But I would wait until the soreness from yesterday's experiment has passed. Is there anything else you would like to…er…ask me?'

'Nothing whatsoever,' she said, and had to get her expression under control. Whatever questions she had about '…er…' she was certain Blake would be able to answer them very satisfactorily. 'I would be grateful if you could reassure my husband that no lasting damage has been done.'

Dr Murray bowed himself out—no doubt to be cornered and interrogated thoroughly by Blake.

Ellie sent Polly away and wandered around her new bedchamber—a room she had spent virtually no time in at all.

Tomorrow, Blake had announced, they would set out for Hampshire. A day late to ensure that she was rested.

She knew it would probably be a while before he would relax and stop treating her as though she was fragile, but he would come to see that she was not soon enough. Last night, and again that morning, he had lost that careful control eventually, and those moments had been as precious to her as the pleasure he had given her body. It was so intimate—experiencing the man stripped to his essential animal nature and yet retaining his tenderness, his instinctive care for her.

Blake did not love her, and she still could not fathom why he had married her, but he was making her very happy and she was determined to make him happy in turn. He was her dream come true—even though she had still to discover the depths and the intricacies of the man if he would only let her.

She shivered, thinking about her casual words to Verity about his inner darkness and her friend's alarmed reaction.

She could grow to love him so very easily, she thought, meeting her own gaze in the mirror. Perhaps she was already falling—tumbling past the point where prudence and self-preservation might keep her safe. The realisation was sobering. Blake could break her heart without the slightest inkling that he was doing so.

Chapter Sixteen

There was a scratch on the door and Blake came in. 'Am I disturbing you?'

Disturbing is certainly the word. But then he has been disturbing me since the first time I saw him.

'Not at all,' Ellie lied.

'Murray tells me that there is no damage done.'

'Yes. That is good news. He warned me that I cannot switch between using the raised shoe and limping, though. I must choose. I have decided that I will go back to how I was before.'

Some emotion she could not read showed on his face.

'I am sorry, Blake. I know it is clumsy, but I will be free to walk anywhere—even barefoot in the bedchamber. It is how I am,' she added awkwardly, unable to explain properly.

This is me—damaged, broken and not very well repaired.

Every item in this house, every garment Blake wore, every servant she had encountered—all demonstrated that he was used to perfection. If a vase was broken then it would be mended by an expert so that no one could tell or else it would be discarded.

He frowned and her heart sank. 'I asked you to marry me as you were—as you *are*, Ellie. I hate the idea of you torturing yourself to try and become something else. You have never deceived me about your limp.'

She was suddenly irrationally happy. 'Then you won't be cross when you discover I have deceived you about my hair and this is really a wig and I am bald?' she asked, trying to look anxious.

'A...? You *dreadful* woman.' Blake strode across the room, picked her up and deposited her on the bed. 'I am going to take every stitch off you—starting with this wig.' He tugged at a curl and she yelped. 'Hmm...glued tight, I see. We will have to see if exercise will shake it loose. And we must test this bed thoroughly while we are about it.'

He really was indecently good at undressing a woman, she thought, laughing up at him while he stripped off his own clothes. There was an entirely new field of fascinating study in watching the way his muscles tightened and relaxed, in the contrast of his skin against hers, of feeling the hair on his legs against her own smooth skin as, naked, he straddled her hips with those strong horseman's thighs and leaned forward on his hands, caging her in.

The thought led to another. 'Dr Murray says I may learn to ride.'

'Does he, indeed? You never have before?' When she shook her head he grinned. 'You can begin now, if you like.'

'Now? But we are—'

'Astride.' He swung his leg over and dropped onto the bed beside her. 'Try it—but not if it pulls at any painful muscles.'

'You want me to…? How does that work?'

'Find out,' Blake invited.

Ellie straddled him cautiously, settled herself with a wriggle that made him groan, and found that although it did make her muscles twinge that was nothing against the delicious feeling of power the realisation of Blake's arousal was giving her. She leant forward to kiss him, her breasts brushing his chest hair, and liked the sensation so much that she stayed bent over, teasing them both, until Blake grabbed her and pulled her down, opened his mouth under her lips.

It felt strange, upside down, and it took her a moment to learn how to kiss him all over again. Ellie thought that she could do this all day—explore the feel and taste of Blake, his body hard and safe and strong under her. Then he began to shift his hips, pushing up in obvious demand, and she sat again, feeling him hot and imperative against her. She was wet and ready for him, she realised, almost shocked at how quickly that had ceased to embarrass her.

'Lift up,' he said, his hands on her hips, so she did. 'Now, put me where you want me.'

She fumbled, making Blake gasp, and she realised, once she was sure of what she was doing, that this kind of thing could be a delicious tease. Then everything suddenly fitted, and instinctively she sank down, taking him deep into her—so deep that she froze, her gaze locked with Blake's, seeing his eyes wide and dark and hot.

'When you are ready,' he said, sounding like a man at the extremity of pain, 'move.'

So she did—gasping at the intensity of it, unable to control the speed, the rhythm, the pleasure, lost in a mutual frantic race to completion that caught them both suddenly, fast, obliterating anything and everything.

I love you.

The words echoed in her head as she collapsed onto Blake's sweat-streaked chest.

I love you.

Somehow she managed not to say it.

* * *

'Eleanor, wake up—we are almost there.'

Ellie blinked and looked around. She was curled up in the corner of Blake's travelling carriage and he was sitting beside her, relaxed in a sprawl that showed off the length of his legs to perfection. If he had been a vain man she would have suspected him of adopting the pose for just that purpose, but her new husband seemed to have no great awareness of his physical beauty beyond paying close attention to the state of his linen and his neckcloths.

'What makes you smile?'

'I was thinking that you look as comfortable as a cat.'

And just as certain that you are lord of all you survey.

Which was probably nothing but the truth, given that what he was surveying consisted of his wife, his carriage and, if they were almost at Hainford Hall, his lands.

'I am—but I am willing to catch mice if there are any around that need chasing.'

The look in his eyes as he watched her brought the heat to her cheeks and he laughed, but not unkindly.

'I love the way your face reflects your thoughts, Eleanor. You have no sly artifice, no tricks. When you are angry you show it honestly, when you are happy you glow, and when you are in my arms and you find joy there I am scorched by your passion.'

Her breath caught at the frankness of his words, the heat in his gaze, at how husky his voice had become as he leaned towards her, reaching for her. Then the carriage slowed and turned sharply and Blake fell back against the squabs, the moment lost.

I love…

But it was her lack of artifice he loved—not her, she reminded herself. And a niggling little suspicion surfaced that whenever she was in danger of coming close to him, to revealing her feelings for him the man, he treated it as physical affection on both their parts. It was as though it was safe to allow her to see that he desired her body, her lovemaking, but refused to let her see his inner thoughts and desires. His soul.

'Most women show their feelings,' she said tartly, almost needing to pinch herself because otherwise she might slip into delusion, into pointless hope, that his lovemaking, his desire for her, meant something else entirely. 'But with the pretty ones, and certainly the beautiful ones, you look at their beauty, not at their expression. With me there is no perfection to linger on, so you notice my mood instead.'

'I notice that your eyes change colour with your mood. I notice—' The carriage stopped and Blake broke off and looked out of the window. 'We are at the hall—those are the lodge gates.' He lowered the window and leaned out. 'Good day to you, Fallowfield. Wife and family well?'

'My lord. Thank you, my lord. All well. My oldest's gone to Fareham to apprentice to the farrier there.'

'He'll do you proud, I have no doubt. Here's my countess, coming home for the first time, Fallowfield.'

He held out a hand to Ellie, who scooted across the bench seat and looked out of the window at the big man with one arm who touched his forehead to her.

'My lady. Welcome to Hainford Hall.'

'Thank you, Fallowfield. I know I am going to be very happy here.'

And I will be, if force of will can guarantee happiness.

'How did he lose his arm?' she asked as the carriage rolled through the gates and then through wide open parkland dotted with clumps of trees. Everything seemed lush and green and fertile. Rich.

'He was our farrier. A big plough horse reared as it was being led into the forge, struck his arm, pinned him against the wall. The arm was too badly crushed to save, so I gave him the lodge here, and charge of all the other lodges, the boundaries and the woodsmen.'

All the other lodges, Ellie thought weakly. *This isn't an estate—this is a small kingdom.*

Then she forgot her nerves at the sight of the house, long and low and golden in the sunlight, as beautiful and elegant in its sprawling grace as its master.

'You like it,' Blake said. It was a statement—he could see her face, her betraying expression, but she did not care if she was transparent.

'I *love* it,' she replied, and for a second thought she saw something in his face.

Pain? Regret? Surely not. Probably annoyance that she was exhibiting such strong emotion. Whatever it was it was fleeting, gone in the blink of an eye, and he was smiling back at her.

'It looks like a home,' Ellie explained. 'I was fearing a palace and this is…this is…'

And suddenly her eyes were blurred with tears. She swallowed hard, fighting them back. *So stupid.* She did not cry, and there was nothing to cry about—only that she had been searching for a word that would please Blake and what she had said had been the absolute truth.

'Eleanor?' Her face had betrayed her again.

'It looks like a *home*, not just a house. It looks like *our* home. I cannot recall feeling that I have had a home—not since my father died. Places to live, yes. But when my mother married again it was not our house, somehow.'

'And then it became dangerous because of your stepfather?'

She nodded tightly. 'And the house where I lived with Francis…that was just somewhere to be. It was perfectly fine, but somehow it was only a roof over my head. I think, if things had not been so difficult there, that Carndale Farm might have become a home, but it would have taken time. I would have had to create it. But this…'

This house will contain you at its heart.

'It was a good house to grow up in,' Blake said.

They had never spoken of children—not explicitly, not in terms of a family. There had just been that joking reference to the Pencarrrow nose. Ellie had a sudden vision of small boys racing their ponies across this green parkland, little girls shrieking with laughter as they chased a puppy and a ball along the wide terrace that was coming into view as the carriage drive swung round.

'The West Front,' Blake said, pointing. 'We came in from the north, but the main entrance is on the South Front.'

As the carriage turned again Ellie looked away from the house and caught a glimpse of a distant tower beyond the trees that edged the park. 'What is that? Another house?'

'The next estate.' Blake's face had become expressionless. 'That is the point where my neighbour's land comes nearest to the house. Two generations ago my grandfather's best friend, Charles Harper, Viscount Trenton, built his new mansion almost on the boundary, so their families would be as close as possible.'

'That sounds like the preliminary to a marriage,' Ellie said.

'It might have been,' Blake said, his voice strangely constrained. 'But my father had only brothers and so did George Harper, the heir of Trenton.'

'And you are the only child of the last Earl? Did the Viscount not have a daughter for you to marry?'

She'd said it lightly, meaning to tease, but Blake had turned away abruptly.

'Oh, I am sorry—that was the home of Felicity wasn't it? How clumsy of me not to realise.'

'She...' For a second Blake closed his eyes, and when he opened them again they were dark, hard. 'As I told you, Felicity had other ideas. When she eloped with that damned poet she broke... she broke her father's heart.'

His reaction to the failure of an arranged betrothal seemed somewhat extreme after what must have been several years. Unless it had been *Blake's* heart that had been broken and not Felicity's father's.

'We are about to arrive. You need to put your bonnet back on, Eleanor.'

You do not care? You expect me to believe that? You must have known her well enough to have fallen in love with her. Was she at least a friend? Did you have no feelings at all for what happened? Or perhaps your nose was so put out of joint by her implicit rejection of you that your pride became more important than your concern for a girl you had known all her life.

That was not a good thought to have about the man who was now her husband. She had considered him better than that.

Ellie found her bonnet, put it on and tied the bow with care while she got her expression back under control. She turned to find Blake perfectly composed and smiling.

He leaned forward and tweaked the bow. 'Perfect. Welcome home, my dear.'

It had been inevitable that Eleanor would mention Felicity. At least he had told her enough to squash any curiosity, any desire to probe his feelings about the girl next door who had been so very rash.

The girl I drove to rashness by my arrogant

neglect. The love I lost. Lost before I realised I loved her.

He had been young. Was that any excuse? Young and privileged and used to having what he wanted when he wanted it. Felicity—petite, pretty, apparently so docile—had been what he wanted. But not then. Not while he had still had his wild oats to sow and a father who had been carrying all the burden of the estate and its responsibilities and had been in no mood to acknowledge his own eventual mortality by handing over any part of that burden and its power to a son.

He'd had money, freedom and no responsibilities.

Except to Felicity.

Now he handed his new wife down from the carriage and wondered if his desire to marry Eleanor had not been some distorted reflection of his squandered love for Felicity. She had been pretty, docile—until provoked past bearing—perfect both physically and dynastically. Eleanor was plain, lame, independent, and came with no useful connections or wealth of any kind.

'My lord.' Tennyson, his butler, was advancing across the carriage drive, managing to hurry without appearing in any way flustered or out of breath—quite an achievement as he was elderly, rotund and red in the face.

The benefits of my best port, Blake thought, his spirits lifting.

He had known Tennyson since the butler had been a skinny under-footman, sneaking him left-over sweetmeats from the adults' dinner table.

'My lady.' Tennyson bent almost double. 'Welcome to Hainford Hall. I am Tennyson. We have been too long without a mistress.'

That was a jab at Blake, as both he and the butler knew full well. How much the servants knew of what had taken place before Felicity had fled with her poet Blake had no idea, although he suspected that staff always knew considerably more about their employers' business than their employers ever suspected. But what they wanted now was clear direction, the kind of stability a family in residence with a countess who ran the household on a fair, firm rein would provide.

He glanced at Eleanor, wondering at the sudden tightening of her features, as though she had just stopped herself from pursing her lips.

Instead she smiled. 'Thank you, Tennyson. I look forward to meeting all the staff, but particularly the housekeeper. Mrs—?'

'Mrs Morgan, my lady. She will be at the front entrance with the rest of the staff to greet you.'

Blake offered his arm and guided Eleanor towards the sweep of steps, keeping his pace slow and pointing out features as they went so that she could walk as smoothly as possible.

'The East Wing—that is the oldest part. The West Wing came next, and then the centre was built to replace an earlier single-storey connection between the two. A strange design, but it seems to work.'

He risked a downward glance, but Eleanor was smiling and seemed quite confident. She obviously understood enough about the management of a great house to know that the housekeeper was her point of contact with the staff and that the butler worked to Blake's direction.

'Mrs Morgan is experienced and capable,' he said, hoping to reassure her.

'Not so capable that she is entrenched and will expect your bride to dance to her direction, I hope?' Eleanor said crisply.

'So do I.' Blake suppressed a smile and recalled what Eleanor had said about the work involved in managing a household. She might have no experience of one this size, but she knew the principles.

Beside him, he sensed rather than felt her take a deep breath as the staff came out and lined both sides of the steps.

He had written to Tennyson a few days before.

The Countess suffers from some lameness. Unless she asks for assistance, or refers to

*it herself, no member of staff in any depart-
ment is to give the slightest indication that
they are aware of it.*

He watched now, intent for any betraying
glance that might embarrass Eleanor, and realised
just how much it mattered to him that nothing
upset or hurt her. It was possessiveness, he supposed. She was his now.

He closed his hand over hers as they climbed
the steps then, at the top, swept her up and carried her over the threshold.

Home—and for the first time in a long time
being here really felt like home.

Chapter Seventeen

'I thought your ladyship would wish to start at the top and work down,' Mrs Morgan said.

'Thank you, but no. From the basement up,' Ellie said firmly. 'A well-run house starts in the domestic offices, as I am sure you agree. My husband can show me the public rooms.'

My husband.

It still felt very strange to say it—almost as strange as being addressed as *my lady*—even though her husband seemed determined to demonstrate his role to her at every opportunity. She had not expected that Blake would want to make love so often and so...*intensely*. Not that she was complaining, despite the fact that she felt a trifle sore and all kinds of unexpected muscles were making their presence felt.

Blake had made love to her twice that morning, allowing her out of bed finally to what had felt like an outrageously late breakfast. Ellie had been sure that all the staff were perfectly well aware that it was not sleep that had detained the Earl and Countess in their chamber, but Blake seemed oblivious to whatever the expressionless footmen might be thinking.

He had shown her the large dining room—they had eaten in the small one the night before—then strolled with her through the gardens closest to the house for a snatch of fresh air, then taken her back into the house to view the Countess's Sitting Room. She must have that redecorated and furnished absolutely as she wished, he had said with an airy wave of the hand, before taking her to the Long Gallery for a tour of the ancestral portraits.

Ellie had felt herself wilting under the haughty gaze of an endless succession of ancestors. Gratifyingly, not all the women were beauties, although the fleshy, protuberant-eyed Countesses of Charles II's reign had doubtless been considered so at the time.

Blake had conducted the viewing in chronological order, starting with the first age-darkened, wooden-looking Sir Giles Pencarrow, who had come out of the West Country to risk all at the side of the Tudor invader and had been rewarded with a barony for his gamble.

Finally they'd got to the end, and the portrait of Blake by George Romney painted ten years earlier. He was shown standing, holding his horse's bridle, while a pair of hounds sat at his feet and Hainford Hall glowed golden under a setting sun in the background.

She'd wanted to stand and look at it for a long time—to study the young, arrogant, beautiful face staring out into the life that awaited him, would shape him. Instead, Ellie had made him walk her back slowly over three generations while she'd tried to learn the names.

'I will come here every day until I have them all fixed,' she'd told him.

'And I have sent to Lawrence for our bridal portrait,' he had replied casually, as though the prospect of finding herself looking down at future generations—*Who's that plain woman next to the handsome man, Grandpapa?*—was not in the slightest bit intimidating.

Perhaps the great Thomas Lawrence would work his magic on her as he had on the Prince Regent.

Now she stood in the entrance hall attempting to assert herself with the housekeeper while at the same time keeping on good terms with the woman.

'Carriage approaching, Mrs Morgan,' the footman on duty by the front door called out.

'That will be the first of the bride visits,' the housekeeper said, apparently quite unaware that she was sending one very inexperienced countess into a nervous spasm. 'Whose carriage is it, James?'

'Lord Trenton—I recognise that pair of leaders.'

'I will go and have refreshments arranged, my lady. Will you receive in the Chinese Salon?'

It was apparently a question simply for the sake of form, because she was already steering Ellie towards a pair of imposing double doors.

'Let his lordship know immediately, James,' Ellie called over her shoulder.

Goodness knew where he was—perhaps down at the stables or, worse, as far away as the Home Farm, leaving her to receive not just her new neighbours but the family of the woman Blake should have married.

With a harried glance around the room—exquisitely papered with Chinese scenes on a duck-egg-blue background—Ellie took a seat opposite a group of sofas and armchairs, then bounced up to check her hair in the mirror over the fireplace. She sat again, then realised she should appear to be occupied, so took a slim volume from a side table, opened it and stared unseeing at the pages.

She was perfectly socially adept, she scolded herself. She knew just what to do and how to do it. But where, oh, where was Blake?

'Lady Trenton and Lord Trenton, my lady.'

'Thank you, Tennyson. Please have refreshments brought up.' Ellie rose and held out her hand. 'Lady Trenton... Lord Trenton. Such a pleasure. Thank you so much for calling.'

They shook hands. He was a bluff, fit man in his sixties, his expansive belly doing nothing to diminish the impression of strength and determination. His lady was a faded blonde beauty, still graceful and charming as she shook hands, then bent to kiss Ellie's cheek.

'A new bride for Hainford Hall—such a joy,' she murmured.

'My husband will be with us shortly, I expect,' Ellie said. 'What a very pleasant afternoon for a drive you have had—although I believe your house is not far distant?'

'A stone's throw,' Lord Trenton agreed. 'Our lands march together along the entire valley.'

Tennyson entered again, followed by a flurry of footmen with tea things, an urn, plates of little dainties. 'His lordship's apologies, my lady, he will be with you directly he has changed. He was at the stables, I understand.'

Ellie was mid-way through an enquiry about lemon or milk and was passing the sugar when the door opened and Blake walked in.

'Sir, ma'am—my apologies.'

There was a flurry of greetings before they all settled back with their teacups. Conversation was general and surprisingly stilted, considering that these were close neighbours who had known Blake since he was a boy. Perhaps it was her presence that had put a damper on everyone's mood, for surely Lord and Lady Trenton would be baffled by Blake's choice of bride.

She looked again at Lady Trenton and thought that if her daughter had inherited her looks she would have been truly lovely as a young woman.

And Blake ended up marrying a hedge sparrow instead of their bird of paradise.

Sheer pride kept her expression bright, and somehow she made conversation and did all the right things with the teapot and cream jug. She might be a hedge sparrow, and one who had not been raised to be a great lady, but she would be a hedge sparrow with perfect deportment if it killed her.

She made determined conversation with Lady Trenton who, as she explained, had just returned from Bath, where she had been attending the deathbed of a distant relative.

Ellie noted that Lady Trenton was not wearing mourning for that relative, and could only conclude that her final attendance had been in hopes of a legacy.

'I am so sorry to hear of your loss, Lady Trenton. Doubtless that is why we did not have the pleasure of your company at our wedding?'

Lady Trenton gave a nervous titter. 'Oh, yes,

of course. We would have so enjoyed being there. Dear Blake…quite like a son to us.' She sighed. 'Such hopes we had.'

Lord Trenton scowled at her, and his wife gave another of her irritating little laughs and added hastily, 'Of our dear Felicity, I mean. She was such a beauty.'

She turned from Ellie with what looked suspiciously like relief as Blake moved over to sit beside her on the sofa.

'Will you be restoring the rose garden, Blake dear?'

'I had not given it any particular thought,' he said. 'It has certainly been allowed to deteriorate since my mother's day. I have had little time or inclination for garden design.'

'Our Felicity loved roses. You remember, of course.' Her voice was low, intimate, as though she and Blake were alone in the room. 'I have never been able to grow them in our own garden—they remind me of her so. That evening when you and she walked out amongst them—'

'Time we were taking our leave, my dear.' Lord Trenton stood up abruptly. 'We should not be monopolising the newly wedded pair.' His smile was ghastly. 'Stop boring Hainford with your everlasting gardening. It will be Lady Hainford's decision now—she who tells her gardener what to grow.'

He had not been fast enough to prevent Ellie seeing Blake's face—that one revealing moment when there had been nothing but memory and pain and loss before he had his expression under control once more.

He had loved Felicity, she realised. Perhaps in his heart he still did, whether he acknowledged it or not.

Her insides seemed to have turned to ice, but somehow polite social behaviour kept her smiling brightly as she shook hands, determined not to look at Blake as he said goodbye.

'How very lovely Felicity must have been. Her mother is still a handsome woman.'

Blake looked down at Ellie, standing beside him, neat, composed, apparently cheerful. *My wife.* And he had not given her a moment's coherent thought since he had walked into the drawing room and found the Trentons sitting there.

Bloody idiot, he snarled at himself now. *You knew they would come—you should have been prepared.*

Because Eleanor had sensed something—he was sure of it.

'...love her?'

'What?' He jerked back to the present. 'I... er...yes, of course. I had known her for years... we were going to marry. Of course I loved her.'

Not that I realised until it was too late.

'I am sure you did,' Eleanor said, with the faintest touch of impatience in her voice. 'What I asked was whether you love her still. Her memory?'

'No.'

It was so abrupt—far too forceful. Betraying. Did he mean it? He found he did not know. But he could scarcely believe that Eleanor had asked so directly.

She looked up, her face showing nothing but that sparrow-like intensity, as though she was studying something that might or might not be good to eat.

'No,' he repeated. 'Of course not. I am married to you, Eleanor.'

'What on earth has that got to do with anything?' she asked, and he realised suddenly that he had no idea whether she was hurt or angry or merely curious. 'I had hoped for honesty from you, Blake.'

Then she walked away, leaving him staring after her, quite incapable of finding anything to say. But he was no longer in any doubt as to her feelings, even if he could not sort out his own. His wife was both very hurt and very angry, and he could have prevented that with a little forethought and by keeping a better guard over his reactions.

And my emotions.

Loving a ghost, clinging to guilt, was a dishonourable way to go into a marriage.

Hell. *Hell.*

He turned and strode after her, around the the West Front and onto the long terrace. There was no sign of his wife.

'Wilkins!'

The under-gardener, who was sweeping up trimmings from the climber he had been pruning, dropped his brush and hurried over.

'Have you seen her ladyship? She came this way a moment ago.'

'Yes, my lord. She went along in the direction of the sunken garden. She was—' He glanced nervously at Blake's face. 'Hurrying, my lord.'

That was probably the man's tactful code for crying, Blake thought grimly. He nodded his thanks to Wilkins and strode off towards the far end of the terrace, where the sunken garden was located. The intimate little rose garden, neglected since his mother's death. The garden where he had proposed so disastrously to Felicity.

He blinked and was back in those moments before it had all gone so horribly wrong. She had been standing amidst white and yellow roses, her blonde hair more beautiful even than the satiny petals, her slender figure more graceful than the sweep of the arch above her head...

He shook himself and found he was looking

down on an overgrown tangle of briars as he stood at the top of the flight of ten shallow steps that led down into the square plot. Somewhere in the centre was an octagonal pond, but that was invisible amidst unpruned rose bushes and sagging vine-swagged arbours. Blake stood listening, but he saw Eleanor before he heard her—just a glimpse of deep rose-red skirts between the stems.

He ducked under low thorny branches, stepped over fallen pergola poles and finally reached the centre, where Eleanor stood looking down into the scummy water of the pond, her back to him. Felicity had stood just there, a single white rose in her hand, and he had stepped forward, pressed a kiss to the vulnerable nape of her neck, She had turned. Turned and slapped his face. Turned and poured out her anger at his neglect of her, his complacent assumptions.

He had made no effort to move quietly but Eleanor did not turn when he reached the paved area behind her.

'Lady Trenton is quite correct—this does need complete restoration,' she said, apparently addressing a mat of pond weed. 'In fact it has gone beyond that. I will have it stripped right out.'

'You will?' Blake said, startled by her assumption of control.

'Certainly. I know that it is difficult to grow roses in the same soil they were planted in before. I have no idea why that is, but I have read about it. So I will have the earth cleared as well, and replaced.'

He made an involuntary sound and she finally turned to face him, chin up, eyes sparkling with unshed tears.

'As Lord Trenton implied, the flower gardens are part of the responsibilities of the lady of the house, are they not? And I *am* the lady of this house, whether you like it or not, *husband*. Wedded and bedded.'

'Eleanor, I am sorry. I do not know what you think, but—' Blake began.

She put up a hand to silence him. 'You are sorry, I am sorry, and Lady Trenton was tactless—which is not your fault. And I should know better than to care about your past, or even what you still feel about it. How very unbecoming of me to feel jealous of a ghost, even if you *are* still in love with her,' she added with a brittle laugh.

'Eleanor, don't joke about it,' Blake said, and caught her hands in his, pulling her round to face him fully.

'No? What else is there to do, I wonder, other than joke and carry on? You have no need to tell me I am being foolish.'

'My feelings are more of guilt and regret than anything,' Blake said, pruning the truth as rigorously as Wilkins had been pruning that shrub. 'I was so arrogantly certain of what was right for both of us that I tried to push Felicity into a decision she was not ready to make, and that sent her into flight, into doing something that if I had been more careful, more patient, she would never have contemplated. Until she had gone I did not realise how I felt about her.'

'And you did not go after her? This woman you loved?'

'No,' he admitted. 'I was hurt… I was angry. She had made her bed and I simply assumed she was happy lying on it. By the time I knew what had happened—that her poet had abandoned her in Rome when Trenton refused to let them have any money—it was too late.'

'Oh, poor thing. To be betrayed like that…'

One tear welled up and ran down Ellie's cheek. Her eyes were red, and he saw that she would never be a woman who could weep prettily. Her eyes would become bloodshot, her nose would go pink and she would blow it energetically on a large, practical handkerchief. She had no pretty little wiles as Felicity had had.

'Oh, Ellie.'

She looked up, seemingly startled by his use of her shortened name, and he kissed her on a wave of affection and guilt and pity. *Betrayed.* Was his failure to find out what had happened to Felicity a betrayal too?

She tasted of salt, and Eleanor, and somehow of anger, and she was stiff in his arms.

Still too thin, he thought, feeling her shoulders under his palms, as fragile of the bones of the sparrow he had likened her to.

For a moment he thought she was yielding, that her lips had softened under his, but then she pushed him away and stood, head down, still in his arms.

'Don't, Ellie.' He couldn't tell if she was still crying, but he thought he would rather she stabbed him.

'Don't push you away? No, I will not—and of course I will be a conformable wife,' she said, still addressing his middle waistcoat button. 'You will just have to give me a little time to… I was not so naïve as to believe that you asked me to marry you because you loved me, but I did not realise that you…that you still loved someone else.'

She put back her shoulders, effectively dislodging his hands, and raised her gaze as far as his chin.

'Just because I do not much want to kiss you right at this moment, it does not mean that I am going to close my bedchamber door to you. It is very foolish of me to behave as though a dead woman is as much a threat as a living one.'

Relief swept through him. She was upset—of course she was. And naturally she wanted time to get over the upset. He *would* stop thinking about Felicity, difficult though it seemed at the moment. But he had received a shock too, Blake told himself, wrestling with the turbulence of his emotions. He had thought Felicity safely in the past—a matter for sadness and regret. Now he could almost see her standing there amidst the roses, could almost hear her voice on the soft breeze, although the words he heard she had never spoken.

Love is pain...

'You need not worry that I do not know my duty as your wife,' Eleanor continued, her voice firmer now. 'I know you want an heir.'

Relief was replaced by a flood of something that was not precisely anger, nor hurt pride, but an unpleasant mixture of emotions that contained, at its churning centre, something horribly like fear.

'Damn it, Eleanor, I don't want you sleeping with me out of *duty*. Children are not the point.'

Her lips moved soundlessly.

Not the point...

'Out of what, then?' she demanded.

Now she was looking him in the eye, and he wished she was not. He was not the only one who was hurt and angry, and *he* had made her feel like that. 'You did not marry me for love, that is clear, and you surely do not think I love *you*.'

'I had rather hoped that you might enjoy making love,' he said through stiff lips, almost unable to believe he was actually asking a woman to approve his bedchamber skills.

'I did,' she said. 'I do. You are very good at it. At least I assume you are. I cannot compare it to anything. It is very...'

'If you say *nice* I will not be responsible for my actions,' Blake said grimly.

Eleanor's eyes widened. 'You would hit me?'

Blake slammed his clenched fist against a sagging pergola support. 'Under no circumstances would I strike a woman, Eleanor. If you don't know that about me by now—'

'Oh, what have you done?'

She reached for him and he realised that his hand hurt like the devil—because he had slammed it into broken wood wrapped in rose briars. Splinters and thorns studded his bruised fist, and blood trickled down his wrist and over her fingers as she held him, the crimson shocking against her white skin as it stained the lace cuff of her gown.

'That must hurt so much. Come inside quickly, so I can clean it and get those splinters out. And it is your right hand too.'

Blake looked down at her bent head, felt the tenderness with which she held his throbbing hand, saw her concern over something that had been his own stupid fault on top of an incident which must have hurt her deeply, whatever her feelings for him. This was one reason he had married her, he realised. She did not sulk or bear grudges. She was honest with herself over her feelings, and she was honest with him too. And she had a heart that was generous and giving.

'Ellie,' he said, and she looked up. 'I married you because I *like* you.'

And that was nothing but the truth.

Chapter Eighteen

'Well, then,' Eleanor began, and a smile flickered over her lips and was gone. 'That is a good thing, because it is why I married you too. Whether you will still like me when I have finished with your hand remains to be seen.'

'Duncombe will deal with it.'

His valet would be exceedingly efficient and aloofly incurious about what Blake had done to injure himself.

'*I* will.'

She walked beside him back to the front door, managing not to fuss over him and without so much as a glance at her own stained cuff. Felicity would probably have fainted, he thought, and realised that Eleanor's practical approach was rather refreshing under the circumstances.

'Hot water to his lordship's dressing room, please, Tennyson, and some linen for bandages and salt. I will see you there,' she added to Blake. 'I must find some tweezers.'

Duncombe came with the hot water and helped Blake, cursing and wincing, out of his coat. 'Do you wish me to remain, my lord? It is rather... gory for a lady,' he added as he rolled up Blake's shirtsleeve.

Blake regarded the throbbing results of his lack of control. 'I have every confidence that her ladyship is perfectly capable of dealing with any amount of gore, Duncombe.'

Eleanor came in, her gown changed, her cuffs turned back, her hands full of items that Blake decided not to look at too closely. She poured salt into the hot water and stirred it.

'Put your hand in that and I will clean it so I can see clearly. I worry that anything left behind will fester.'

Blake submerged his hand, thinking ruefully that if the doctor or Duncombe were doing this he could curse and relieve his feelings at will, whereas stubborn masculine pride was going to keep him tight-lipped for however long this torture would take.

'Put your elbow on the towel and hold up your forearm,' Eleanor said after a few minutes. 'The light here is perfect.'

She sat down, picked up a pair of tweezers and

leaned close to his hand, her nose almost touching it as she squinted at the splinters and thorns.

'I never really thought you would strike me,' she said after a minute. 'I rather lost track of who you are for a moment.'

She said no more, and he could find no words to answer her.

It took almost half an hour and another soak in fresh water before Eleanor was satisfied that every last fragment was removed, and then there was a tussle over just how much bandaging was necessary.

His wife won, of course. She tied off a neat knot and put down the scissors. Her hands were shaking, and she did not meet his eyes as she began to tidy up the equipment.

'Eleanor? Ellie?'

She looked up and her eyes were bloodshot, just as he had predicted, her cheeks were tear-streaked and her hair, even in its modish new crop, was a mess. She must have been weeping silently all the time she had been tending to him.

'Eleanor, why are you crying?'

'Because I was hurting you,' she said as she dumped the bandages and picked up a square of linen. She scrubbed at her eyes—not improving things one iota—then blew her nose defiantly.

'You were much gentler than Duncombe would

have been,' Blake said. 'And in any case I deserved it.'

'I think it was a disproportionate punishment for not looking at what you were punching,' she said, and the ghost of a smile touched her mouth.

Blake stood up, pulled her to her feet one-handed, and kissed her. This was his wife, and his bedchamber was just the other side of that door, and his senses were full of the taste of tears and newly awakened sensuality and the now familiar essence of Eleanor.

She made a noise like a startled kitten and blinked up at him. 'Blake...?'

'I want you, Eleanor,' he said with brutal honesty, and waited for the rejection those tears promised.

Blake was braced for a slap, an angry outburst, even more tears—although he was beginning to see that Ellie wept more over other people than she did over herself. Instead she reached up and curled her arms around his neck, then raised her face to him, eyes closed, lips parted.

He seized the silent invitation, kissed her, took her in his arms and began to walk her backwards, pushing open the door as her back touched it. Kissing, kissing until she was against the bed.

She fell backwards with a gasp as the kiss broke, and tried to scramble up, but he caught at her skirts and tossed them up in a flurry of petticoats, then fell to his knees, his hands on her bare thighs.

'Stay there,' he growled as she batted at the smothering fabric. Under his left hand her skin was warm and smooth, and he cursed the bandages covering so much of his right. But his fingers were free...

'Blake? What are you *doing*? Oh!'

Ellie subsided backwards as he pressed her legs apart and nuzzled into the nest of hot feminine curls. She was still moving, but then her hands found his head and clung on, her fingers burying themselves in his hair, and he smiled against her secret flesh, aroused by her frank acceptance of his actions.

Did nothing daunt Ellie?

What was Blake *doing*? Surely not kissing her *there*? Ellie felt shock, embarrassment, and then sensation so intense and so focused that she stopped thinking altogether.

Vaguely at the back of her mind was pain and hurt and anxiety, but somehow she could not hold on to them—not when her entire world was focused on the sensation of Blake's lips and tongue and teeth, on the texture of his hair between her fingers, the shape of his skull, the overwhelming masculinity of him. How did he know the precise point to drive her out of her mind?

And then she stopped thinking altogether, and surrendered to the wave of fire and darkness sweeping through her. She was vaguely aware of protesting as the heat of Blake's mouth left her, and then the mattress shifted as something pressed down on either side of her head. She felt pressure and then yielding as he sheathed himself in her and began to move.

She reached up and found him, opened her eyes onto the intensity of his gaze, saw the sudden lack of focus as he lost himself in her and the tension that was almost pain as he surged and gasped and fell forward, his face buried in her shoulder. She tightened her arms around him and held on—held him while he was hers and only hers.

His eyes had been open as he'd taken her, found his release in her. Surely that meant he had been seeing *her*, thinking of her and only her, in those moments? Or had his imagination conjured up another face, a beautiful face, to superimpose over hers? A lush, feminine body instead of her angles and bones?

Oh, my love, see me. *See the one who loves you.*

It was a very polite marriage, Ellie thought bleakly on the fifth morning as she passed Blake the marmalade and he thanked her punctiliously. Ever since that afternoon when she had realised that he still held deep feelings for Felicity—the day when he had made shocking, desperate love to her, fully clothed—they had been scrupulously careful of each other.

Blake had shown her over the parts of the house she had not seen, had set aside a couple of hours a day to explain the estate, the tenants, the work of the Home Farm. She'd learned about the holdings and the business interests of the earldom and been stunned. No wonder Jon had smiled when he'd said that Blake kept him busy—and that Blake himself worked hard.

They'd entertained the local gentry when they'd called to pay their respects, and she'd met the vicar and the congregation on the third day, which had been Sunday. The Trentons had been there too, in their pew, the tops of their heads visible over the top of their high panelled enclosure, before Eleanor had sat in the Hainford pew and had been able to see nothing but the arches and the pulpit.

Polite greetings had been exchanged and nothing more said. Blake made no reference to the neighbouring estate and neither did she.

He came to her room at night and made love to her with skill and care—and a consideration that made her want to shake him and demand the fierce passion of that afternoon. But she never found the words to talk about their marriage and her dreams for them before he kissed her and left her alone in her big bed.

Blake seemed to feel that good sex and mutual politeness was what made a satisfactory marriage, and that was all. And he seemed worryingly off-hand about children. He wanted an heir, she knew that, but it was almost as though 'an heir' was an abstract object, quite removed from a real child. Was that how *he* had felt? An heir to be pushed into a suitable dynastic marriage?

But he had loved Felicity...

Eleanor had made herself a list of things to achieve—learn to ride; restore the gardens, beginning with the sunken rose garden; work through the house turning it into a home; visit all the tenants. She wrote that list down, but she kept another list in her head: never let Blake see how uneasy and unhappy she felt; never betray her love for him; find a way to fight a ghost for the love of her husband.

She did not let herself dream about a baby.

Finally the miserable weather cleared and she thought about that first item on her list. She had ordered a riding habit before her marriage, but she had not shown Blake, and nor did she intend to involve him in her riding lessons, provided the head groom was prepared to teach her.

When Blake found out she would tell him she

had intended to surprise him, but the truth was that she did not want him worrying about her leg and fussing over her.

'Polly, have you met the head groom yet?'

'Finch?' Polly blushed a deep and surprising pink. 'Um…yes.'

'What is he like?' Ellie probed, diverted by the blush.

'He is young to be head groom, but everyone speaks well of him and he's very…manly.'

Teasing would be unkind, so Ellie nodded, and merely said, 'I will change into my riding habit and go down to the stables to see for myself.'

Somehow she was not surprised when Polly caught up with her in the stable yard with a better pair of gloves than the ones she had originally selected.

Finch was certainly *manly*, she decided, feeling interested that being in love with one's husband did not prevent an appreciation of tall, blond, well-muscled head grooms. From a distance, naturally.

He was refreshingly matter-of-fact about the whole business when she explained that she needed riding lessons. 'Does your leg pain you, my lady?' he asked when she was seated in the saddle, and, when she assured him it did not, made no other reference to her limp.

She had been afraid that he might insist on

consulting Blake first, but he seemed to assume that she had permission to ride as she wished. He found her a stolid brown pony named Toffee, and spent an hour a day with her in the paddock, patiently teaching her. Polly soon gave up finding excuses and simply tagged along, perching on the mounting block or sitting on the paddock fence.

'You're a natural, my lady,' Finch pronounced after the third lesson, and let her off the leading rein.

By the end of her third week at Hainford Hall Ellie was trotting and cantering, and good-natured Toffee was obediently following every one of her directions. It was a revelation to be able to go at speed—albeit the pony's paces were not exactly breathtaking—without the awkwardness of walking or the passiveness of being a passenger in a carriage.

She and Toffee made a good pair, she decided as she ventured out on her first exploration away from the paddock, with Finch a tactful distance behind and Polly abandoned at the stables. Neither she nor the pony were anything but what they appeared—plain, straightforward and practical rather than decorative—and she liked that.

It was a lovely afternoon. She had left Blake closeted with Jon and a pile of estate papers and told herself to think about nothing but her posture in the saddle, the beauty of the parkland and the plans for the sunken garden which were gradually taking shape in her mind.

The sight of another horse jerked her out of her abstraction and she stared at the pretty bay mare and its black-clad rider. She was close to the Trenton estate boundary, she realised, even as she guessed who the rider was.

Ellie let Toffee walk on until the two horses met. 'Good afternoon, Lady Trenton. Have you come calling?'

'Why, yes. I had hoped to find dear Blake at home.'

The other woman put back her veil. Ellie had not troubled herself with one, feeling that her complexion was unlikely to be damaged by the country air, but then, she reflected bitterly, it was not roses-and-cream-perfect in the first place. Lady Trenton's features seemed more haggard than before, and there was a suspicious redness around her eyes.

As if conscious that Ellie might have noticed something, the older woman smiled brightly. 'What a dear little pony. Is it any particular breed?'

Her own mare curvetted a few steps, showing off her arched neck and flowing tail. Lady Trenton was an accomplished rider, it seemed, and not above patronising *dear Blake's* plain little wife.

'None whatsoever, I imagine, but he is perfect for a beginner,' she returned with a warm smile.

'Oh? You did not ride before?'

'No, but I am learning fast. I do, you know. I like to be competent at everything I turn my hand to.'

'Including marriage and a great estate? It is not something that I imagine you are used to.'

'Marriage? No,' Ellie agreed, holding her smile with difficulty.

'You are older than I was when I married, of course. And doubtless more experienced.'

Ouch, Ellie thought, schooling her expression to show that she was taking *experienced* at face value. 'I believe Blake is at home—although I left him and Mr Wilton buried in a pile of estate work. Perhaps I can take a message?'

Lady Trenton produced a handkerchief and touched it to her eyes. 'If you would. I find myself too... I will write, of course, but please tell him that we have decided to put up a memorial to Felicity at the church. It is a long time since her death, but...'

But the scandal is old history now, Ellie supplied, then chided herself for being uncharitable. But was it a coincidence that they were doing this now that Blake had returned home with a bride?

'I am sure that will be a great comfort to you,' she managed.

'There will be a small ceremony. I will write

formally, but I know Blake would wish to be there—would want to know as soon as possible.'

'Yes, of course,' Ellie said blankly as Lady Trenton put down her veil and turned her horse back towards her own house. 'Of course.'

It makes no difference, Ellie told herself an hour later.

She had retreated to the Long Gallery to memorise more of Blake's illustrious ancestors but had given up, unable to concentrate. Now she sat in one of the window seats instead, feet up on the cushions, arms curled around her legs, chin on her knees.

But it did. All Blake's feelings about his lost love would be stirred up again, and a belated ceremony was going to bring back all those feelings of guilt he so obviously held on to.

Oh, for goodness' sake, Ellie, pull yourself together. Of course Blake will be affected. After such a tragedy involving a close neighbour he would be heartless not to be. It does not mean that he is becoming obsessed by his feelings for Felicity.

She stared at the haughty Elizabethan dame opposite her.

I hope.

The painted eyes seemed to speak of an infinite mistrust of the entire male sex.

Movement outside caught her attention and she twisted to look down through the old glass to the inner courtyard. Blake was standing talking to Jon, one hand on his half-brother's shoulder. They were laughing over something in the sunshine. Then Blake shook his head, still smiling, and they turned and went inside.

That is Blake, the real Blake, she thought. *That straightforward, honest man. That honourable man. I can trust him. I believe that. He is too good a man to neglect me for a ghost and I will fight with everything I have to make him happy in this marriage.*

'Is your maid entangled with my head groom?' Blake asked over dinner that night.

'"Entangled" with Finch?' Ellie laughed at his choice of word. 'She is very taken with him—and who can blame her? He is exceedingly good-looking, only in his early thirties, and has a good position. As for him, he seems glad to see her but is being very discreet. Why do you ask? Would you disapprove?'

'Not at all. I only ask because they are not being quite as discreet as you imagine. Hay lofts are tempting spaces.'

'Then he is going to have to marry her,' Ellie said briskly. 'She's a respectable girl—or she was until she encountered Finch.'

'He isn't casual about that kind of thing,' Blake observed. 'I am sure he means to do the right thing by Polly. There's a whole set of rooms over the harness and carriage wing if they want to set up home.'

'That would be kind of you.'

Blake shrugged. 'Why not? He is a good man and she is loyal to you. Why shouldn't they be happy and be able to stay here if they want?'

'No reason at all,' Ellie agreed.

People in love ought to be happy and secure and together...

She had meant to tell Blake about her riding now that she was off the leading rein and venturing into the park, but somehow that afternoon's encounter had taken the shine off her achievement. She had meant to give him Lady Trenton's message as well, but had kept putting it off.

Coward, she told herself. *You have to do it before Lady Trenton's letter arrives.*

Chapter Nineteen

The footman put the brandy decanter on the table, but Ellie did not rise and leave Blake to his solitary drink. 'Thank you, William,' she said. 'We do not require you further.'

Blake looked at her, eyebrows raised. All the sections had been taken out of the dining table, so she was close enough to see the question in his eyes.

'I met Lady Trenton riding in the park this afternoon,' she said, before she lost the will to speak. 'She asked me to give you a message.'

'Not a very urgent one, it seems.' He was frowning now.

'Upsetting rather than urgent.' Ellie realised that she was twisting her napkin and smoothed it out. 'Lord and Lady Trenton are putting up a memorial to Felicity in the church and will be holding a ceremony to which you will be invited. She is writing.'

'Upsetting?' Blake poured two fingers of brandy into the glass and swirled it around, apparently focused on the golden brown liquid in the candlelight. 'I am sure it will be a comfort to them.'

'For you, I meant,' Ellie said. 'It will bring back memories that can only be painful.'

Blake's hand was steady as he raised the glass to his lips. 'It will be sad for everyone who remembers her.' He looked her straight in the eye over the rim of the glass. 'I am not holding on to the memory of a dead woman, Eleanor. I regret the way I dealt with her, that is all.'

'But you love her still.' It was not a question.

'No. You are wrong. I do not love her—not even the memory of her, Eleanor. I give you my word.'

His eyes were the deep grey of old pewter and he did not smile.

'Of course,' she said.

He has given me his word and he is a man of honour.

Yet she could not but recall that conversation with Verity.

'He has such darkness inside,' she had said of Blake.

And Verity had replied, *'Do be very certain that it is a dark space that you can bring light into and not a black emptiness that will suck you in too.'*

Much as she hated the thought that her husband was still obsessed with this woman from his past, her suspicion that he might lie to her about it was even worse. And it was unworthy of her. This was the man she loved—her husband. She must believe him and must hope that one day he might find it in him to love her. Love their children. Want to make a home.

How would he feel about her when she was big with child...ungainly? How would their marriage survive when this easy lovemaking which sometimes seemed the only glue holding it together became restricted by childbirth and small children?

'Of course,' Eleanor repeated. 'And the Trentons will be grateful for your support at a very difficult time for them.'

It was a relief to be able to focus on someone else's marriage for a change, Blake thought as he stood in the stable yard and talked to his head groom.

'I'd be very grateful for the accommodation—and the approval, my lord,' Finch said as he heaved the saddle onto the back of Blake's new hunter. 'I never thought of settling down, but you know how it is with the females, my lord. One minute there you are, fancy-free and not an idea in your head about wives and babes, and the next you're knocked on your back by a fine pair of eyes and it's all up with you.'

'I hope it's more than a fine pair of eyes,' Blake remarked as he ran his left hand down Tuscan's neck. There had been a brisk exchange of views with Ellie that morning, when he had appeared with his right hand unbandaged, and he had finally submitted to a light strapping.

Just for the sake of domestic harmony, he told himself, ignoring the fact that he had enjoyed watching her solemn expression as she concentrated on getting the bandage just right, her lower lip caught between her teeth in fierce concentration.

'Upsetting?' he suggested.

'It is that.' Finch tightened the girth and straightened up. 'She looks no more than a piece of fluff, but she's got a backbone, has my Polly.'

Like mistress, like maid, Blake thought as he swung up into the saddle, automatically adjusting his balance as the big horse snorted and sidled.

'He's fresh, my lord. Needs the fidgets shaking out of him.'

'I'll take him down the drive to the hay meadows,' Blake said. 'Do you want to come? Try him against Romulus?'

'Thank you, my lord, but there's something I

need to do. Another time, perhaps? They're well matched.'

Blake turned through the archway, keeping the horse to a controlled trot until he stopped pulling and settled obediently, then let him canter. By the time they reached the long drive and he gave Tuscan his head he was as ready as the stallion for the freedom of a thundering, flat-out gallop. Tuscan was too full of oats, and Blake was too full of thoughts and emotions and conflict.

He needed this, he realised as he put the big bay at the hayfield gate and they soared over. He felt like hell.

The ceremony in the churchyard the previous day had been devastating, but not for the reasons he suspected Eleanor believed. Felicity was gone. She was the past. The upright figure who had stood next to him in her elegant dark grey ensemble, her hand on his arm, was his future. The best amends he could make to Felicity's shade was to be a good husband to this living woman.

The memorial was a six-foot handsome column of white marble. An oval plaque had Felicity in profile on it, and on top was an urn draped with swags and ivy. Her name and 'Beloved Daughter' with the dates of her birth and death was its only inscription.

Lord and Lady Trenton had obviously been deeply moved, but he had been able to tell they were comforted by this symbol that their daughter had their forgiveness and acceptance at last. For himself he supposed it had drawn a sharp line under his history with Felicity. It was time to stop feeling regret, stop feeling guilt, and concentrate on making his wife happy—because she certainly deserved it.

Eleanor must be hating this, he had thought as he had stood there, looking down at her calm, serious expression. But she had been there—out of compassion for her new neighbours and to support *him*.

He had wondered if one day she would she grow to love him, because he was beginning to suspect that the feeling that warmed his heart when he looked at her, that made him want to whip himself for every unconsidered hurt he inflicted on her, might just be love. Not that he could tell her that, burden her... Eleanor would feel it her duty to love him in return, and love, he was discovering, was not something you got by wishing for it.

He did not deserve that she loved him, of course. She would love their children, if they were fortunate enough to have them. Would he be jealous of his sons and daughters when she rocked them in her arms?

'Blake.'

Eleanor had nudged him and he'd realised that

he had drifted off into his own thoughts. The few friends and relatives who had been invited to the ceremony had started laying flowers at the foot of the memorial, and Eleanor had moved forward to lay a spray of yellow and white roses and ferns.

He had pulled himself together and given her his arm for the short walk back to the hall and Trenton Grange, steadied by her calm tact.

Now Tuscan jinked at a hay stook and Blake cursed, made himself concentrate on what he was doing. The far field was still uncut, delayed by the weather, and he wanted to go and check that it was ready to be scythed tomorrow. He steadied Tuscan to an easy canter and headed for the distant boundary hedge.

The stallion's powerful stride was soothing, and Blake let his thoughts drift back to Eleanor. He could not even curse the Fates for bringing him and Lytton and Crosse together that night in White's, because if that fatal card game had not happened then he would never have met Eleanor.

There was one more thing he must do to clear his conscience as far as Felicity's memory was concerned. Then he could concentrate entirely on convincing his wife that she had made the right decision when she had said *yes* to his proposal.

From her eyrie in the Long Gallery window seat Ellie saw Blake come in from the stables.

Usually he went to the front door, sought her out, told her what he had been doing. Today, walking rapidly towards one of the side entrances, he seemed almost…*shifty*? The glimpse she'd had of his face had revealed an expression not precisely grim, but certainly deadly serious.

The ceremony in the churchyard must have hurt him more than he had allowed her to see. Neither the hurt nor the fact that Blake had hidden it from her was a surprise. She had promised herself not to mention Felicity unless he did, but if he needed her then perhaps she should just happen by and see if he said anything.

She reached the landing in time to see the tails of his coat vanish in the direction of his suite of rooms, so she followed along the passageway, through the open door of his sitting room, and paused outside the bedroom door. That was open too, and she could see that he was not inside, but she could hear someone moving in the dressing room.

Her kid slippers made no sound as she walked across the carpet and halted in the doorway. Blake had his back to her as he stood at the dressing table. One drawer was open and he lifted something out and stood with it in his hands, quite motionless as he looked down at it. His body, intensely still, blocked it from her view.

'Blake?'

He turned, his hand behind his back.

'I thought I saw you come in,' she said. 'A good ride?'

'I was looking at the hay fields. There will be a better crop than I feared after all this rain. Have you had a pleasant afternoon?'

'An idle one,' she confessed. 'I felt rather tired, for some reason, so I went to the Long Gallery and have been learning some more ancestors. I was daydreaming in the window seat when I saw you.'

She could have kicked herself for mentioning tiredness when she saw Blake pick up on the word.

'I am perfectly well. I simply spent too much time investigating the linen presses, that is all.'

He tugged on the bell-pull. 'I will take a bath. It is a trifle early to change for dinner, but I must smell of the stables.'

'What were you looking at just now?'

'Nothing of importance.'

'Blake, don't lie to me, please.'

He stiffened, but she was too suspicious now to worry about any insult to his honour.

'If it were of no importance you would not be trying to hide it.'

'I have no wish to distress you.' He brought his hand from behind his back and held out a miniature portrait.

'Felicity…' Ellie breathed.

Lord but she had been beautiful—ethereal, almost—with an innocent fragility that took the breath. No wonder Blake had kept the miniature. No wonder he could not resist looking at it, whatever he had promised her, his wife.

'She was lovely.'

'Yes,' he agreed, his voice flat.

'No doubt you would have fallen in love with her whatever your parents had arranged.'

'My feelings did not enter into the arrangement.'

'No? Did you not resent that? When you were younger, I mean? Before you fell in love with her?'

'I was the heir. That is what heirs do—marry appropriately. My father saw that as my duty and his was to arrange the match. It was hardly his fault that I made a hash of proposing and drove her away.'

'And you will expect to make the same kind of arrangement for your own son when the time comes?'

'Of course.' Blake sounded surprised that she had to ask.

'Despite you own marriage not being to the advantage of the earldom?'

He shrugged. 'Despite that.'

This is our child you are talking about as

though he was a piece of property, she almost shouted at him.

Then she saw his fingers close around the miniature and more immediate worry surfaced again. 'You told me you were not holding on to the memory of a dead woman, and yet you have to hide her image away so you can brood over it in secret.'

'Eleanor, I am not brooding over it. I was not hiding it away. As I said, I simply did not want to upset you. It is over. Felicity is the past. I swear it.'

Can I really trust you? she wanted to ask.

The words died unspoken as she heard Duncombe clear his throat as he entered the bedchamber.

Ellie turned on her heel and walked out.

'Are you quite well, my lady?' Polly put down a cup of hot chocolate on Ellie's bedside table and went to draw back the drapes to their fullest extent before she came to study her mistress's face.

'I had a bad night,' Ellie confessed.

A night she had spent alone, after telling Blake that she needed an uninterrupted sleep. What she had got was seven hours of uninterrupted fretting, and telling herself that she should be grateful that Blake was not carrying on an affair, or out carousing every night, which was what many wives had to endure, had been no help at all.

He had given her his word that he had put his

thoughts of Felicity behind him and quite clearly he had not. But promising to control emotions and thoughts was apparently an impossible undertaking.

There were times when she wished she did not love Blake, but wishing it did not make it so. She could survive without his love—she had married not expecting it, and had never been promised it. But the children… She had begun to look forward to children as a joy in themselves, both for her and for Blake, but now it seemed that obtaining his heir, and controlling that heir's future life were paramount in his ambitions for fatherhood.

If he thought like that about his oldest son, would he simply ignore any other boys and girls as of lesser importance? He would never be cruel to a child, she knew that, but children needed love…unconditional love…

'Your chocolate is getting cold, my lady,' Polly prompted.

'Oh.' A skin was beginning to form and, looking at it, she felt distinctly queasy. 'Can you take it away and bring me tea, please, Polly? Chamomile.'

She sipped the clear liquid, ignored the maid's anxious looks and began to feel a little better. 'I need fresh air, I think. Send word down to Finch to saddle up Toffee and I will ride after breakfast.'

When she got downstairs she discovered that

she would be eating alone. Jonathan had ridden out
to deal with some emergency involving collapsing drains, and Blake had taken an early breakfast
and also gone out, the butler informed her. No,
his lordship had not vouchsafed his destination.

'But doubtless his lordship will not be long or
he would have given me a message for your ladyship.'

'Of course—thank you, Tennyson.' At least
she was able to ignore the laden buffet and nib-
ble at some toast without being urged to eat more.
'Please send down to the gardens and ask for a
small posy of roses to be made up immediately.'

She was ashamed of herself for feeling as she
did about Felicity, and for finding it so hard to
forgive Blake for his continuing attachment. She
should be willing to forgive his attempts at de-
ception too, she knew. Perhaps a little penitence
would ease her conscience and her emotions. And
if she achieved some inner calm then she would
speak to him about the children she hoped the
future would hold.

'I want to follow the stream today,' she said to
Finch as he mounted the steady grey gelding he
used when he rode out with her.

He had tucked the small posy of roses into one
of his saddlebags, where it looked almost comical
against the battered leather.

'There must be some lovely spots for a picnic, and his lordship said something about trout fishing. I thought to surprise him with a little expedition if this better weather holds up. Then I want to go on to the church.'

'It's a fine trout stream, my lady,' Finch agreed. 'I can show you the best fishing spots. But as for picnic places—you'll be the best judge of those. If you turn left under the arch we can cut through the spinney to the riverside path. If we're quiet you might see kingfishers,' he added.

It was a joy to amble along the riverbank, with rare sunshine sparkling on the water as it chattered in its shallow gravel bed. The willow trees made shade, wild flowers spangled the turf, and they passed one delightful little bay after another—all of them, Finch assured her, excellent fishing spots.

It was almost time to turn and cut across the meadows to the church when Finch saw the kingfisher. 'See, my lady? There on that bare branch over the water. That's his fishing spot. If we walk slowly we can get a bit closer.'

They reached an open patch of grass where a track from the hay fields met the riverbank and stopped there while the tiny jewelled bird dived and came back to his branch, beak empty. He tried again and this time brought back a fish.

After perhaps ten minutes it flew away, a blue

speck vanishing upstream into the shadow, and Ellie turned Toffee's head towards the village with a sigh of pleasure.

'That was magical.'

She felt so much better, so much more tranquil and at peace as they rode up to the churchyard gate. Finch helped her down and handed her the nosegay, then took the horses off to the water trough on the green.

Ellie saw Tuscan as she turned the corner of the church's western end. There was no mistaking the big stallion. He was tied up at the gate that led towards the Trentons' house and she drew back behind a large table tomb at the sight.

Blake was standing in front of Felicity's memorial, hat in hand, one hand pressed against the stone urn. He seemed deep in thought. Then he put down his hat, took something from his pocket and stretched up to move the ornate lid of the urn that topped the column. Even at his height Blake could hardly reach, but he dropped the object in and moved the cover back.

Ellie was not sure how she got there, but she found herself sitting on the broad wooden bench inside the lych gate. *How could he?* Leaving tokens like that could only mean that, far from being put aside, Blake's love for his lost beauty must be as profound as ever.

I swear to you, he had said, only yesterday.

He had lied to her, and all the closeness that she had thought was growing between them, all the trust and hope that one day he might even come to love her, his wife, was simply self-delusion.

Her skimpy breakfast churned in her stomach, and Finch found her a few minutes later retching miserably behind the wall.

'I'll take you along to the vicarage, my lady, and ride back for the carriage,' he said when she straightened up and accepted the red spotted handkerchief that he had soaked under the pump.

'I am all right now, thank you, Finch.'

'I'm not at all sure you should be riding, my lady. Not at this stage of things.'

'What things?' Ellie blinked at him, trying to make sense of his words while she fought not to give way to tears.

'Why, you are with child, are you not, my lady?' he asked in his straightforward manner.

For the second time in her life Ellie fainted.

Chapter Twenty

$$\mathcal{O}\!\!\!\!\!\!\sim\!\!\!\!\!\!\mathcal{O}$$

Ellie recovered consciousness almost immediately—in time to stop Finch shouting for help and carrying her off to the vicarage.

'How do you know?' she demanded.

'My ma and my sisters have all had plenty of babes,' he said. 'There's a look that women get. And then you were sick.'

'I will ride back,' she said. 'Toffee is as steady as the coach would be, and I do not want any fuss.'

Finch did not speak again until they were back at the stable yard. He helped Ellie dismount, then stood there, whip and hat in his big hands, and just looked at her. 'My lady…'

'Don't speak of this, Finch. Except to Polly.'

She patted Toffee and went inside, up to her bedchamber, and rang for the maid. 'Please tell anyone who asks that I have a headache and do not wish to be disturbed.'

'My lady? What is wrong?'

'Go and talk to Finch.'

Ellie locked the doors behind her and went to sit in front of the dressing table mirror. She was in love with, and married to, a man obsessed with a past love, and now she was carrying his child. Which would be a miracle if only she could feel happy about anything else in this marriage. She should have realised sooner, but it was very early days and she had explained the irregularity in her courses to herself as being due to the excitements and changes of the past few weeks.

But she was pregnant, and somehow she had to come to terms with the reality, because this marriage must be saved for the sake of the child. And for Blake's sake.

And because I love him and I will not give up on him.

And yet she would be bearing a child whose father saw it as a dynastic pawn, just as he had been.

'Do not leave me, Eleanor,' he had said in jest.

And she had promised. *'No, I never will. I keep my vows...'*

And when she had agreed to marry him she had asked for his fidelity, and Blake had said, *'While we agree that the marriage is real then you will have my fidelity, not only the appearance of it.'*

While we agree...

Well, what she had seen was presumably as

clear an indication as she could ever receive that for Blake the appearance of their marriage and what lay in his heart were two quite different things. How did that make a real marriage? The kind she had dreamt of, hoped for? How could she trust him to treat his children with the love and warmth she wanted for them?

Ellie took off her hat and her gloves and contemplated her reflection in the mirror. Strangely, she felt no desire to weep. She still loved him, so the human heart was obviously more resilient than she had imagined. But she could not face Blake just now—not with the news that should have made her so very happy.

She could not force him to change so she must learn to cope, and that was hard to face while she felt weak and ill and unhappy. She needed time to herself, time to become stronger both in body and spirit, and then she would return and somehow build a family from a hollow marriage. Now, feeling as she did both sick and betrayed, she would only lose her temper, say things that might never be forgotten or forgiven.

For a moment she hesitated. Stay? Confront him with his broken promises? What good would that do other than to humiliate her? No. She was Countess of Hainford and she had a farm—even if it *had* been absorbed into Blake's estates on their marriage—and money in the bank. All she had to do was to get to Carndale…so far away, so peaceful and uncomplicated.

Ellie began to stand and realised that she was shaking and very cold. If she just lay down for a while… *No.* If she did that she would weep, and she needed to be strong—had to be strong. She tugged the bell-pull and then remembered that the door was locked. She opened it just as Polly reached it.

'My lady! James has told me! Such wonderful news! I had begun to wonder…but then you often are irregular so I didn't like to hope, but—'

'Thank you, Polly. But not everything is… There is some trouble between the Earl and myself. I need to be by myself for a while, just to… to think, you understand?'

Polly obviously did not, but she nodded. 'Yes, my lady.'

'Is the Earl back yet?'

Polly shook her head.

'Then please bring Finch here.'

Polly blinked, opened her mouth as though to protest, then left without asking questions. Ellie began to rummage in drawers to find her pin money.

'My lady.' Finch came in, closed the door and stood, stolid as always, as though he was used to being summoned to the Countess's bedchamber.

'I need to travel to Lancashire immediately. Is

there a carriage and horses I can use to get me to the nearest posting inn to hire a chaise?'

'There's the Countess's travelling carriage, my lady, and a second team of horses. You've no need to go post.'

'But how would I return it?'

'It is *your* carriage, ma'am. And I will drive.'

'No, Finch, his lordship—'

'You are, my lady, in a delicate condition—if I may be so bold as to mention it again—and I'll not have it on my conscience that I let you clatter about the country in a hired chaise without your own men at your back.'

His weatherbeaten face was set in an expression of grim determination.

'His lordship might not like it, but he can only sack me, and I can always get a job with horses somewhere. I want to marry Polly and she'll go with you, which is only right, so I'm coming to Lancashire one way or another. I'll go and get the carriage ready now, my lady,' he added, and he strode out without waiting for her reply.

Ellie took a deep breath. 'Help me change, Polly. Then we will pack. I do not know how long we will be away, but take only sensible, practical stuff. I'll have no need of ball gowns and evening dresses. Hurry.'

'But his lordship will follow us—catch us,'

Polly said, even as she began to help Ellie out of the riding habit.

'I will misdirect him,' Ellie said grimly, her brain spinning with the effort of remembering everything she must do.

'We *are* coming back, aren't we, my lady?'

'Of course we are, Polly. Of course.'

Blake rode away from the churchyard with a sense of liberation, as though a weight had been lifted from both his spirit and his back. He had carried that portrait of Felicity like a talisman and like a punishment ever since she had fled with her treacherous poet. It had been months since he had looked at it, although at the back of his mind he had been as aware of it as he would have been a monk's hair shirt fretting at his flesh.

It had taken him far too long to realise that he should have talked about what had happened with Felicity before. He could have confided in Jonathan and come to understand his own feelings a lot sooner. Guilt, he was sure now, was an unhealthy emotion unless one learned from it and moved on—instead of romanticising it as he had done.

It had taken him far too long to realise how he felt about Eleanor as well. He had gone from hostility and guilt—guilt *again*—to reluctant admiration and then liking.

I married her because I like her, because she is brave and honest and her passions are genuine, not some act, he thought as he rode. *There is beauty in her eyes and her soul and her passions. I love her.*

He intended to tell her now—to go home, explain the feelings that he had hidden from everyone, himself included, for so long. He had taken that miniature and in a way given it back to Felicity by hiding it within her memorial. Now he felt free to go to his wife and open his heart.

Blake turned towards home and sent Tuscan off in a flat-out gallop across the hay fields, taking gates and hedges and ditches as though in a hunt after some phantom prey. He gave the big horse its head, hardly seeing where he was going, thinking only of Eleanor and holding her in his arms, somehow making her smile with happiness.

He rode by instinct until part of the park's herd of deer panicked and plunged out of a thicket in front of them.

Tuscan shied, then reared. Blake got the stallion's head down and had him under immediate control. And then one of the does careered back towards them. Tuscan backed, stumbled, and Blake, his balance all on the wrong side, was pitched to the ground.

He was conscious of pain in his head, and then everything went black.

* * *

The setting sun blazing in his eyes woke him and he struggled into a sitting position, feeling sick, dizzy and disorientated. Tuscan grazed calmly, broken reins trailing, taking no notice whatsoever of the herd of deer close by.

'Stupid horse,' Blake said, and Tuscan's ears twitched as though the last thing he would dream of doing was to shy at a herd of deer.

He should get up, mount, ride home. Eleanor would be worrying about where he had got to and he had so much to say to her. His head was aching, but that was not why he felt so sick—that was from the remembered shame of betraying Eleanor by clinging to that illusion that he loved Felicity, had loved her for years, when all the time it had been nothing but a spell cast by a lovely face and his own sense of guilt for neglecting her so long.

Blake hauled himself to his feet and made his unsteady way towards the horse. He couldn't see his hat, but his head hurt too much to put it on anyway.

Love her.

That was the important thing. Confess first—all the muddled thinking, all the clinging to the memory of a woman he had never really known, never truly understood. And then tell Eleanor about the realisation that it was she whom he loved.

Could she love him in return? He would be a

luckier man than he deserved if she did. They had got off to a dreadful start, and then he had insulted her, kissed her in a field, married her out of hand and brought her to the one place where she would come face to face with all the memories of his past.

Blake gathered up the broken reins, stuck his foot in the stirrup and got into the saddle—then sat there swaying while the familiar landscape swayed and circled around him.

Concussion.

Perhaps it would be better to wait until he had stopped seeing double before he tried either confession or lovemaking.

He was half a mile from home, riding on a loose rein and letting Tuscan find his way, when he saw two riders galloping towards him. They became one as he forced his eyes to focus, then resolved into Jon, hatless and grim.

'Thank God. What has happened to you? You are bleeding like a stuck pig.'

'Am I? Scalp wound, I suppose. Fell off...hit my head,' Blake said concisely, wondering if he was about to cast up his accounts. 'What's the panic—I haven't been gone that long, have I?'

'Hell, no, I wasn't worried about *you*.' Jon rode alongside and leaned across to peer into his face. 'But I am now—you look dreadful.'

'Concussion.' Blake put up a hand and probed

the sticky patch at the back of his head. 'Nothing cracked, I don't think.' The wave of sickness passed. 'Who *are* you worrying about, then?'

'Eleanor.'

'What? What's wrong? Is she hurt? Ill?' He kicked Tuscan into a trot, and then into a less skull-jarring canter.

'No. Gone. So are Polly and Finch.'

'What?'

'They've taken the small travelling carriage and the team of four bays. When Frederick asked Finch where he was going, expecting to be needed to drive, he said *he* was driving the mistress.'

'What?'

'Eleanor came in from her riding lesson with Finch—'

'Her *what*?' Blake shut his mouth—hard. Asking questions was only going to slow down the explanation.

'Apparently she was white as a sheet. Sent for Polly, then Finch. The next thing they're carrying bags out to the carriage. Tennyson asked Eleanor what he should tell you and she simply handed him two letters. Blake, what the hell's going on?'

Blake stopped swearing long enough to snap, 'I have no idea. And *what* riding lessons?'

'Finch has been teaching her to ride on Toffee. I thought you knew.'

He didn't shake his head because it hurt too

much—but not as much as the realisation that he hadn't even noticed that Eleanor was learning to ride.

Tennyson was pacing up and down in the hall when Blake went in. 'My lord! Your head—'

'Give me the letters.'

The blue wax that Eleanor always used splintered under this thumb and he forced his eyes to focus on the few lines of writing.

Blake,

I saw you at the church by Felicity's memorial. Even after I saw the portrait miniature and you promised...

I want to be a good wife, to make this marriage work, but I need to get away, to think how to do that.

I am not feeling very well, but I know where to go for advice.

Please do not follow me. I will come back. I keep my promises.
Eleanor.

'London. She has gone to London—she must have. She says she is feeling unwell and knows where to seek advice and she liked Dr Murray, trusted him. Hell, *why* isn't she feeling well? I hadn't noticed anything.'

All the more reason for leaving him if he hadn't even noticed that she was feeling ill enough to flee to London.

'Tennyson, tell Duncombe to pack and order the stables to get the travelling coach ready. You had better come too, Jon. I may need you.'

'You're damn right you need me. But you need a doctor first.'

Blake snarled at him but he stood his ground. 'What does Finch say?'

That letter was sealed with a cheap wafer and addressed in Finch's round, painstaking hand.

My lord,
Under the circumstances I think it best if I
am with her ladyship. I will guard her with
my life, be certain of it. I will ensure that the
carriage and horses are returned to your
lordship when her ladyship no longer re-
quires them.
Jacob Finch

'Thank God he is with them,' Blake said, handing the letter to the other man.

Had Finch been with Eleanor at the church? Had he seen what *she* had seen? It seemed that little episode must have looked truly damning if Finch, with no emotional involvement, had immediately sided with Eleanor's demands to leave the house without telling him.

'But why has she gone?' Jon demanded.

'Because she saw me leaving what must have seemed like a token inside Felicity's memorial—because she knew I was still carrying a miniature of Felicity and I suspect believed I loved the memory of a dead woman more than my wife and she could not trust my word.'

Blake spoke before he realised that he had an audience—not just his half-brother but Tennyson and now Duncombe.

'You...' Jon expressed himself in language that made the butler gasp.

'Quite. Duncombe, sort my head out—I haven't time for the doctor. Then get me a clean shirt and pack.'

The valet came down the remaining steps and peered at Blake. 'You are concussed, my lord. Your eyes... You should be resting.'

'I will rest in the carriage. *Hurry.*'

Duncombe washed the cut on Blake's scalp and bandaged it, then started to pack while Blake, unable to sit still, searched Eleanor's rooms.

The family jewels were still there, and all her evening finery.

'She's packed for practicality,' he said to Jon, relieved by this evidence of rational thought and not simply hysterical flight. 'And Polly must be with her as well as Finch.'

Talk about snatching at straws... She is sick. Oh, God, I ought to be with her.

'This is locked.' He tugged at a drawer and then, when it failed to open, forced it with a paper knife without even thinking why he was violating his wife's privacy. It was locked but he could not afford to overlook anything she had tried to hide from him in case it held a clue.

The drawer was full of paper covered in Eleanor's handwriting. He picked it up, expecting it to be more of Oscar's adventures. A phrase caught his eye and he stared. Not Oscar... But what the devil...?

Another straw?

There was no time now. He pushed the whole lot into a portfolio.

Jon infuriated him by taking his arm down the stairs, then producing a rug as they got into the carriage. 'Rest, damn you!'

What else was there to do? Nothing until he found her. Certainly thought was beginning to be difficult through the pounding waves of headache and nausea.

Blake suffered Jon and Duncombe to thrust him down full-length on the seat with a pillow under his head.

He closed his eyes.

She saw. What must she be thinking? I promised her... She promised she would not leave me. But how can I blame her? She doesn't love me, but I must have hurt her so much...

Chapter Twenty-One

Finch hired a coachman and a groom in Lynd-
hurst, so they could drive through the night, and
sent the team back to Hainford Hall with a groom
from the livery stables.

'There is no way anyone could know which
way we'll go from here,' Finch explained when
Ellie protested about giving up the strong team
so early. 'This is on the way to London just as it
is to the North.'

Hopefully her reference to seeking medical
advice would make Blake think she was going
to London, as she'd intended him to think. She
would write to him once she was settled at Carndale, Ellie thought. There was no reason to hide
from him—not if they were to find some way to
save this marriage. But she did not want to see
him. Not yet. She did not think she could cope
with it, if she was honest with herself. Quiet re-

flection was what was needed. She would write eventually…tell him to write back.

'His lordship hasn't let Carndale, has he?' Polly asked suddenly. 'I only just thought of that. What are we going to do if he has?'

'There is no need to worry—they haven't finished the roof repairs or the bore hole for the well yet, Jonathan was telling me that only the other day. It will not be let until everything is complete.'

It was strange how the old farmhouse represented a haven of calm now. Security. Perhaps it had even stopped raining.

It took them four days. Without Jon to book ahead and secure the best accommodation Ellie had been reluctant to arrive anywhere late in the evening and chance finding rooms, so she and Polly were both sick of the sight of the coach interior by the time it drew up in front of Carndale. The journey had not been helped by the fact that there had been absolutely nothing they'd felt like talking about.

The past was too painful—especially the recent past—and the present too uncertain.

Her nausea persisted, worse in the morning, which Polly told her was the usual pattern. 'My ma used to suffer from it something awful,' she confided. 'But it stops after a bit.'

'I hope so,' Eleanor said wanly. She was making herself eat for the baby's sake, although keeping breakfast down was proving a lost cause.

She felt relief at the sight of Mr Grimshaw's craggy face as he crossed the yard to meet them. With his dour unflappability he seemed like a rock in a storm, utterly reliable.

'Miss—my lady, I should say. We weren't expecting you.'

'No. I have come to stay for a while, Mr Grimshaw. Are the family all in good health? And the farm? I hope the well is finished soon for you.'

'Aye, my lady.' He held out a callused hand to help her down. 'That's just finished today, and they'll be done with the roof come next week. No need to worry, though. It's sound enough, and we'll not have any rain for a few days.'

'That seems like a miracle,' she said, looking at a clean, dry yard under a blue sky. Even the plain old house looked warm and welcoming. 'Do you think Marjorie will be able to lend a hand again?'

'She will that, my lady.' He dug in his pocket and produced the key. 'I've been letting the men in and out to do the roof.'

'Thank you.' Ellie took the key. 'Have you anywhere my men can sleep? Mr Finch, my steward, Phipps, my driver and David, the groom.'

'Aye, I can house them if you want, my lady. But there are rooms over the stable at the back.

Needs a clean-out, but I reckon it would suit bachelors.'

Finch's eyebrows had risen at his new job title, but she had to do something to reward him for his support and loyalty. Hopefully he would be marrying Polly soon, and they could have their own rooms in the main house. She could only hope that Blake was not going to dismiss him. Surely he would not do that? She had to trust that she was not *completely* wrong about him.

Although that might be easier to bear, she thought as she waited for Finch to unlock the front door. If she *had* been utterly misguided about Blake, if he *was* simply the arrogant rakehell intent on only his own pleasure and interests that she had taken him for in the beginning, then she could surely learn to fall out of love with him—which would make it so much easier to endure this marriage.

The old house was warmer than she remembered. It smelt of woodsmoke and dust, but not of damp or neglect. She could take refuge here until she found the strength to go back and discover some way to exist and create a family.

A refuge, *not* a hiding place, she repeated to herself as she walked through the dim rooms. If she ran, as a cowardly little voice inside her urged, then they would never be able to reach any way forward. And besides, tempting as the idea of hiding somewhere and pretending to be a widow with a child might be, it was a coward's way out.

This baby deserved to know his or her father. And Blake had the right to be the kind of father she knew he could be if he could only forget he was an earl and think like a plain man. But just now the last person she wanted to see was her husband.

When he arrived in Berkeley Square that evening the house was as Blake had left it—empty except for a skeleton staff busy draping the main rooms under dust sheets as Turner directed a campaign of deep cleaning and repairs.

'Her ladyship?' Turner stood amidst the table silver in the strong room, surrounded by metal cleaner, polishing cloths and tubs of steaming water. 'There has been no word from her, my lord.'

'Obviously a misunderstanding,' Blake said. 'I understood her to be coming to Town on some business, but she must have gone to… Oh, what the hell? If I cannot trust your discretion, I cannot trust anyone's. Between you and me, Turner, my wife has left me. I thought she would come here.'

'It seems we must put on our thinking caps, my lord.'

The butler opened a cupboard, produced two glasses and a bottle of brandy.

Blake sat down with a thud on the chair on the opposite side of the table and reached for a glass. 'Does nothing throw you off balance, Turner?'

He took a gulp of brandy and decided that he did not want to know what spirits of this quality were doing in the strong room.

'One would hope that a superior butler will always rise to the occasion, my lord. I collect that her ladyship is upset—some misunderstanding, no doubt. But she has no close relatives, I think?'

'None. Oh, come in, Jon, join the party.'

Jon came in, sat down and twitched the brandy glass out of Blake's hand. 'You know what the doctor said about alcohol and concussion. I have the wedding invitation list here.' He brandished a sheaf of papers. 'That has all Lady Hainford's close friends on it—although quite how we go about asking if she is with any of them without starting the rumour mills going... I can set an enquiry agent to find who is living in each house... that might be the most discreet way. I won't say who we are looking for. It will take a day or so.'

'I had better start with Dr Murray. She liked him when he saw her about her leg, so he's the most likely medical man she will have gone to for advice.' Blake shoved both hands through his hair and winced as he knocked against the bandage. He tried to think, tried to focus on something other than the sickening fear that he had lost her.

'And if we do not find her in London?' Jon asked, downing the brandy in one go.

'I'll cross that bridge when we come to it,' Bake said.

Or throw myself off it.

'Dinner,' Jon said decisively. 'We are both bone-tired and you are concussed.'

It was sensible, and Jon was right. There was nothing to be done tonight. Blake went upstairs to bathe and change, ate dinner, then swallowed the foul potion that Duncombe produced—'For your headache, my lord,'—and retreated to his study. He felt drained, beyond tired and yet achingly beyond sleep even as his eyelids dragged down.

What about heartache, Duncombe? Have you a potion for that too?

On the table was the portfolio of papers that he had taken from Eleanor's locked desk drawer. What had possessed him to break into her private things? It was most definitely not the action of a gentleman, even a desperate one, but instinct had driven him—some small nagging voice that he had promptly forgotten in his haste to reach London.

Now he opened the leather flaps and began to read. After a page he sat up straight. After two all desire for sleep fled. Blake laid the papers out on the desk and began to sort them into order because—bless her orderly soul—Eleanor had dated most of them. Dated, and noted the place where each part had been written.

The faintest glimmering of hope crept into the aching void that was his heart.

'Yes, I am happy to confirm that you are in an early stage of pregnancy, my lady.' Dr Eldridge, the doctor Ellie had gone to on the advice of Mrs Grimshaw, beamed at her.

'I thought I must be,' she said faintly. She was pleased—of course she was—and happy, but she wished she might be *joyful*.

The doctor was a jolly soul, unused to aristocratic patients, and cheerfully frank in a way that Ellie suspected many a London doctor would not be. He explained all the symptoms she might encounter, was encouraging about the morning sickness, and prescribed country walks, fresh air and a lack of worry for anything else that might ail her.

'But summon me at any time you feel the slightest need, my lady.'

Finch was waiting with the carriage and helped Ellie and Polly in. 'I bought some newspapers, my lady. I thought you might find them of interest,' he said.

'Thank you, Finch.' He climbed into the carriage after them as Ellie insisted—he was her steward now, after all—and settled next to Polly as Ellie picked up one of the papers and tried to read.

The print blurred and danced before her eyes. So she must not worry and all would be well, would it?

Where was Blake now, and what was he doing? Did he miss her even a little? Was he worried about her? She swallowed, turned the front page—all advertisements as usual—shook the pages of newsprint into order and made herself focus on the first item on page two.

She had reached the foot of the fourth and final page by the time they drew up in front of Carndale. And if she had been challenged to recount a single item of news she knew she would not have recalled one of them.

'Eleanor is not in London.'

Blake pushed back his chair and began to pace up and down the study.

'The agents have turned up nothing, Murray dithered about his patients' confidentiality, but it was largely to save face, and he couldn't hide his surprise when I told him I thought she had been to visit him, so she hasn't been in touch.'

'So where else?'

Jon looked as tired as he felt, Blake thought as he sat down again. Neither of them had slept much over the past three nights, and he had noticed that Jon had been pushing his breakfast around his plate as much as he had just now. At least his head had stopped aching. His doctor had pronounced him free of the concussion—not that it seemed to have done his thinking powers much good.

Eleanor had some money, but not much, and she had respectable servants. If anything serious had occurred they would have let him know, surely? She did not know his other properties but—

'Of course—Carndale. She is familiar with it, it is a good long way away and it is not mine. Or rather she would prefer not to think of it as mine.'

'I will order the carriage.' Jon pushed away his half-eaten breakfast and stood up.

'No, the curricle. Just you and me and a bag apiece. We'll drive turn-about, if your arm can stand it.'

When Jon began to protest—something about Blake resting because of his head, the distance— Blake said flatly, 'No. I cannot bear to think of her believing that I would hurt her deliberately. But I *have* hurt her, Jon.'

'All right.' His brother nodded agreement. 'But we are taking your tiger, so we've a third to spell us with the driving—and do not tell me that the entire staff doesn't know what is going on, because they do. With you looking like there's been a death in the family and no funeral, they don't have to use their imaginations to know what the cause is.'

* * *

Nine days since Ellie had left Hainford Hall. Long enough, surely, for her to have decided what to do, she told herself as she tried for the third time to draft a letter to Blake.

The part concerning Polly and Finch was easy—praise for their loyalty to her, a word about how carefully Finch had looked after her, a statement that she was certain Blake would not be angry with him for following her orders…

What was difficult was how to make him understand that she needed time before she could return to the marriage, but that she *would* come back, that she had every intention of honouring her vows. She set out how she had felt about his prevarication over the miniature, how she had come upon him in the churchyard unintentionally and how she felt hurt, angry and…lonely.

In a way, it would have been easier if you were in love with a living woman. I would be able to fight, then. But all I have now is the knowledge that I am so far from what you need and want, let alone desire, that staying in your past is easier for you than making a present with me.

I have to come to terms with that, and now I must discover how to forgive and to understand because I—

She almost wrote *love you*, then jerked back her hand, blotting the page. That was too much like emotional pressure.

I want this marriage to work so much. For the—

For the baby's sake. No, she could not mention the child either.

The letter was almost right. She had told him why she had left, assured him that she was coming back, and done her best to safeguard Polly and Finch from his anger. Now all she had to do was finish it appropriately—however that might be done—and then work out how to cope with a loveless marriage and a baby on the way and go home again.

There was the sound of hooves in the front yard. Mr Grimshaw's gig, by the sound of it, although the dogs were barking, which was odd. Polly was upstairs, changing the bed linen, so Ellie put down her pen and went to the front door herself.

It was a high-perch curricle with a team of four steaming horses, a tiger perched up behind and two men…

The tiger jumped from his seat and ran to the leaders' heads and the driver climbed slowly down.

Blake.

He looked gaunt and grim, there was stubble on his chin, and his heavy driving coat was thick with white dust. For a moment her treacherous heart sang with relief and joy. He was here, he had come for her, and she took two running steps before joy turned to dismay.

What am I going to do now?

She stopped dead, began to back away—as though getting behind the door, closing it, would make him disappear, like a child playing hide and seek.

If I cannot see you, you will not know that I'm here.

'Eleanor.'

He came across the few feet between them faster than she could back away.

'Eleanor, don't run from me. Please.'

Be civilised about this, she told herself as she put up her chin and turned. *Be dignified. He knows you are hurt, but do not let him guess how you feel about him.*

She went back inside, held the door open for him and walked in front of him into the parlour.

Chapter Twenty-Two

Ridiculous to have forgotten how Blake seemed to fill a room, how he took her breath. Idiocy to want to touch him, to kiss him, to be held.

'Please sit down,' Ellie said.

Dignity. Be civilised.

'I will stand. I am relieved to have found you. I thought you had gone to London.' He sounded as though he was giving evidence in a court of law. 'You said you were not well.'

'That—' Her voice cracked. She moistened her lips and tried again. 'That is what I hoped you would believe at first. I am all right. Only… tired.'

'You knew I had kept that miniature and then, at the church, you saw me put some token into the monument. You believe that I hold Felicity's memory more dear than I hold my marriage to you, than my promises and vows to you.'

'Yes. I thought… I had told myself that she was in the past and that we could build our marriage together, be honest with each other. I saw I was wrong and so I left. I *will* come back, Blake, I swear it. I just couldn't… I did not know how to pretend that I had not seen and somehow hide the hurt, and I dared not speak of it and end up saying things that neither of us would ever be able to forget.'

'I am not surprised,' he said, startling her with his ready acceptance. 'I can only wonder at your restraint. If the positions had been reversed—if I had seen what you did, thought that you felt like that for another man, alive or dead—I could never have controlled my tongue or my temper. Marriages have broken apart for far less.'

He held out one hand to her, then sat down abruptly without touching her, even though she was still on her feet.

'You have no reason to believe anything I tell you, Eleanor. Certainly no reason to trust me now. But will you let me explain?'

I do not want to hear you telling me how lovely she was, how tragic it was!

For a second she thought she had shouted it aloud. 'Very well.' She sat down too—it felt easier to control herself, somehow.

'I told you how I put off asking Felicity to marry me after my father died. I hadn't realised how I felt about her—I suppose I had come to take her for granted. She refused me. I became persistent…angry. I kissed her and she started crying. I stormed off, expecting her to come round in a day or so. I was too proud to go and beg. But I had been taken by surprise at how very beautiful she was, how she had felt in my arms. It was a lightning strike of realisation— Eleanor, please, do not look like that. Hear me out. I need to explain this properly. I am not trying to hurt you.'

Are you not? You are succeeding very well so far.

'Go on,' she said to the log basket.

'I found I was in love with her and realised that I had never looked at her properly before— that is the truth. I had been away a lot, and she had been an awkward fledgling girl. Now she was exquisite—far more lovely than any of the ladies I had seen in London. And she was *mine*. I told myself that she had only to get over her fit of pique at being neglected and all would be well.'

He put his elbows on his knees and ran his hands through his hair. Then he looked up, his face bleak.

'So I gave her time—and she reacted by running off with that damn poet.'

He was just out of arm's reach. Ellie lifted a hand, shifted on her seat, then let her hand drop.

She wanted to touch him, wanted to be in his arms, holding and being held. But that was too easy for both of them. Blake had to finish.

'She left a note, you know. She said I had been a brute, a ravening beast without sensitivity or sensibility. She could not bear to be married to me. I could well believe that she had been frightened and shocked because I had kissed her—probably with far more passion, far more demand than I should have. Her father picked up their trail, but it was a week later. They had taken a ship for Italy and it was far too late to do anything about it.'

'So your heart was broken,' Ellie said.

'My heart was broken, my pride was in tatters and I knew damn well that I had completely mishandled the whole thing—I should have come home sooner... I should have wooed her properly. I reacted by behaving as though it hadn't happened. I should have followed them—found her, made certain she was all right, told her I was sorry and asked her to forgive me for my crassness. And then, if she had been content with her poet, I would have learned to live without her, to be happy for her. Instead I made a shrine in my heart for my lost love and carried on. And somehow the news that she had died, unhappy and alone, only made it worse. I managed to nurse my broken heart and found it armoured me very effectively against Cupid's arrows and the inconvenience and uncertainty of a new courtship.'

He looked at her and his smile was wry and self-mocking. It did not touch the darkness in his eyes.

'And then you met me.'

'Yes.' Blake's voice warmed. 'I met you. And you baffled me, infuriated me, provoked me and challenged me—and I found I *liked* you. Liked you a lot.'

'So you married me. A safe, plain bride who was not going to run off with anyone else.'

He had the sense not to deny it.

'I was very happy with you, Eleanor. I was beginning to hope that you were happy with me. And then we went home to Hampshire, where there was so much to remind me of her and what had happened. I hadn't examined that statue on its pedestal, hadn't looked at my own feelings for so long. I just assumed that somehow I would always love the memory of her, and that I would never feel that way about anyone again.'

Ellie looked down and found that her hands were crossed over her stomach, cradling the baby that had not even begun to swell her belly yet. 'Go on,' she whispered.

'I felt so strange. Guilt for the way I had acted was still there, but that feeling that I had always thought was love had become unwelcome, bitter. I couldn't recall her face any longer, but that didn't bring me any peace. And I was hurting you, and I hated it that I was. I wanted you—only you—but I didn't realise just what it was that I felt. All I knew was that when her parents put up that memorial it felt as though a blindfold had been ripped from my eyes. I did not know whether I had *ever* truly loved her.'

'Ever?' Ellie shook her head, trying to clear it. 'Eleanor—'

He ran his hands through his hair again and she almost smiled. It was so characteristic of Blake to do that when he was frustrated or impatient.

'I had been telling myself a story all this time since I had proposed to Felicity. I was in love with her—an impossible love—and she was my beautiful ideal, my lost destiny. But that was all it was—a story. I married you telling myself that I had to marry, and that I liked you, I could be happy with you and I hoped make you happy too. Everything I was beginning to feel for you—it was like smoke blowing across a puzzle that I had almost solved. I couldn't read it any longer.'

He came out of the chair, down on his knees on the faded hearthrug at her feet.

'I had no time to think. You were there—and

real. And yet I was hurting you because I could not let go of the guilt and the memories.'

Blake held out both his hands and Ellie took them in hers.

'Yes,' she admitted, 'it hurt that you still had the portrait. It hurt that you seemed to need to go to her memorial.'

'I had that miniature all this time. I cannot recall the last time I looked at it, but it had become part of the things that Duncombe always moved from house to house. I remembered it and knew I must get rid of it, because she was no longer part of my life and I did not want you to see it and misunderstand. I could not give it back to her parents because that would have been like an admission that I had never loved their daughter, so putting it into the memorial seemed the best thing to do with it. When I did it—when the stone lid grated back on to that urn—it felt like a door closing on the past, Eleanor. All I could see was how futile it was to feel guilt over it when it was blighting what you and I had, what we *could* have.'

She had been so wrong about what she had seen. 'You were coming home to me?'

'Eventually.'

That smile was the old Blake. Still rueful, but with a healthy self-mockery there now.

'I rode hard. I gave Tuscan his head and galloped and I felt free for the first time in a very long time. I needed to think, to feel, to listen to what my heart was telling me about you.'

Her fingers tightened involuntarily on his but he kept talking.

'Tuscan shied at a deer, unseated me because I was hardly thinking about what I was doing. I hit my head, knocked myself out. By the time I came round and got home you were gone.'

'*Knocked yourself out?* Blake, you should not have been travelling.' She released his hands, ran her fingers into his hair, found the lump on the back of his head and the healing wound. 'Did you see a doctor?' she demanded.

'I was concussed, that was all. Duncombe dressed it, I rested, then saw the doctor in London.'

'You went careering about the countryside with concussion?'

'Trying to find *you*,' Blake said flatly. 'What the hell were you thinking of, Eleanor?'

'Me?' she demanded, jerking her hands from his head with more speed than caution.

Blake winced, but she found that with relief so many other emotions were bubbling up—and amongst them anger.

'I was thinking of how to make this marriage work—how to make something meaningful out of a *ménage à trois* with a ghost.'

Blake made the fatal mistake of laughing. 'Will

you come home and we'll carry on as we did before?'

For a moment she'd thought he was going to tell her that he loved her, that *that* was what he had meant about understanding his feelings for her.

'As we did before?'

She should be happy. *So* happy. Blake did not love Felicity's memory, and had finally worked out just how his past had haunted him. He had come for her, searched for her, wanted her home again. But it was no longer enough.

'I… I do not know. We can never be as we were before.'

She loved him, and courtesy and kindness and his remorse at having hurt her would simply be coals of fire because now—selfishly—she wanted so much more. She wanted it all, and anything less would break her heart. But she would have to endure for the child's sake.

Ellie got to her feet and the solid flagstone floor felt unstable beneath her. 'I do not think I can—not yet.'

How could she be a good wife, having to hide how she felt because she was too much of a coward to tell him? Suffer his kindness and his pity and probably, because he *was* a kind man, his lies about how he felt for her?

She walked past him, out through the door before he could stop her, out through the kitchen where Jon and Polly and Finch scrambled to their feet as she passed. Out across the yard past the chicken coop and the privy and out onto the hillside.

She did not know where she was going or what good it would do. She knew only that she could not be in the same room as Blake, seeing his face, seeing his expression change when he realised his plain, lame wife was foolishly in love with him and wanted more than a fresh start or for things to be as they had before.

'Eleanor!' Blake stood unable to comprehend it as the door banged closed behind her.

Hell, had he failed to apologise enough? Had he not managed to communicate how deeply sorry he was that he had hurt her, how wrong he had been, how much he loved her?

The dark green of her gown moved across the back window of the parlour and he strode across to see her weave her way, limping rapidly, through the outbuildings and out of the gate into the hillside meadow beyond.

And then he realised just what he had not done.

The catch on the window was old and stiff, and he had to thump it hard with the flat of his hand before it opened, but he was in no mood now to find his way out of the house. He wanted the fastest route to Eleanor.

A coat seam split as he climbed through the casement and dropped to the ground, and a strong smell of mint wafted up. He had landed in the middle of the herb patch.

Kicking the crushed leaves and earth off his boots Blake ran, scattering chickens as he went. He lost sight of her for a moment, and then he was through the gate and running up the hill.

'Eleanor!'

She stopped on the crest of the ridge, where a clump of windswept trees made a small spinney, and stood waiting for him, her back turned. She looked...weary.

Blake slowed, getting his breath as he walked round to face her. 'You are unhappy because you love me and you think I do not love you. But you are wrong. I *do* love you,' he said.

No time now for elaborate explanations that might be misunderstood.

'You *love* me? Why didn't you say so?' she demanded, staring at him.

'I meant to and then I got too tied up in explaining. Concussion, male stupidity, guilt... I don't know, Eleanor. I have never told anyone I loved them before.'

'You *love* me,' she repeated, and this time it was not a question.

Blake nodded, instinct telling him that this was not the time to protest too much.

Then the rest of what he had said seemed to reach her. 'You believe that I love *you*?'

He pulled a folded paper from his inside breast pocket. 'I found all of these in your room when I was searching for clues to where you had gone and I read them. You are writing a novel, aren't you?'

She shrugged, the colour high in her face. 'I was trying to. It is no good—I realise that. I couldn't send it to a publisher.'

'Because it reveals too much about your own thoughts and feelings. And the hero looks just like me. I was jealous until I recognised him.'

'You *are* very good-looking,' she said tightly, still blushing. 'I saw you with Francis once and you seemed so right for the hero.'

'I sorted them into order,' he said. 'You start off with what I flatter myself is sensual desire and as the story progresses something else happens. You were writing about your feelings for *me*, weren't you, Eleanor? Why didn't you tell me that you loved me?'

'When you married me because I would *do* as a wife and you *liked* me? How could I have borne it if I'd told you and you were *kind* to me?'

She could not meet his eyes now, and that was probably a good thing—because otherwise she would see the look of triumph on his face. He hadn't been certain, was not such a coxcomb as to have fully believed what he was reading, but she had fallen for his bluff and admitted it.

'Why didn't you tell *me*?' she demanded, but her voice shook with something more than anger.

'I didn't realise until I rode away from the church and saw things so clearly.' He risked moving close—so close that her skirts brushed his boots—and reached out gently to turn her face to him. 'I love you, Eleanor. My Ellie. I love you with all the incoherent clumsiness of first love— because that is what this is. You will have to forgive me while I get it right. I have never loved before and I will never love again.'

'Blake…'

She reached out and rested her hands on his shoulders, looked up into his face, and he wondered how he had ever thought her plain.

'You *have* got it right and I do love you—so very much.'

He bent and kissed her, and for the second time went down to his knees in a field with a woman in his arms—but this time he knew she was *his* woman.

'Blake? Blake! We are in a *field*.'

But somehow she was not struggling very hard as he freed his arms and shrugged out of his greatcoat.

'It hasn't rained for days, by the look of it. There don't appear to be any bulls, and I can't see anyone. Besides, this spinney makes a nice screen, don't you think?'

'Screen for what?' she asked, but she was smiling and her eyes were sparkling. 'Are you going to kiss me in a field again?'

'Kiss you and make love to you—which is what I very much wanted to do that first time, even with the bull watching. Come here and lie down.'

He got her settled on his coat, fully dressed, then unfastened his falls with one hand and threw up her skirts with the other, coming down over her to stop her laughing protests with his mouth.

Blake's mouth was hot and demanding and exactly what she wanted. That and him inside her.

Ellie wrapped her legs around his narrow hips, opening herself to him, and he slid home and then went still except for his mouth, silently telling her how he felt, how he had missed her, how he had worried about her. How he loved her.

She tried to answer the same way, her tongue slipping languidly over his, and the taste and the smell of him, even with confusing overtones of mint, was so familiar, so precious.

He began to move within her, very slowly, and she used all the muscles that she had discovered in their few weeks of marriage to answer him, rocking to the rhythm he set, feeling the long muscles of his back flex under the silk of his waistcoat and the linen of his shirt. His buckskins were rough and arousing on the tender insides of her thighs and Ellie began to move more urgently, needing him, needing to feel his passion as she tried to show him hers.

Blake answered her with his body, stroking into her with hard, demanding thrusts, challenging her to respond, taking her higher as she followed him.

He freed her mouth to gasp her name and then, 'Come for me, Ellie. Come with me, my love.'

And she did, breaking apart to become something different with him. His love, her love, one person…and then she lost the power to think, only to feel.

Distantly someone was shouting, calling Blake's name. Ellie blinked and opened her eyes and found she was in Blake's arms, held against his chest, and that somewhere above them a lark was singing in a blue, blue sky.

'Awake, my love?' He sat up, bringing her with him, and then stood. 'I think we had better take ourselves down the hill before the search party comes near to us.' He reached down and helped her to her feet. 'All right?'

'My legs are shaky,' she admitted. 'And I am worried that this has all been a dream.'

'What a very vivid imagination you have, Ellie,' Blake said, his grin wicked. 'I wish I could dream like this every night.'

'You can. *We* can,' she said as he picked up his coat, shook off the grass and grimaced at the torn seam. 'Every night.'

Then she remembered.

'Well, perhaps we had better make the most of it, because in a while I think that running around in fields making love like this might become a little difficult.'

'You mean with the weather closing in for autumn?'

'No...'

She stopped and tugged him round to face her, laid his hands on her midriff.

'Blake, your feelings for Felicity are not the only reason I left. What you said about the way your father expected to direct your marriage, your future, and how you would expect to do the same for your eldest son. That chilled me to the bone, my love. Children deserve to be loved for themselves, not as dynastic pawns. Your heir will be a child who deserves to find his own way, his own love. And the others will be just as valuable, will deserve to be valued as much as your heir. My emotions might be all over the place at the moment, and I know I was upset—but, Blake, I had to find some way to make you realise that. Because otherwise how can we make a loving family together?'

He looked down at her, and then at her hands. 'You weren't feeling well... Ellie?'

'There's nothing to see—nothing to feel yet. But the doctor says that there is the beginning of our family snug in there.'

'Oh, Ellie. My Ellie.' He swung her up into his arms and kissed her. 'My clever girl. I don't deserve any more than to get you back safely, to know that you love me. But this—'

He set her down gently on her feet but kept his arms around her.

'All my adult life I have told myself that my father had the right to direct my choice of wife and that it was part of my duty as the Earl to think like that too. But what if our son found a woman to love who was simply Miss Brown of nowhere in particular? Would I say to him that I found true love but he must forgo it? And as for his brothers and sisters—they will be ours, and they will be loved, because you have taught me how.'

Eventually he took her hand and they walked up to the crest and then down the slope to the farm, where Jon was standing with Polly in the yard, looking around. Blake raised a hand and waved to his brother. He waved back, then, reassured, went into the house.

'Don't sell this place,' Ellie said as Blake bent and picked a buttercup and tucked it in her hair. 'Please.'

'No, we will keep it as our place of escape for when we do not want to be the Earl and the Countess—just Blake and Ellie. All our children will like the animals—'

'*All* our children?'

'We have made a start,' he said, holding the gate for her. 'And now we have the knack of it we ought to keep on, don't you think? Imagine all those little boys and girls, chasing the chickens and getting covered in mud.'

'Idiot.' She elbowed him gently in the ribs. 'I missed you so much,' Ellie added, suddenly shy. 'I told myself that if I could only have the space to think I would be able work out how to have a happy marriage.'

'Of course you would,' Blake said. He closed the gate and swept her up into his arms again. 'You can do anything, my Ellie.'

'When you look at me like that I believe you,' she agreed as he carried her across the yard and stopped just before the door. 'I was meant for you.'

'And I for you. And when I carry you over this threshold—that is when our *real* marriage begins, my love.'

Blake shouldered the door open and stepped
over the threshold, and Ellie finally allowed herself to believe in happy endings.

* * * * *

*If you enjoyed this story, you won't want to miss
these other great reads from Louise Allen:*

*HIS HOUSEKEEPER'S CHRISTMAS WISH
HIS CHRISTMAS COUNTESS
THE MANY SINS OF CRIS DE FEAUX
THE UNEXPECTED MARRIAGE OF
GABRIEL STONE
SURRENDER TO THE MARQUESS*

*And make sure you look for Louise Allen's
short story—ON A WINTER'S EVE—in our*
ONCE UPON A REGENCY CHRISTMAS
anthology!

MILLS & BOON®

& HISTORICAL

AWAKEN THE ROMANCE OF THE PAST

MILLS & BOON®

EXCLUSIVE EXTRACT

Georgiana Knight accidentally auctions her innocence to ex-soldier Frederick Challenger. In order to protect her reputation, she must marry him, but if Frederick hopes to tame her he'll have to think again…

Read on for a sneak preview of
A CONVENIENT BRIDE FOR THE SOLDIER
by Christine Merrill
the first book in the daring and decadent series
THE SOCIETY OF WICKED GENTLEMEN

Mr Challenger dropped to his knee before her. 'Miss Knight, would you do me the honour of accepting my offer of marriage?'

Georgiana had heard the phrase, 'without a trace of irony'. This must be the opposite of it. The proposal was delivered without a trace of sincerity. And yet, he did not rise. He stared at her, grim-faced, awaiting an answer.

'But, I do not want to marry you,' she said, staring back at him incredulous.

'Nor do I want to marry you.' If possible, his expression became even more threatening. 'But as you said before, if word of this gets out, I will be called to offer for you. I see no other way to save both of our reputations.'

'Your reputation?' Did men even have them? Of course they did. But she was sure that it did not mean the same thing as it did for girls.

'If you do not marry me, I will be seen as the villain

who threatened you, a seducer of innocents. Bowles, on the other hand, will be cast as your rescuer. In either case, your future is set. You will have to marry one of us to avoid ruin.' The statement was followed by the audible grinding of teeth. 'Please, my dear Miss Knight, allow me to be the lesser of two evils.'

The idea was insane. 'But then, we would be married,' she reminded him. 'For ever,' she added, when the first statement seemed to have no impact upon him.

'That is the way it normally works,' he agreed. 'You must have understood the risk when you undertook this desperate mission. As I told you before, if you do not marry me, then you shall wed Bowles.' He looked at her for the length of a breath, then added, 'For ever.'

'For ever,' she repeated. It sounded so final. Eventually, she had known she would have to marry someone. She'd just never imagined it would be to a man who had never been willing to give her the time of day, much less a proposal.

MILLS & BOON®